DRAGON BONDS

Return of the Darkening Series Book Three

AVA RICHARDSON

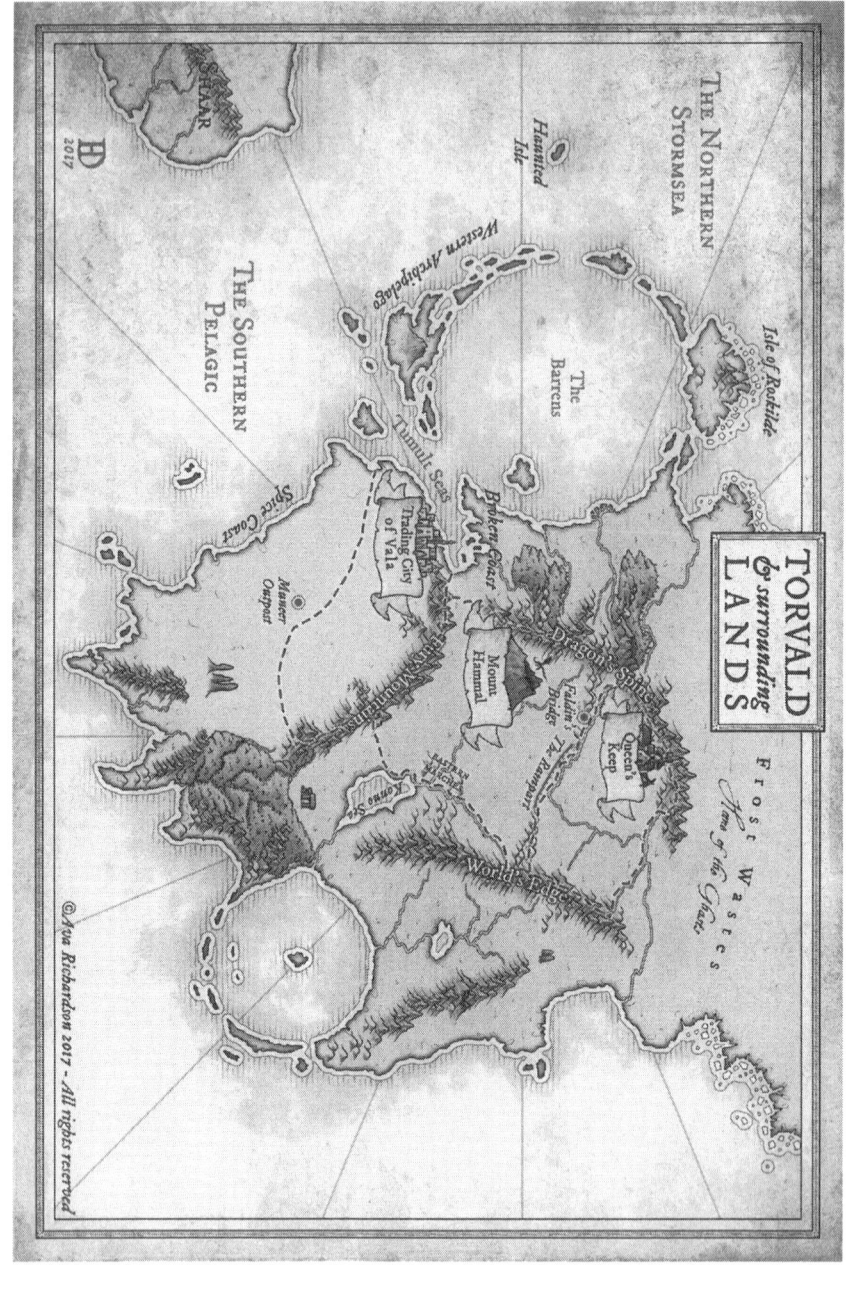

TORVALD
& surrounding
LANDS

THE NORTHERN
STORMSEA

THE SOUTHERN
PELAGIC

The
Barrens

Hassdal
Isle

Isle of Roithild

Western Archipelago

Tumult Seas

Spice Coast

Broken Crown
Peaks

Trading City
of Vala

Manser
Outpost

Mount
Hannal

Dragon Spine Mountains

Calim Wood

Queen's
Keep

World's End

CONTENTS

THE RETURN OF THE DARKENING SERIES

Dragon Trials

Dragon Legends

Dragon Bonds

DRAGON BONDS

RETURN OF THE DARKENING SERIES
BOOK THREE

BY AVA RICHARDSON

BLURB

The Darkening has risen...

Agathea Flamma and Sebastian Smith now face an overwhelming enemy. The rapid spread of the Darkening, a threat arising from the mists of legend, looms over the entire land. With both their families torn apart by the conflict and betrayal lurking around every corner, one mistake could doom the kingdom.

They'll have to decide where to put their faith: blood ties or newfound friends?

After the destruction of the Dragon Academy, it's up to Thea and Seb to gather their loyal comrades—and forge uneasy new alliances—to quell the ancient menace and face the evil Lord Vincent. With civil war raging, the Dragon Riders must race against time to find the legendary Dragon Stone, the only tool they have to fight against the endless darkness that threatens to swallow them all.

MAILING LIST

Thank you for purchasing 'Dragon Bonds'
(The Return of the Darkening Series Book Three)

I would like to thank you for purchasing this book. If you would like to hear more about what I am up to, or continue to follow the stories set in this world with these characters—then please take a look at:

AvaRichardsonBooks.com

You can also find me on me on
www.facebook.com/AvaRichardsonBooks

Or sign up to my mailing list:
AvaRichardsonBooks.com/mailing-list/

CHAPTER 1
THE TORN CITADEL

"Dobbett? Is that you?" A rustling and snuffling in the darkness ahead put me on alert, and I set a hand on my sword.

Since the attack on Torvald, things had changed in the Flamma household. Luckily, most of the house had been spared from direct damage—but that didn't mean that any of it was safe. Bands of Wildmen could be heard in the streets, and the Darkening-controlled wild dragons flew overhead, passing like a shadow and swooping down on anything that moved.

Not as many as there were.

Ten days ago, Prince—no wait—*King* Justin had ordered us back to the city to help anyone we could find. We couldn't approach the mountain; the air was so thick with the vicious, black wild dragons controlled by Lord Vincent. They'd torn apart the city, their claws scraping away roofs and their snouts breaking apart grain houses, inns and homes. But the wild dragons were growing tired of destruction—most had left. There were only so many cobblestones even a feral dragon can eat before it's had its fill. And only so many orders they could take before their wild nature took over again and they headed back to the wilds.

Perhaps it cost too much to control them all?

I didn't know, but I needed to find out.

Pausing outside my family's sweeping staircase—the one that had once led to my own bedroom— I could see the window was thankfully unbroken. My parent's had returned to Torvald so they might salvage what they could. Now I just wanted to get them out of the house and gone from the city.The view looking down over the different tiers of the city was a sad one. Smoke still drifted up from several fires, and I could see the ruinous smears of crumbled buildings, bridges and walls. No movement in the sky today. I remembered how Seb had suffered when he had been trying to control the wild dragons. He'd been exhausted, too tired to even speak afterward. How much energy must it have cost Lord Vincent to control so many wild dragons?

How much willpower does the Darkening have?

A huff and a snarl from the darkened room ahead of me snapped my attention back to the present. Just what on earth was wrong with me? You would have thought I would be at least a little wary of where I was about to set foot in such an uncertain situation.

I tried to breathe, remembering the mental exercises I'd been taught at the Dragon Academy, taking time to flex my hand around the hilt of my short sword, draw it without a sound and feel its weight as I edged closer to the darkened, half-open door.

What was I about to find? A Wildman, a raider from the South or some other horror?

"Thea?" The word came out a worried hiss from behind me. I looked down to see my mother, the Lady Flamma, standing at the bottom of the stairs, brandishing a heavy iron skillet. *That is probably the very first time she has ever had to pick up one of those.* Guilt for being a little unkind bit at me. I could see the fear in my mother's pinched face—she just wasn't used to this kind of thing. And yet she still had gone off to find the biggest, heaviest thing she could use to help her daughter.

As if I still need protecting.

I was the one who'd had training as a fighter—just as all Flamma children had been trained. My oldest brother, Reynalt, was now commander of the Dragon Riders, and Ryan was the King's Navigator. I was a Dragon Rider, too, along with Seb, my navigator. But, to be honest, I didn't know which, if any of us, I would put money on winning in a fight against the Lady Flamma when she was armed with an iron skillet and an iron will. The events of the past few days had marked her—I had heard of hair turning white overnight, but I had never seen it before, and Mother's hair had done just that. She had given up elaborate hair dressings and now wore her silver-white locks in a simple braid. Her gown was simple, too—blue wool with no decorations. Her hair and dress made her blue eyes seem even brighter. They glittered right now with a battle lust.

Flapping at her with one free hand, I whispered as loud as I dared, "Go back. Father needs you to keep him safe."

My mother frowned, and I was sure she was about to refuse. Amazingly, she turned and left, hurrying back to the drawing room where she had left her husband.

"First time for everything," I muttered. But I felt strangely sad, instead of pleased. It was odd not to have Mother fussing over me like I was still a girl. Not that I wanted Mother to spend the rest of her life trying to get me married to a nice, wealthy boy —far from it. Besides, there probably weren't many nice boys left.

That thought was still too sharp even for me. I veered away from what that actually meant for the many noble suitors I might have once had. Even the Westerforth boys, Terence and Tomas, horrible as they were, didn't deserve to be eaten by a dragon. But was a dragon hiding here?

Something snuffled and growled inside my old room. It was now or never.

With a yell, I kicked aside the door and swept in, my short sword low. Something small, wiry and fanged barked and snuffled. The furry white land-pig growled, snapped and got caught in the ruined bed sheet.

A wave of relief crashed through me. It felt like years since I'd last seen her. "Dobbett, where have you been? Have you been up here this whole time?" I sheathed my sword and extricated her from the voluminous white sheets that had once been part of my bed.

She excitedly licked my hand and tried to snuff at my face.

"They thought you had run away!" I scolded the land-pig, who looked a little like a cross between a small, pug-nosed dog and a fluffy cushion. Her big, rolling eyes regarded me with the love and undying admiration that only a pet can give. I sat down, sighed and allowed Dobbett to climb up onto my lap with snuffles, snouts and sneezes.

"There, girl." I patted her thick fur as I had done a hundred times before in this very room.

But it had looked quite a bit better than this.

The wooden board windows to the balcony had been left or blown open, allowing the winds to ravage the small room. Smoke tainted the air and even a few leaves littered the floor. A wardrobe had been overturned, spilling out a collection of sugary dresses and blue robes, jerkins of fine fawn and a mass of shoes. They looked like they belonged to someone else and to a very different time.

My old writing desk had fallen over and had deep gashes on its surface—doubtless from Dobbett's scrabbling and not from a dragon. The wall hangings and blankets were spread around the room and pulled from the walls. Despite all the destruction, what struck me the most was how the room seemed too much space for anyone.

Have I changed so much? Have the years of cramped living at the Dragon Academy, sharing a room with Varla, changed me so much?

Small, finely-embroidered cushions lay scattered over the floor. They'd been made by a great craftsman from the Gabbon Heights. They were still nice to look at, but they were useless.

They'll keep my father warm, at least. I gathered them up in a blanket that was still mildly clean.

On a still-standing bedside cabinet, I saw my small dragon figurines, baring fangs or in noble stances. They had been carved by a master woodsman from the South and although they had certain elegance it was clear the carver had never ridden a dragon.

These are the sorts of things people carve when they think about dragons and Dragon Riders.

I picked one up, looking at its fierce snarl, with one claw raised high. "Kalax doesn't look like that, does she, Dobbett?" I asked the land-pig, who had closed her eyes and was wuffling happily. A *really* fierce dragon didn't bother to strike a pose before it struck.

"I was such a stupid little girl," I told Dobbett, who agreed with a pleased whine. She started to make a husky, almost purring snore. I urged her up to follow me, stepping over a spilled pile of dresses, breeches and other old clothes.

Growing up as the only girl with two big brothers, one couldn't help but be a bit rough around the edges. But I had also been the darling daughter of Lord and Lady Flamma and therefore had been expected to dance, recite poetry, play a musical instrument and practice the art of dressing well.

I much preferred my Dragon Academy jerkin, the tunic, breeches and heavy riding boots. I cringed when I thought back to the girl I had been. I must have been so naïve, so arrogant. What must Seb and the others have thought of me when they'd first met me?

Another fearful whisper rose up from the stairs below. "Thea?"

Sweeping up Dobbett under one arm and clutching the cushions and blanket under the other, I stepped out to the landing. "It's just Dobbett, Mother."

"Oh, by the First Dragon!" Mother swore while shaking her head. "You gave me a fright. Come back to the drawing room. Your father has almost decided."

"And I bet I know *what* he has decided," I muttered, trying to keep it under my breath but to no use. Mother had always had *very* sharp hearing.

"Agathea, that is no way to talk about your father."

I hung my head. She was right, of course. My father had been through enough without having a disobedient daughter as well. They had seen their home and the city of Torvald destroyed, the old king was dead, and now most of the land was in the hands of an enemy. The Darkening had returned. A good portion of the population was presumed dead, and still others were under the strange effects of the Memory Stone and had forgotten almost everything that had once mattered to them.

If there was *anything* that we could give thanks for, it was that Lord Vincent had other things occupying his mind than individually controlling the ordinary citizens of Torvald.

Most of those affected by the Memory Stone had been left where they stood, to be taken away by friends, neighbors and family to be looked after. Lord Vincent and the Darkening had other battles to fight. Now, I needed Father and Mother to come with me and join the refugees heading to the king's camp. Ryan, I knew, would have been saying the very same thing to them.

"Come on, you'll catch a chill out here that will be the death of you!" Mother's voice took on a stern tone. I headed down the stairs.

Without the servants or any supplies, my mother had seemed mortified that we couldn't keep the house heated or even clear up the mess from the recent battle.

I clambered past our small barricade of tables and chairs and slipped into the room.

Believe me, Mother, the very last thing anyone should worry over is dying from a cold.

❦

King Justin had ordered us back to the citadel of Torvald after the attack on the refugee camp, when Lord Vincent's vast dragon had succeeded in destroying most of our provisions, injuring a score of Dragon Riders and breaking the spirits of most foot soldiers.

If not for Seb holding back the dragons with his Dragon Affinity, the last hope for Torvald would have died there. Amazingly, we had survived and regrouped near the mountains in a lonely, broken gorge that not even Merik had on any chart. But we had all been affected by Lord Vincent's Memory Stone. Some were now prone to periods of confusion and forgetfulness, but most could at least remember who they were fighting and why.

King Justin—and it still felt odd calling him king, since I had grown up with him and had known him as a boy I could beat at archery—was set on a counterattack. The forces of Lord Vincent were only wild dragons and Wildmen after all, hardly organized or disciplined, but after that attack on our camp, everyone had to admit there was a far bigger enemy at work here than any of us could counter easily—The Darkening.

It seemed that Lord Vincent might even be something from legend—a son of an ancient king who had broken through the veils between the worlds, a man who had gone mad with his own need for power and the taint of the Darkening; maybe even due to the Dragon Affinity having affected him.

I shivered. I didn't like thinking about that last bit, for Seb had that same affinity—and I knew how much it cost Seb each time he used that skill. It left me worried for him. And for the future.

I'd never believed the old stories. But they all seemed to be true. Lord Vincent...the traitorous lord who had served the old king had somehow managed to reawaken the Darkening, to channel its power with the help of the three Dragon Stones—the Memory Stone could command others, the Healing Stone, and the Armor Stone, the black stone that could make dragons and riders impervious to injury. Lord Vincent had all three. With his powers vastly amplified by the Darkening, he could command almost every wild dragon in existence.

But King Justin wanted to fight. At least some of his advisors had convinced him we wouldn't be able to do it without help, and he had agreed to venture back to try to recruit those who still could stand.

There were still an awful lot of people holed up in their homes just as my parents had been, waiting and watching the skies for rescue. King Justin wanted to let them know that there was a new king, and that he was strong. Maybe then they would come out and fight with the rest of us.

At least, that was the plan.

In the drawing room, I dropped the blanket and pillows on the floor and faced my father. He stood by the huge fireplace with his back to the flames. I'd gotten my red-gold hair from him. He wore his hair long so it brushed his shoulders, and as I walked in he was smoothing his mustache. Like Mother, Father had seemed to age years in just a few days. Lines marked his face around his eyes, but he was still a strong, tall man dressed in a fine jerkin of leather edged with gold threads and leather breeches and boots.

Ryan, who looked very much like a younger version of Father without the mustache, had built up the fire. He bent now to feed it one of the table legs—there would be no woodsmen delivering wood. Ryan kept the flame low so it would not attract too much attention from any marauders in the city. The drawing room was a defensible space—the windows faced an inner court-yard and just now the long drapes were drawn over them. The room seemed dark and a little dingy—and huge—with a small pile of spindly tables that Ryan was slowly burning. He had come with me from King Justin's camp, and Seb had traveled part way with us before splitting off to see if he could find his own family.

Straightening, Ryan shot me a worried look from behind our

father's back. He was letting me know that this wasn't going to go easy.

Clearing his throat, Father gave me a nod and tucked one thumb into his wide, leather belt. "Agathea, we've been discussing matters. King Justin is being hot headed. His father would never have advised a counterattack, not with the city in ruins and uncounted numbers missing, dead or injured. I cannot condone his throwing the lives of our people away in this fashion! I will give his plans no support. No…the people must leave Torvald and go into hiding."

I glanced at Ryan, who winced and shook his head. Glancing back at my father, I told him, "You defy your king and speak treason?"

My mother stamped her foot. "Agathea, we may not have many windows left to us, or servants left to the house, but I would like to think the House Flamma can still carry on a civil discourse!"

My face started to burn, and I was back to feeling as if I was ten still. "I'm sorry, Mother, Father." I nodded to where he was glowering at me. "I'm used to plain speaking in the Academy, sir." I clasped my hands behind my back and hoped I wouldn't get myself into more trouble.

Father turned and spread out his hands to the fire. "But that is my point, child. The Academy failed us all. So did King Justin. His folly cannot be allowed to continue."

I glanced at Ryan for help, but he had turned away as well and was staring at the pile of tables that were about to become kindling. I had to imagine he was tired of arguing with Father. I wasn't. Near me, Dobbett settled onto one of the pillows from my room. I wished I could do the same, but I needed Father to see sense. "But…Father, King Justin needs us—all of us." Frustration and anger made my voice higher than it should be. I took a breath and tried for a more reasonable tone. "Where would it be safe from Lord Vincent's dragons? What if he sends worse after us?" I didn't really know what could be worse than those wild, black dragons, but I had vague memories of seeing Lord Vincent's dark figure at the palace. He had commanded the king and others with the Memory Stone. His powers would be even stronger now that he had the three Dragon Stones.

Mother huffed a breath, but Father held up a hand and said, his tone reasonable, "Do you think I have so little care for this city? What I am suggesting is that we leave with the other families. We can hide deep in the woods. Once everyone has had a chance to rest, to gather our strength and mourn our losses, *then* is the time to prepare for battle. But not now. Not now."

I couldn't believe I was hearing my father say these words. It was as if a different man had stolen his skin. My father, Lord Flamma, was head of the second most important family in the kingdom. There were even sayings about us—*Easier split an egg from dragon than a Flamma from their mount. Always a Flamma, always a Dragon.* Our family was entwined with the cobblestones and masonry of this city, with the Dragon Academy, and the royal family. We had fought for generations to protect the city and serve Torvald. I couldn't believe Father wouldn't take up arms against the worst enemy we had ever encountered.

He shook his head and smoothed his mustache. "I know what you must be thinking for I can see it in your eyes, and it breaks my heart, too—to think that we must abandon the city, the Flamma estates...all the lands we have held for centuries."

I was speechless; tears stung my eyes.

"But you have to see I am right. Why throw our lives away for King Justin, who seeks one last, desperate moment? He is a boy and barely older than you." He glanced at Ryan, who stood with his arms folded and a dark frown pulling at his face. As the King's Navigator, Ryan must hate that Father was forcing him to choose between his family and the king. And then it hit me—did I have to choose, too?

A pounding on the front door echoed through the house. The servants had fled during the battle—or so I'd learned from Mother. I reached for my sword and turned, hearing Ryan step forward as well as he uttered an oath.

But Father waved a hand at us. "Weapons down. That is our code—six knocks, one for each letter of our name." He stepped out of the drawing room and came back with his arm over Reynalt's shoulders. Grinning, Father said, "I sent for Reynalt. Our family is complete once more."

Mother threw herself into Reynalt's arms. Commander Reynalt, I should say, for he was the aerial commander of the Dragon Riders. I didn't know if I should salute or offer him a sisterly embrace.

He was looking harried and a little pale, but he was still easily the tallest. He was also wearing his moustache as long as Father's, attempting to imitate him, I thought.

"Mother." He kissed her cheek and patted her shoulders. She let him go at last, and Reynalt scrubbed a hand through his hair.

Mother glanced from him to Ryan to me and pressed one hand to her heart. "All of my children here safe and under one roof."

"A roof that currently has several new holes from wild dragons," I muttered.

Ryan and Reynalt shook hands and thumped shoulders. After a moment, Reynalt glanced at me and gave me a nod.

Reynalt was almost ten years my senior, and we had little in common except a love of dragons. I had always viewed him as stuck up, and I think he had always thought I'd been spoiled.

"Good to see you, Thea—you've put yourself through a lot." Reynalt gave me another nod. I could decipher the hidden message that he thought I'd done well for a mere girl, but the kindness in his voice touched me. He had always been there, looking after me and Ryan.

"How is the king?" I asked.

Reynalt frowned. "Well, Justin is… still affected by having been under the control of the Memory Stone, I fear." Reynalt glanced around for a place to sit. Other than the floor, there wasn't much of anything. He glanced at Father. "Some mornings he forgets he is to inspect the riders, and other times he forgets the plans he has made and the orders he has given. All he truly remembers is his desire for revenge on Lord Vincent."

"And the Darkening?" I added. "Tell me now you still disbelieve the old stories of its return?"

"Now, Agathea…" my mother warned. I glanced at her and

saw the worry in her eyes. She must be fearful of yet another fight between us. We'd once bickered far too much.

Reynalt huffed. "I think there are more pressing concerns, such as the status of our troops and our city."

Ryan gave a sharp laugh. "Half the command—or what's left of it—is here."

Reynalt pulled at his moustache, but Father spoke up. "And that is why we must begin to do things differently, why we must *think* differently. There are few leaders, but House Flamma still stands. The royal family has been compromised by accursed magic."

"By the Memory Stone…one of the three Dragon Stones," I said. No one seemed to hear me.

Father clapped a hand on Reynalt's shoulder. "We cannot rush into battle with an enemy who has left us weakened—both physically and mentally. That is why I am taking this family out of the city to regroup with some of the other nobles. We will come up with a better course of action. One that is clear sighted."

"Father…" Ryan started. A sharp look from Father and a pleading one from Mother stopped his words.

Putting his other hand on Ryan's shoulder, Father shook him. "Ryan, you must come with us. Our family will make the best stewards, the best leaders, for those we can save."

"Father, we can't abandon King Justin! The people need stability. They need one ruler, not the Flammas announcing themselves as…as stewards," I cried.

Frowning, Reynalt stepped away from Father and came over to face me. "Thea, even you cannot call Justin king and have it sound commanding. That is because he is a boy…a boy left devastated by his father's death and by a crushing defeat." He glanced at Ryan. "And you, Ryan, as his navigator and second, you will be expected to command the squadrons in battle. But what squadrons do we have left. One? Two? Perhaps a third, but most all of them were cadets only a short time ago. Are you ready for that responsibility? Do you wish to lead children to their deaths?"

Flushing red, Ryan pushed Father's arm off his shoulder. "I'll have you know—"

"No, Father is right." Reynalt slashed the air with a hand. "The people need us. We have to look after each other now and show the world that we are strong, together. That is what the people need—we must lead them to safety."

"Well said." Mother dabbed at her eyes with a silk hand-kerchief.

At that moment, I saw the plan that must have been in the works for a very long time.

Mother had been so happy when the old king had danced with me at the Winter Ball—she had wanted me to marry Prince Justin, which would have put a Flamma on the throne. And Father was so proud of all that Reynalt had achieved—he was second-in-charge of the army.

I didn't think Father or Mother had wanted to scheme against the old king or against King Justin. But there was one thing they cared about above all else—House Flamma. If they thought this was good for the Flamma family, they would do it.

But what about me?

I didn't know where I fit into this new plan. I thought of Seb, out in the city somewhere, maybe dodging Wildmen or raiders and even dragons. He had come with his folks as well, also intent on trying to help others or save what they could. How could I stay with my family and leave Seb to some uncertain fate? And how could I abandon my family?

My family means everything to me. I am proud to be a Flamma—but what they are asking...they're asking me to leave the Dragon Riders, to give up Kalax, my dragon, and Seb, and my friends. Ferdinania. That's everything I worked so hard to get.

"I-I can't go." The words fell out. My father frowned. Mother gave a gasp. And Reynalt stared at me, terrible disappointment in his eyes.

But Ryan stepped over to my side and slipped his hand into mine. "Neither can I. My place is at the side of my sister, and with my king, for I am the King's Navigator."

I gave a nod. Ryan was right. We couldn't abandon our king —but I saw that was just what my father, Reynalt and Mother planned to do. Shame washed through me. Suddenly, I wanted to run from the house—run and find Seb and Kalax. I wanted to get back into the fight against the Darkening.

CHAPTER 2
FIRES IN THE CITY

Monger's Lane was gone. But any thought of this place being my home— with its broken buildings and heavy smell of dust and smoke in the air—was burned from me. The small street where I'd grown up looked different, and felt different, too.

I recognized a few parts of the rubble-strewn street—a corner well I had fetched water from every day was now being used by a human bucket-line to put out fires. And the tiny marketplace still stood.

The wild dragons of Lord Vincent had come through here, setting some houses on fire and knocking the roofs off others. The shabby houses of Monger's Lane were home to some of the poorest in all of Torvald, with many made only of wood, not stone. Timbers lay in the streets, some smoldering. I could hear the cries of children, and the moans of those hurt. A few men ran past, bags over their shoulders, either carrying what they owned and fleeing or stealing whatever they could take.

It was a mess.

Even so, I owed it to my family and neighbors to try and help in some way. The city might be ruined, but there was still some hope. People were alive. We had rallied, and King Justin had recovered from the enchantment of the Memory Stone. I still wasn't sure what I thought of the new king. He barely talked to me or anyone under his station in life, which was pretty much everyone. But maybe he had never been forced to deal with the poor. I wondered if he even knew places like Monger's Lane existed.

Had existed, I reminded myself. The rubble that crunched under my boots—broken cobbles and shattered glass, fallen walls and cindered roof slats—could hardly be called anything but a ruin.

Still live! Hunt… fish!

Kalax's thoughts flashed suddenly into my mind. It was becoming easier with every passing day to live in a sort of shared space with the dragon, internally at least. Sometimes it felt as if there was not that much difference between Kalax and me. Often I would dream of flying and hunting over distant moonlit lakes, or seeing stars wheeling overhead as I spun through the sky.

It was confusing at times and made my head ache. I wondered if Varla was right to be worried when she'd said the Dragon Affinity had always been regarded as more of a curse than as a blessing. What had Jodreth the wizard said? That the Middle Son—the one who brought forth the Darkening—had had a strong ability with the Dragon Affinity? And that was how all of this had started.

Kalax not Seb. Seb not Kalax. Seb is too small. Kalax's mirth flashed across my thoughts—a dragon's sense of humor. I knew she thought nothing of doing this. She was also much better at joining my thoughts or of closing herself off from me than I was.

Of course. Dragons think clearly. Humans all muddled and fogged!

I stopped where I stood and thought to her, *Can all dragons talk to all other dragons—as we are now?*

A snarl of laughter shook me. I looked up but I couldn't see the large, red dragon, though I knew she was shaking her head in amusement. The scent of pine and the smell of fresh mountain water rose up. Kalax must have hidden herself near a river in a thickly wooded area to avoid detection from the occasional wild dragons.

Only humans need chatter. Dragons just know. Smell it, growl or roar. Dragons rarely talk. You, Thea, and I are special.

I felt oddly pleased by that—although I also knew Kalax was being sarcastic. She'd often thought at me that humans, although useful, were frightfully slow and weak. We had to put on armor and it wasn't thick enough, we got cold or hot too quickly and cried often over matters that didn't matter. For Kalax, life was simple. *Almost.* She thought about fish a remarkable amount of time, as well as danger, sleep, warmth...but rarely about the things that worried me.

Such as why I feel so guilty about my family.

I sighed. I could feel Kalax withdrawing her mind to focus on the stream and scenting for fish. Dragons seemed to have no need for guilt.

It's my fault Monger's Lane looks like this. I should have fought harder…should have warned them.

But how? I'd been caught in fighting to save the old king—and in trying to save what we could of the Academy. I'd done all I could, but my throat tightened and my heart beat harder. I still felt I should have done more. What if my family all lay dead under the rubble of our home? What if all I'd had to do to save them had been to fly here sooner, have Kalax scoop them up and fly them out of the city to the woods? But I knew the answer.

Torvald would probably have fallen a lot faster if I hadn't been at the palace.

The night of the battle felt like it had been years ago, not a few weeks at most. We hadn't been able to stop Lord Vincent—he'd gotten into the royal palace and used the Memory Stone on the old king. Lord Vincent had unleashed his forces against the palace—wild dragons had attacked the Dragon Academy and the city, and the main squadrons of the Dragon Riders had been lured far to the north. It had been only a few of us who could do anything.

Thea, Merik, Varla, myself and a few other riders had done our best to keep the wild dragons occupied so people could escape the city or find shelter. But even we'd had to admit defeat. The Dragon Affinity I'd used against the wild dragons to force them away was only so strong.

Kalax's senses suddenly mixed with my own—I could *smell* a cobblestone as it hurtled through the air toward me, covered with a patina of soot and ash. Kalax's warning followed. *Seb...danger!*

I ducked, turning and drawing my sword in one swift movement. The rock hit the spot where I'd been standing. Across the square, I saw a glint of sunlight on metal and then movement in the shadows. I leapt forward, then tucked and rolled across the ground, ignoring the pain of hot cinders on my shoulders. Leaping up, I ran to the other side of the ruined square. The buildings were still standing there, and that's where my attackers were hiding.

"Wait!" a woman shouted, her voice fierce.

I stumbled to a halt, my breath ragged and my lungs burning. I knew that voice.

At the mouth of the alley to my right, small shapes—none of them larger than I was and all covered in heavy, shapeless clothes —shifted and moved.

I'd worn rags like that once.

The voice I'd heard reminded me of mornings spent running to and from the market, repeating errands over and over to myself as my father ordered me to collect more wood or coal for his smithy, or buy cheap drink for him. I thought of weary evenings after I'd done a day's work and was shutting up for the day.

Was it? It couldn't be...Widow Hu?

She stepped from the shadows and I recognized my neighbor from when Monger's Lane had enough houses to have such things as neighbors. She was still bowed and ancient. I'd once taken her wood or a few pieces of bread if we had any to spare.

She had always seemed to me near blind and slow. She looked different now.

"Sebastian Smith! I thought there was something familiar about you. Always that terrible hair sticking up, looking browner than it should. And arms and legs longer than they need to be. You've grown, I see—and even filled out into that jerkin they have you in!" She stood as straight as she could, given the hunch at the top of her back, and peered at me through thick goggles obviously taken from one of the abandoned shops. She still wore her usual robes of gray and black, but had added a thick, leather belt from which hung pouches, bags and a long knife. She clutched a stout staff in one hand.

"Widow Hu? And who taught you the quarterstaff?"

Coming up to me, she snapped, "Did you never meet old Alf, my husband?" Her voice was as dry as I remembered.

"Uh, no?" She had always just been the Widow Hu, with no husband or man in her house.

She thumped the bottom of the staff on the ground. "Wall guard, he was, man and boy. Signed up and served through the bandit raids, the wild dragons, and when that uppity duke what's-his-name wanted to grab Thuland from us. Alf was adamant I learn to use this thing, even though I thought him a fool." She sniffed.

From the dark, ragged forms behind her, a voice barked out, "Who is he?"

I glanced at them. Street kids stepped from the shadows. Some of them I even recognized from my years in Monger's Lane. Fat Joachim had grown into a sizable brawler, and Sparrow

—the girl who'd never been caught stealing bread from the market—now had a livid scar across her cheek.

"Wot?" she asked, accusing and surly. She had seen me staring at her face and touched her cheek with a grubby hand. "Got it from a bleedin' Wildman, didn't I? But I put his eye out." She grinned fiercely.

From the back of the gang, a small figure stepped forward. "Seb?" The voice held a familiar raspy tone.

"Elena!" My little sister—still barely large enough to hold that short bow she carried—ran to me and threw her arms around me. I hugged her back. She wiggled free and wiped her snotty nose on her sleeve. Frowning at her, I said, "Elena, where have you been? Where's Da?"

I'd wanted everyone to stay together when we'd returned to Torvald, but da wouldn't listen to me and wandered off, looking for his friends. Mother and Elena had gone after him, and I had my hands full for a few days just trying to help a few neighbors put out fires. It seems as if every other day, the raiders or the dragons that remained would light a new building on fire. Just for fun, as far as I could tell. Well, at least I'd tracked down one of my kin.

Elena looked at me with large, dark eyes. She'd ever been a watchful, quiet one. "Da's gone. Don't know where. And Mum..."

"She be in the shelter, Seb," Old Widow Hu said, patting me on the shoulder. She glanced up, her mouth pulling down as if a shadow had passed overhead. "Sent her there soon as I came across her, and her looking for her man. Haven't seen your da, but Elena's proving she's got sharp eyes when it comes to spotting black dragons."

One of the many things to say for a city like Torvald, one that had grown up next to Hammal Mountain and the Dragon Academy, was that we were used to dragons in the sky—but they were usually friendly. Sometimes, a dragon from the enclosure might get dragon sickness, or could be more than upset at losing its riders. But such things were rare. Dragons by nature were loyal creatures—but they also didn't like other dragons challenging the order. So the first line of defense was always other dragons. But this was a new world—one run by Lord Vincent. And his wild dragons were still in the skies. I didn't trust any shadow.

I didn't see anything—and Kalax wasn't sounding the alarm, so I turned back to Widow Hu. Relief eased my shoulders. "It's good to hear about my mother. But Da—?"

"We just don't know. Look over there." She nodded to the area where the smithy and the widow's house had once stood. Nothing more than smoke and blackened timbers remained. The devastation stretched for streets and streets. Rows of houses were still shouldering and collapsing in on each other as their floors and roofs gave way. No one had been able to put out these fires, and I wondered if da had seen this and become disheartened—perhaps he'd even gone back to the bottle. Why hadn't he listened to me when I'd said we should stay close?

Widow Hu patted my shoulder. "We were heading back to the shelter when our scouts said they saw movement—you. Just one of the wild dragons set off that fire right a night ago. It spread as far as you can see."

My chest tightened. I hoped my father wasn't under the rubble. Despite all, I didn't wish him ill.

Feeling oddly numb, I glanced back at Widow Hu. "There is hope," I said quietly. "We can get you out of the city."

Hu looked at me sharply. "We're not staying to fight them off?"

"The king—King Justin—sent us back here ten days ago. Didn't Elena tell you? He's ordered us to try and save who we can and what we can so we can prepare for another battle." I wet my lips. I wasn't sure of such a decision. I wasn't sure we even had enough forces for another battle against the Darkening. Even without the magical powers Lord Vincent had, we'd be outnumbered.

"Good!" Hu said swiftly with a savage look I'd never expected to see on her face. "We'll show them Torvald's a force to reckon with."

I nodded and told her, "The king has our forces hidden in the wilds a few days away."

What's left of our forces, anyway.

"We'll be ready." Hu looked at the kids around her.

I glanced at them. Even little Elena looked as serious as any soldier. I didn't want to see any of them hurt, and they were no match for Lord Vincent's army—not for the Wildmen or the raiders from the South. I struggled to find the words to tell them these children were not really fit to join King Justin's army. "I came to help you all get out. To try to show you a route away," I said.

Widow Hu frowned. "Seb, you've been gone from Monger's

Lane for a time, but know this—this was our home. It's broken and battered, but this is a war. These folks don't just need a king to believe in, they need to stand up and stand on their own." She stared at me, her eyes magnified by the thick goggles. "Monger's Lane has always been a bit of a law unto itself, and now...now we've all suffered. And we aim to give some of that back." With a nod, she took a breath as if there was no more to say.

Turning, she started down the littered alleyway. The children followed her, so I did as well, all the while keeping an eye on the sky. I could hear distant clashes still—swords rang out or cries sounded. And sometimes the faint roar of a dragon carried to us. The Widow Hu's ragtag band followed her as fearlessly as I might have followed Commander Hegarty.

They really were a sort of family. Just as the Dragon Riders had become my family.

Kalax sent me a sort of snort, and thought to me, *You, me and Thea. We clutch.*

She was right—she and Thea and myself, the three of us had shared a lot. We had flown together, slept side-by-side and kept each other alive. Wasn't that the very definition of a good family?

"Come on, slowcoach!" Elena called out. She had stopped at the end of the alleyway and shouted back to me, waving a small arm. I picking up my pace and jogged to keep up with the fighters of Monger's Lane.

Around the next corner, the hairs stood up on the back of my neck. Kalax didn't so much think at me as she sent a feeling of uneasiness. My nose was filled with the sooty smell of hot air

27

and ash, but the breeze shifted and I smelled something else. The unmistakable musky scent of a dragon.

A dragon was near—I could sense it. It wasn't Kalax or any of the other dragons from the enclosure. This feeling was alien— it was wild and its mind was…different. I glanced up, but I couldn't see the shadow of the wild dragon…I couldn't hear it, yet.

I knew the affinity could be a two-way line of communication—if I could sense the wild dragon, it could sense me. I tried to clamp down on my thoughts, pushing away everything that might give me away as a Dragon Rider. If the wild dragon thought we were harmless, it might fly elsewhere, looking for a better fight.

"Seb?" Widow Hu glanced back at me.

I had stopped and now I crouched down low. I could hear the dragon now, a sharp rasp of a croaking, alligator-like roar from behind the buildings in front of us.

"Dragon," Hu muttered. The children around her knew enough to be silent. They stopped and ducked into any bit of rubble that might hide them.

I could sense the wild dragon searching and I worried that it must have felt me at the same time that I had felt its presence. I wanted to reach out to Kalax, but I had to stay still and quiet. But I could feel that she had sensed the danger that I was in and was about to take flight.

Kalax, no! I warned her.

Of course, a dragon does what a dragon wants to do. I might be able to use my affinity to command dragons—but it was only a powerful suggestion. Kalax would make up her own mind.

A sibilant, triumphant hiss filled the air as the wild dragon picked up on my thoughts to Kalax. I wondered if that would get the attention of other wild dragons—or was this one just angry about another dragon being near? I just had to pray that Kalax did not come to me. That would attract the attention of Lord Vincent and the Darkening. If that happened, we'd all be lost.

The wild Northern dragon was a creature I could handle. I wasn't a match, however, for the forces of the Darkening.

I wondered if this one dragon had decided to nest in the cinders here—maybe its wild nature had taken over and it just wanted to eat and rest.

"Children, back!" Hu muttered, her voice low.

I winced. Dragons had good hearing and even better sense of smell. The dragon would hear her words. I could only hope that the smoke from the fires had masked Kalax's scent.

The dragon's guttural hiss sounded again. Wood splintered and cracked as the dragon rose up, shaking itself from the rubble where it had been resting.

"To the shelter?" asked Joachim, his face pale.

I nodded and told Widow Hu, "Hurry. Take them with you. Get to the shelter and hide."

She shook her head and glanced at Sparrow and two gangly-looking boys I didn't know. The boys had slings and bows they had loosed. "You three, you know the drill," she said.

How many dragons have they faced already?

The three stood and hurried off in different directions.

Sparrow and the boy with the bow ran to the right, and the boy with the sling edged through the rubble toward the dragon.

I headed to Widow Hu and whispered, "Are you mad?" Another loud crunch sounded and I heard the wild dragon snuffling, as Kalax often did after a late daytime snooze.

Rolling her eyes, Widow Hu pointed to the corner just ahead of us. "We can head it off there. Unless you, Sir Dragon Rider, have a better plan?"

Before I could stop her, she hurried toward the gap in the houses ahead of us. I couldn't believe the half-blind, old Widow Hu was about to try to fight a dragon with only children to help her.

Even I wouldn't try to fight a dragon on my own. I headed after her, determined to stop her from making a very bad mistake. But she stopped, raised her staff and struck it hard against the cobbles. The sound echoed around us. I stopped and held my breath.

Just past the rubble, glittering, onyx scales shimmered in the sunlight. The wild black dragon was turning toward the Widow Hu.

The dragon roared again, its voice echoing through the wreckage. I could see its sinewy form. Compared to Kalax, it was thin, but barbed scales fanned out around its neck and jaw, and horns spiked its head. That head lifted now and I could see the dark eyes. Its head turned from side to side like a snake's.

This black was truly wild. I knew that at once. The Darkening wasn't controlling its actions right now. I wondered if it had broken free of Lord Vincent's control, or was this just a temporary freedom for the wild dragon?

Widow Hu lifted her staff and struck it against the cobbles so hard a flare of blue sparks came from the end. The wild black dragon couldn't resist the sudden noise and movement. Something strange had moved—it would attack.

Sword in my sweating hand, I braced for the worst.

CHAPTER 3
SEARCHING

Staring at the fires in Monger's Lane, I wondered how I would ever find Seb or any of his family. I wasn't even certain where his home was—or had been. In the time I'd known him, he had never talked much about his past and had never invited me to his house. He hadn't even wanted me with him when he'd escorted his family back to Torvald.

For me, on the other hand, it seemed as if everyone knew not just my family name but all about my brothers, my father and mother and, of course, the instructors had expected me to live up to House Flamma's reputation for producing the best Dragon Riders.

Your name or your skirts won't change what I need from you, Flamma! Instructor Mordecai had once shouted that at me—which was ridiculous really, because I had never asked for any special treatment. I had proven myself one of the best fighters, a solid protector. Growing up with two brothers, I'd had a lot of practice holding my own.

But while my family name had been impossible to escape from at the Academy, Seb's background as a nobody from Monger's Lane had singled him out for everyone expecting him to fail. He hadn't. He was the best navigator—and he had the Dragon Affinity. Not many could claim that. He'd even been teaching me how to communicate with Kalax with thoughts. But I could see why he'd never invited me to see where he'd once lived.

Monger's Lane looked a wreck now, but I could see from the tight press of ruined houses and the narrow streets that this had never been pretty. And it stank. I'd known it was the poorest part of Torvald. And everyone had heard you didn't go to Monger's Lane wearing rich clothes if you wanted to keep your money and life. My father had often muttered darkly about how it should be burned to the ground and rebuilt.

Well, now he'd gotten that wish.

Monger's Lane and all streets around it looked gutted by fire. Around it, the houses built from stone had mostly survived the dragons, the Wildmen and the raiders. Down here, the whole neighborhood had been crushed, and not just during the battle but over the past short time of looting and strife. Blackened piles of things that might have once been buildings littered the streets. The narrow lanes wound through the piles of charred wood as if they'd been planned by a demented, mostly blind spider. Tiny alleyways gave way to the entrances of now hollow warehouses. Streets didn't seem to lead anywhere. I could see no open plazas, gardens or public buildings—this wasn't anything like the wide streets I was used to. In the distance, I could hear the clash of metal on metal—fighting still going on. Cries echoed around us, but so far away from this place of desolation.

I was never going to find Seb.

Nudging my arm, Ryan asked, "When do we give this up?"

I glanced at him. "I didn't ask you to come. You invited yourself along. You can give up anytime. I won't. Seb's my navigator."

He gave me a crooked smile. "What? Leave all the fighting to you? And what else would I be doing—joining Father and Reynalt in their crazy thinking?"

"Thinking about treason," I muttered.

Ryan put a hand on my arm and stopped me. "I am *not* going to be telling King Justin any of what they said. I don't think you should, either."

I pulled away from him and started walking again, but I said, "Don't worry, I still hope it was only talk. I just can't believe Reynalt would ever consider trying to depose the rightful king. As for Father and Mother…?" I let the words trail off.

That was the entire problem.

I'd been at the deathbed of the old king when he'd declared Lord Vincent—his enemy—to be his rightful successor. The old king had obviously been under the influence of the Memory Stone. Luckily for us, the only other people to have been there had been Seb and Instructor Mordecai, who'd sworn us to silence on the matter.

Not that it should matter—King Justin had been the only heir to the throne. The only true heir. But he was young, and he, too, had come under the influence of the Memory Stone. What if Lord Vincent killed King Justin, or brought him under control of the Darkening? Or was King Justin still under the influence of that dark magic? Was his plan to attack Lord Vincent's forces just a way to lead us all to a final defeat?

Shoulders slumping, I glanced around at the ruined part of the city. We were headed into even more trouble, and I didn't want my family to be caught up in the midst of what could be a civil war on top of the war with the Darkening.

Ryan kicked a broken brick and said, "You know Reynalt. He always had a stick up his backside. He probably thinks he's doing right thing, and —"

The guttural croak of a dragon cut off his words. We both stopped and looked at each other.

Not one of ours? I mouthed the words.

Ryan shook his head and put a finger to his lips. He already had his sword in hand, as did I. King Justin had wisely asked us to enter the city on foot as our dragons could attract the enemy. I felt lost without Kalax at my side, and I was wishing this was a dragon from the enclosure—one of ours. But if Ryan did not recognize the dragon's call, this had to be one of the wild black dragons. We could only hope it was not serving Lord Vincent and the Darkening.

A crunch and the sudden bang of rock cracking against rock had me turning to see a building wall as it crashed to the ground. Dust choked the air.

Another sharp bang followed. I held up my hand and waved

that we should run to the other side of the street. Ryan nodded, and we ran.

The roar of an attacking dragon echoed over the ruined streets. I wasn't quite sure what we could do against a dragon with only our hand weapons—I didn't have my bow with me—but we had to do something. That wild dragon was attacking *something,* which would probably turn out to be a *someone.*

"Now!" A woman screamed the word.

We reached the other side of the street and saw an old woman standing at the far end of what had once been a narrow lane. A black dragon bore down on her, crushing houses and breaking glass as it advanced. I opened my mouth to shout to her, to tell her to duck behind the rubble. The dragon reared up and flexed its ruff of spines.

Suddenly, something struck the black dragon's nose. The dragon paused and shook its head. Another small rock bounced off the beast's head and dropped to the ground. The dragon was being pelted with cobblestones. The dragon blinked and shook its head.

More stones struck the dragon against the head, neck and hind quarters, pelting it like a hail storm. The dragon turned, whipping its barbed tail low across the street.

The old woman had just enough time to duck behind fallen wood timbers. The dragon's tail swept over the top of her, crashing into one of the few standing buildings. Walls exploded, the roofs fell in and dust billowed with a deafening thunder.

I gasped, but the old woman stood and shouted, "Now! Now!" Two figures jumped up from the top of a pile of wood that had once been a structure. They were children really, but they ran toward the dragon and threw nets over the beast's head before jumping and sliding down the wood timbers.

The dragon bellowed a roar and thrashed against the rope nets, rubbing at them with one foreleg. I realized they were fishing nets, the sort that river workers might use for a big catch. The dragon tore the nets off, but its jerky movements showed it was becoming flustered.

"They're only succeeding in annoying it. Why anger a wild dragon?"

"They're trying to scare it away!" Ryan pointed to where more tiny darts and rocks shot out from the rubble to hit the dragon.

The tactic never would have worked on a trained dragon, but the wild dragons liked easy hunting and resting grounds. Maybe this could drive it off.

Flinging the nets off, the black dragon reared backward on its hind legs. It looked as though it might tear into the sky. Suddenly, it rammed its claws down onto the ground with a thud that vibrated up my legs. "Oh, no. It's decided to fight."

The wild dragon shook its shoulders and wings, snapping off the remnants of the fishing nets. Now it was ignoring the stones that drummed against its scaled hide. It turned and headed for the old woman, its tail swishing like an angry cat.

The old woman slammed the bottom of her staff into the ground. "No, you don't."

A shout echoed over the ruins of Monger's Lane, but also in my mind. "Halt!" I felt the word in my chest. The dragon stopped, almost as if it had been frozen. I had only ever witnessed that kind of power before from two people—one had been Lord Vincent, or the Darkening working through Lord Vincent, and the other was…Seb.

Glancing around, I saw Seb step up to stand in front of the old woman. He put out a hand, palm toward the wild dragon. I could feel the wave of power radiating from him, as if he was a taut bowstring waiting to be released. I wondered what would happen if he did let go of his control. Could he command a dragon to do anything?

But I could see Seb's hand shaking. It had to be taking a lot of effort to try and wrest control of the wild beast from itself, and from the Darkening. I'd seen Seb use his Dragon Affinity to sense and interact with dragons, or to drive them away or pull them toward him. But how could he fully control a dragon that had no training—and no bonding with any human?

I hoped this would work. I didn't want to see anyone die today, not even a wild dragon. But this skill—controlling dragons and bending them to your will—was what the Darkening sought to do. It left me wondering just how close Seb's skills were to those of Lord Vincent. That wasn't a good thought. Lord Vincent had almost killed me. With a shiver, I kept watching.

The dragon's eyelids lowered. A tremor went through it as if it was fighting against Seb's affinity. Its black eyes twitched, flared to almost yellow and turned deep red once again.

Could the Darkening sense what was happening through the dragon? I hoped not.

"You will return to your mountain and never bother the

human world again," Seb commanded, his thoughts once again making that weird echo as I heard it in my mind and my ears.

The black dragon blinked and shook its head. It swayed as if trying to fight the suggestion Seb had given it. Even from this distance, I saw sweat glisten on Seb's face. The shaking of his hand spread to his arm.

The wild dragon's eyes flared again... and then all tension fled from its shoulders. Its wings relaxed, its mane of spikes settled back. It dropped its head, turned to sniff the air above as if scenting the best current to take. With a rattling noise, almost the sort of chirrup that Kalax made when pleased, the dragon leapt into the air.

Rubble clattered to the ground behind the dragon. The black shadow circled once. I thought it would fly north, but Seb gave a cry and fell to his knees. The dragon above us screamed as well.

"No!" Seb shouted.

"What is he doing? What is going on?" Ryan yelled. I ran for Seb's side, and Ryan matched my pace.

I crossed the ruined street in a moment. Seb knelt on the ground, holding his head with both hands. "Seb, snap out of it!" I held his arms and glanced at my older brother. "Ryan, where is the dragon?"

Ryan dropped his sword and picked up a long, broken beam of wood to use as a makeshift spear. He was doomed. We all were if the dragon came back to attack.

The dragon circled once more, cried out, then fell from the sky as if it had been struck by something. It hit the ground not one street over from us. Smoke billowed into the sky. I stared at Ryan and he stared back.

"No. no. There was no need… No need," Seb muttered. He looked up at me. He wasn't shaking as much, and he wiped the tears from his eyes. "They killed it. The Darkening killed it for disobeying." Seb looked up at me through eyes shining with tears, and I knew at once who he meant.

The Darkening and Lord Vincent. They had somehow snapped the mind or the heart of the wild dragon rather than let it submit to the will of another.

"Come on," I said, helping Seb up to his feet. "We have to get you out of here, and your friends, too."

ॐ

"You sure he'll be well?" Ryan asked once more.

"Seb will be just fine," I said, making the words firm. I was certain I hadn't even convinced myself. "But, uh, you know what you were talking about not talking about?"

Ryan rolled his eyes. "You don't have to remind me. Does the king know of…of your navigator's skills?"

I shrugged. "Remember all the chaos and confusion at camp when we were attacked by that massive black dragon and Lord Vincent?" His face tightened, but he nodded. "Well—most of you woke up from the enchantment then because of Kalax, Seb and me. So I am fairly certain King Justin knows, as does Reynalt and Commander Hegarty. They've been trying to find ways to put Seb's Dragon Affinity to the best use." *Or they're ignoring it altogether.*

He glanced at Seb. "Just don't spread it around too much that my sister is partnered with a freak."

"Ryan!" I thumped his shoulder, but he was already grinning.

He held up his hands. "Joke." He shook his head.

"Haven't we got better things to do right now?" I muttered, looking toward the ruined fortifications.

The sight of the palace, or what was left of it, deeply saddened me. The defenders had done a valiant job of trying to defend it, but many of the towers had been destroyed, and the vast scale of the structure left entire wings that had to be abandoned during the battle. Parts of it still seemed to be smoldering. But, after ransacking it, the Wildmen and the Southern Raiders had left the palace. It was about the safest place to be since most of the gates and walls still held strong.

I was worried about Seb. We'd gone with him to the shelter where he had found his mother again after having been separated from her. The shelter had been crowded with people—and it stank. I'd been glad to leave it. I hadn't wanted to tell Seb anything about my parting from my own family. I'd just made it clear that we needed to get back to the king. And anyone who could walk needed to head for the hills and safety. Seb's family had seemed to understand that he had Dragon Rider business, and it would be safer for them to stay with the other citizens. Besides, Seb's mother was intent on staying long enough to find her husband—if she could.

We gave them directions to follow, but when we turned to go, too, Seb's little sister had clung to him. When we left, he was looking pale and glum. I'd asked him if he was all right. He had just shrugged and said in a low voice soaked with misery, "I don't belong here anymore."

He meant Monger's Lane—not the shelter—and he was right. The others were treating him as if he had grown wings and a tail. Some of the children watched him with rounded eyes, whispering behind their hands until scolded.

"And I am not Agathea Flamma, a lady waiting to make an alliance that will improve my family's standing," I'd told him.

I'd wanted to tell him that these people respected him. I'd wanted to reason with him. In the shelter, I saw things I had never seen before. Those people were pulling together—the noble families weren't.

Seb had just muttered doubtfully, "Family isn't just who you're born as, it's who you find. Down in Monger's Lane, they found each other when they had to rely on someone."

As we strode toward the palace, I thought about that. It was a far cry from everything I had been brought up to believe. Your blood ties were supposed to be the most important thing about you—and who you married. The house name had to be kept alive through the centuries. This was something I'd been taught to respect and never question. In a way, that was what Reynalt, Mother and Father must be thinking. They could abandon Torvald if that could keep the future of the Flamma name secure.

There was a certain logic to it. But what would happen to those people down in the city if King Justin lost another battle?

Would they be punished by Lord Vincent as that wild dragon had been? Would Lord Vincent enslave them?

I didn't know. In some ways, it was nice to know that we had our orders. We were Dragon Riders first and had to trust that Commander Hegarty and the new king had a plan of attack against our enemy—the Darkening.

Unfortunately, I knew the new king a little too well. He wasn't going to be happy that we didn't really have anyone from the city who wanted to join in the king's offensive.

"Next stop, the palace," Ryan announced, pulling me from my thoughts. "We'll meet King Justin and see what luck he has had in trying to gather the nobles." He shot a dark look at me and said, "We'll also see what we have left of the Royal Trove."

Torvald Palace had been the seat of the ruling family for hundreds of years. It had stood almost as long as the Dragon Academy, which had taken over from the Draconis Order monastery, the original builders. Over all those generations, the palace had grown as each monarch added their stamp. Multiple wings, galleries, walls and towers housing everything from royal astronomers to aviaries covered acres of land.

Now, however, fire blackened the gray stone. Towers lay toppled in the gardens. Dragons had scampered across the roofs and turrets, scattering slate tiles and leaving huge holes. But even an invading army couldn't completely destroy the palace—the central three keeps, the oldest part of the palace, still stood, tall and proud, and, for the moment, quiet.

Ryan lifted a hand to give me the signal. I cupped my hands around my mouth and gave a high, shrill whistle.

We waited.

An arrow streaked up into the sky, white and red ribbons fluttering from the shaft. It struck the ground a few feet from us.

The colors meant nothing new to report and all was safe to enter. Those in the palace had to be as worried about where the enemy might be—we still had Wildmen and raiders roaming the city.

Glancing back at the city, I thought of the shelter where Seb had met up with his family. The building had been more of a cellar. They had food and water, but most were too old, too hurt, or too young to join King Justin's attack. They needed to hide—they needed us to keep them safe. Would the king see that, too?

I also wondered what the Darkening would think of Seb's skills. Would they be interested in him? I hoped not.

"So we go in?" I asked.

Seb shrugged, but Ryan nodded and said, "They didn't answer with three reds."

"Maximum threat," Seb muttered.

It was my turn to shrug. I knew enough flag and symbol navigation to help my navigator spot things, but I'd trained as a protector. One of the few female protectors ever. I could fight. I left reading maps to Seb, so I asked, "What are we waiting for?"

The gates were all guarded now and barricaded. We headed to the south wall and found the rope that had been thrown over and left for us. I went up first and stopped at the top to scan the area. All looked safe. Seb came up next and then Ryan. We shifted the rope to the inside of the wall and slid down it and into the garden below.

Gravel crunched under foot. Statues had been smashed by the Wildmen. I noticed the head of a cherub looking up at us mournfully from the shallows of one fountain.

Inside the palace walls, all seemed quiet. The Wildmen that Lord Vincent and the Darkening were using seemed a long way away. It was odd to be in the quiet gardens without hearing music or fanfares. The royal court was certainly no longer in attendance on the king.

Heading to the central towers, I thought it looked mostly deserted. We headed up the stairs. To the right, I could see what had once been the main ballroom—most of the wall was gone and the checkerboard marble floor was strewn with broken chandeliers and the stubs of candles. The Wildmen marauders had clearly spent time ripping down the tapestries and curtains, but they had not stopped to rest. They were nowhere in sight.

Lord Vincent must be driving them pretty hard.

I'd heard childhood stories that the Wildmen liked bright colors and metals. Had they stopped to take what they could, or were they under such tight control through the Memory Stone and the Darkening that they could only fight? If they had been bought, that might be something that could work in our favor one of these days.

Inside the central towers, the atrium of the First Dragon had once held a statue of an immense dragon—the First Dragon. Twin staircases led upward. However, the First Dragon was no more. It looked as though it had cost considerable effort, but the statue had been brought down to shatter on the floor. The marble lay scattered and chipped into piles.

Something teased at my memory, but I couldn't quite place it. Something about this statue? No, it was gone. I followed after Seb and Ryan as they headed up the stairs to the first landing.

A friendly voice called out. "Hey!"

Looking up, I saw the welcome sight of Varla's pale face and sunlight glinting off the optics Merik wore to see better. He had his flying goggles pushed up on his head. Varla's red hair glinted bright and she waved down at us, her dragon armor looking as if she had polished it. Merik held what looked like a meat pastry in one hand, and I realized then I was hungry.

I waved back as we clambered to the second landing where they stood. After a brief round of hugs and much clapping of shoulders, I asked them what the situation was.

Merik grimaced. His dark skin looked even darker, stained as it was with soot from the fires. He hadn't washed, but Varla must have, for no soot stained her cheeks. "Not the best," he admitted, looking to Varla.

She nodded. "Other riders have returned—they became separated from Commander Hegarty and the king before the battle. They claim they traveled to the Academy to see if they could help, but they're...they're still struggling when trying to recognizing people." Varla stared at a very nondescript patch on the floor. I could tell she wasn't happy with this.

"So? That's good news if it means more help. What of it?" I said, but I could see there was something else that she wasn't telling me.

Merik waved his meat pie. "Come on. Come eat. And you might as well know all—it's not just that they must have come under the influence of Lord Vincent's Memory Stone…they kept on talking about the rightful king."

My chest tightened. I shared a worried look with my brother. *Please don't let them be saying Reynalt, please don't let them be saying Reynalt Flamma!*

Next to me, Seb shifted on his feet, and he said, "Who do they say is king?"

"Lord Vincent." Varla huffed out a breath. "They keep on babbling that Lord Vincent is the rightful High King of the Three Realms by dint of conquest."

My shoulders eased down. "Is *that* all? We can deal with that, can't we, Seb?"

Lines creased Seb's forehead as he frowned even deeper. "You saw what happened out there when I tried with that poor wild dragon. What if the Darkening does the same thing again—but with someone?"

"So…we just give up and let them win us over one by one?" Ryan said.

"Ryan is right, Seb—we still have to do what we can." I turned to Varla and Merik. "Who's been saying this?"

"Beris and Syl," Varla said. She turned to lead us deeper into the palace. "You'd better see this."

❧❧❧

Of all of the people I wouldn't have minded turning against us, Beris and Syl were top of that list. That pair of bullies had taken joy in stirring up trouble. But we were all Dragon Riders, and we needed each other.

Beris and Syl were each tied to a chair in a small—by Torvald Palace standards—room. A round mahogany table stood next to the narrow tower windows, built in the days when only arrow slits were added to any tower. Plush carpets as yet undamaged lay on the floor and a few paintings had been saved and stacked in one corner. That was better than having them destroyed—but how many other things would we never recover? And would that list include more riders?

Struggling against his bonds, Beris glared at me, his small dark eyes seeming half-empty. He no longer wore his armor and his tunic had been torn at one shoulder, as if he'd been in a fight. Syl had a bruise on one cheek and while he still had his armor breastplate, he had lost his helmet—just like Beris. Both of them had dusty boots, and I wondered where their blue dragon was right now.

I could no longer hate either Beris or Syl at that moment. It wasn't their fault they were under the control of the Darkening. It *was* their fault that they were such awful people generally, but maybe they would learn something from this after Seb brought them 'round.

I highly doubted it, but still I held some hope.

Beris grunted again, struggling so much that he jostled Syl, who sat next to him. They had been gone, along with most of the other Dragon Riders, to be a part of Commander Hegarty's doomed mission to the north. That mission had left the Academy and the city nearly defenseless, and I was sure that had been Lord

Vincent's doing, acting through the Memory Stone to give Commander Hegarty the idea that he could win if he took a large enough force of Dragon Riders north.

The truth was they had encountered the enemy—but the Memory Stone and the Darkening itself had cast a terrible enchantment over the cavalcade, scattering them into the wilderness while Lord Vincent's Wildmen and wild dragons attacked Torvald. Seb and I had managed to break the spell, but it seemed Seb hadn't managed to help all the riders.

I still don't know what part in the attack on Torvald Beris and Syl played, or even if they had been part of that battle. Had they merely stood back, confused and forgetting everything? I'd seen that happen to those under the control of the Memory Stone. I was just glad now that Varla and Merik had them tied up.

"Release them," Seb said. He knelt on one knee before them. I could feel the waves of something like pressure, like a stiff breeze, coming from him. He was trying to break the enchantment that the Darkening had on them, trying to return them to their normal selves through his Dragon Affinity. If he could connect them to their dragon, Gaxtal, it might work.

I wasn't really sure how Seb did what he did, but he'd helped me connect to Kalax so I could share thoughts with her. And I could definitely feel when Seb used his affinity, but was that because I had spent so long training and riding partnered with him? Or was it because we were both bonded through Kalax? I looked at Ryan, who stood in the doorway, his arms crossed over his chests and a frown tight on his face. He looked as if he didn't like any of this obviously unnatural stuff.

"Back off, tinker!" Beris snarled in a voice thick with venom. I shuddered. That wasn't his voice. He sounded too much like Lord Vincent. Goose bumps lifted on my skin, and I had to push back the memory of when Vincent had tried to kill me.

Seb closed his eyes. Sweat slicked his forehead. His breathing became faster, and he put a hand to his forehead. For a minute, Beris' face seemed to blank, and Syl held very still. But then Seb opened his eyes, stood and shook his head. "It's no good. I can't reach them—they aren't dragons. Their minds are…are too fragile."

Said humans have small minds. The thought came to me from Kalax. She had made it clear long ago she thought humans were extremely useful but weren't a patch on dragons.

"That's right, tinkerer and Lady Flamma." Beris snarled the words, sending a chill down my spine. Beris Veer from the House Veer would never call me *Lady* Flamma. He thought I was lowering myself to ride with Sebastian Smith, and he didn't think any female should be a protector.

Beris tipped back his head. "You have no power over us because you are not the rightful heir. You have no authority. No crown. All of you—a bunch of usurpers! Where is that pretender? Bring him and I will remind him who is his rightful master."

So that was the plan—Beris and Syl had been sent to try and pull King Justin under Lord Vincent's control again.

Ryan let out a low growl and stepped into the room, fury in his eyes. I could see now just how deep his bond was to his protector and fellow rider, the king.

"Ryan," I said with a tone of warning. I put a hand on his chest. "It's not his fault—he doesn't know."

A new voice from the doorway interrupted. "Doesn't know what?"

I spun around to see King Justin, flanked by two of his men-at-arms. He looked older than he had only a short time ago—silver hairs had appeared in his light hair. He was still handsome but lines now marked grooves around his mouth and eyes and on his forehead, and his eyes seemed a paler blue. He didn't seem like the young man who always used to be laughing. He gave a nod to Ryan. Varla, Merik, Seb and I all gave low bows.

"All hail the king!" We all chanted the words; well, all of us except Beris and Syl.

Beris gave an ugly snicker. "The *king?* This pup? What your former playmate hasn't told you, Prince, is that your father announced his successor as Lord Vincent."

I glanced at Seb. He looked pale. No one else except Mordecai knew of this—and that meant Beris must have gotten that information from Lord Vincent himself.

King Justin's voice grew very quiet and he held very still. I had seen this quiet anger from him many times before when we were growing up. Justin had been raised a prince and taught to keep his emotions in check. But whenever I had bested him at archery or in a race, he'd grown quiet like this. "I beg your pardon, rider?" His hand fell to the hilt of the fine sword hung in a scabbard at his side. He glanced at me.

I glanced away, for I knew he would see the lie in me if he questioned me. But then he spoke again and I had to look back.

"If we cannot make use of this little traitor, my men will see to his fate." The king started to turn away.

Seb stepped forward, one hand held out. "No. I mean, King Justin, forgive me, but this is just what the Darkening wants—to drive wedges between us, to squabble when we should be uniting, to turn on our own."

The king paused. I could see he was weighting Seb's words. "Rider Smith, what would you have me do? Set free someone who clearly harbors ill intentions toward me?"

"He's ill, sire." Seb spread his hands wide. "Just as you were, as we all once were, when the Darkening made us forget almost everything."

Bad move, Seb. Never remind a king of his own weakness.

The king glanced at Beris, then at Syl and back to Seb. I held my breath. Justin's hand fell to his side. "Then you had better make him well again. We have a war to win!" Turning, the king left, his men following him. He called Ryan to attend him, saying, "We have maps to chart."

I looked at Seb, who shrugged. "I couldn't let them just execute them."

"No, you couldn't." Rubbing a hand over my face, I wished now that I'd taken Merik up on his offer of food. Merik and Varla stood in the far corner of the room, trying hard not to be noticed by the king. "We need to remember how we broke the enchantment before. Didn't we have the Armor Stone?"

Seb nodded. "We used it to protect *all* the dragons we could, and through them, their riders. But we don't have the Armor

Stone or the Healing Stone, and my affinity just isn't powerful enough."

"That's it, give it up. You never liked me anyway," Beris muttered. I thought I heard a hint of fear in his voice. Was the real, pugnacious bully that was Beris trapped somewhere behind Lord Vincent's control, able to see what was happening, but unable to do anything other than as he was commanded? It was a terrifying thought.

Not hunt enemy? Kalax's voice sounded in my head. Seb had told me once that dragons have no word for execution. They hunt and will fight for territory or to protect their kin. They never decide to kill someone just because it might make their life easier.

I saw Seb flinch and wondered if he was trying to think to tell Kalax about what our king wanted to do with Beris and Syl. I felt rather than heard something pass between Seb and Kalax, and then an angered rasp echoed in my mind, making me wince.

Never kill clutch-mate rider. The king thinks that Beris and Syl are a threat. I thought the words to Kalax.

Riders not threats. Take weapons, leave in the wilds. There. Done. Make their own territory. But this—this is wrong.

I felt the powerful uplift of our dragon as she took to the night air, gliding soft and low over the landscape toward us.

I will come. Take them to Gaxtal. Seb and Thea not do this.

I felt a surge of intense gratitude and pride that Kalax was willing to save us from ourselves. *Save us from ourselves...* The thought struck me and I looked at Seb.

He was grinning, nodding. "Kalax?" he said out loud.

"Didn't you tell me that all dragons can think to each other? Even from long, long distances?"

Dragons have many ways and more languages than humans, she answered.

"Could you *talk* to Beris and Syl or to Gaxtal? Reach them?" Seb glanced at me. "It wasn't *my* special powers that broke the enchantment before, it was all of us. Kalax, you, me...all of us reaching together!" He turned to Varla and Merik and waved them over. "We need everyone."

The two of them swapped an uncomfortable look, but they headed over to Seb's side.

Yes.

I didn't know which of us had thought that one word—me, Kalax or Seb—but I wanted this to work. I grasped Seb's hand, Varla took my hand and Merik took her hand and then put a hand on Syl's shoulder. He cursed. Seb put a hand on Beris' shoulder.

"Get your hands off your betters." Beris struggled against the ropes holding him.

Shush, little human, Kalax snuffled at Beris, and then her dragon senses unfurled through me.

For a dizzying moment, I could almost sense as a dragon does. She could smell every stitch of cloth that still hung from the walls, and the smoke from the fires warmed her. The smells of battle and blood were nothing to her. But another layer bubbled up from underneath that sense—as if everything had color and shape. It was as if she sensed every memory or feeling or thought.

Can dragons smell minds?

I felt Seb drawing closer to Beris' mind and calling out, but a shadow hung between us. It seemed almost like a dark fog that was hard to see through, but Kalax could see past that. I started to sense Syl and Beris, and suddenly a connection snapped to Gaxtal, who I could sense was waiting for them not far from the city. The connections between us seemed to sharpen—like colored lines appearing out of the fog. I thought of all the times I had sparred with Beris, or the times Syl and I had struggled in training. These connections, these threads and attachments, made them who they were.

A gasp sounded, then another. I snapped back into myself. Blinking, I opened my eyes—I hadn't even known I'd closed them.

Beris sat in the same chair, blinking rapidly, his eyes wet with unshed tears. Syl had his head down, but I could hear him gulping in air as if he'd run for miles.

Beside me, Seb gave a groan and started to slump down. I grabbed for him and so did Varla. We caught him and got him stretched out on the floor.

"Is he okay?" Varla asked. She glanced at me, her forehead wrinkled.

I shrugged and kept one hand on Seb's chest. At least he was still breathing and I could feel his heart pounding. "It just seems to take so much out of him."

Seb's eyes flashed open. "The Dragon Stone—the king's stone."

I glanced at him. He had his eyebrows pulled tight as if he

had a headache, and I wondered how much more of this he could do.

Even Varla and Merik swapped worried glances.

Sitting up, Seb started talking fast. "I saw it. The dragons remember it. There is one stone that controls them all—the Memory Stone, the Healing Stone, the Armor Stone. There is one King Dragon Stone that controls them all. The old monks knew of it—the Draconis Order."

I glanced at Varla, who shrugged, and Merik, who was staring, wide eyed, at Seb. But Merik's eyes always looked big behind the optics he wore to help his bad eyesight. Looking back at Seb, I said, "The king is busy preparing for a war—a battle. We don't have time to go chasing legends right now." Even just talking about that one Dragon Stone left me worried. The other stones seemed to have hurt us more than they'd helped.

Beris gave a groan. "Why am I tied up? What's going on?"

Syl muttered, "I think I'm going to be sick."

I nodded to Varla. "Can you untie them?"

She bit her lip but she nodded.

Glancing at Seb, I asked him, "Are you sure about this?"

He was looking pale—even more so than Syl. He pushed my hands away and stood. "We need to get back to the Academy. We have to find out everything we can about the Dragon Egg Stones —all of them."

I shook my head. "Our duty—to the king?"

Seb rubbed a hand over his face. "Me and Merik—we'll cover for you. You and Varla go. Find what you can."

"If there are still any books left," Varla muttered. She'd

untied Beris and he was untying Syl now. They were going to have a lot of apologizing to the king, but maybe they'd be able to make up for what had happened with some information on Lord Vincent.

Merik gave a nod and patted Seb on his shoulder. "We'll cover."

I opened my mouth to protest, but Seb was already waving his hands for us to clear out. "Go on, Thea. This really can't wait. Get back as soon as you can." Varla grabbed my arm and started for the door, pulling me with her. I shot a look back to see Seb leaning on Merik. Behind them, Beris and Syl were just starting to stand, both looking as if they might be sick; their skin was so pale and their hands shaky. Seb didn't look much better.

How is Seb going to be able to cover for anyone, in his state?

But Seb wanted information, and I had to help Varla get safely back here.

❧

"The Academy," Varla said, pointing to a dark shape.

The sun had set and before the battle, the Academy would have had torches lit. There should be guards and noise and the sounds of irritable dragons trying to get some sleep. Tonight, I could only see darkness. The lonesome screech of an owl echoed from somewhere over the brow of the hill that led up to the Academy.

"Weapons," I whispered, raising my sword in one hand. I

wore a small, buckler shield high on my other forearm, near the elbow. I didn't know what we might find.

Beside me, Varla nodded, pulling her long sword, which she held two-handed. I had seen Varla fight many times before, but usually in practice. I still hoped we could get in and out without trouble. We'd decided walking would be safer than bringing dragons into this—we were trying to be quiet and stealthy.

I stumbled on something and looked down. A wickedly curved claw, almost as long as my sword, lay on the ground—it must have been torn from a wild dragon. "Curse him," I muttered.

"Who?" Varla hissed.

"The Darkening. Lord Vincent. Leading people and dragons to their deaths." It wasn't right. We had to find some means to defeat the Darkening forever.

The front gates of the Academy lay on the ground, broken into splinters. They'd been by an iron-shod collection of poles, bound together to form a giant battering ram. I was just glad I couldn't see—or smell—any bodies. The Wildmen were said to carry off their own dead, and to eat the dead of any enemies. I was hoping that last part wasn't true.

With a shudder, I stepped over the rubble and into the main yard, which had once been our practice yard. Moonlight glinted off broken weapons and battered armor. Again, I didn't see any horned helmets or cloaks of the Dragon Riders.

"Someone has cleared away our dead," I said, knowing with certainty that we had lost lives that night.

"But why would the Wildmen do that—bury their enemies?" Varla said. "You don't think the old stories are—"

"Let's not think. Maybe it's some strange tribal custom of theirs?"

"Look!" Varla pointed up to the map tower, which was now a blackened spur of rock. Merik would hate to see that—the map room had been his retreat and domain. "They set fire to it?" Varla's voice held a tremor.

Glancing at the blackened stone of the keep, I said, "I think that they tried to set fire to the whole Academy—only most of it is made of stone. If the map room is gone, what's left?"

"There might be some books left." Varla's voice sounded stiff. The Academy had been her home for far longer than it had been mine. She was technically only a couple of years ahead of me, but she had lost her first flying partner and been forced to wait and study, until her dragon accepted Merik. It had been a rare thing for a dragon to take a rider in place of a first choice.

"Varla?" I hesitated, wondering if I had been wrong about her before. Maybe she *wasn't* as strong as I thought she was.

"It's okay." I heard the leather of her jerkin creak as she straightened. "It's just—it's just that I always thought...you know our room is gone."

I nudged her shoulder "It was too small for us."

She gave a hard sniff. "It was here that—that I finally had friends."

"Oh, for…" I slapped an arm around her shoulder. "You still have that. Now—where do we search? Seb wants anything we can find on the Dragon Stones."

Pulling away, she said, "I think we should split up. I'll take the keep. The commander might have kept some books in his rooms, or up in storage."

"I'll check the staff's old quarters. Maybe one of them had something that could help us out."

"Done. Meet back here as soon as we're done?" Varla said. To my surprise, I found myself agreeing with her as if she was the one giving orders now.

Let her feel strong. The First Dragon knows that we all need that right now!

She jumped easily over the shattered wooden beams and scattered stones and disappeared inside the keep.

I turned in the opposite direction, heading around the side of the main keep, heading for the buildings at the back. I didn't want to tell Varla what I'd *really* come here for—somewhere in this rubble lay the body of the old king and perhaps that of Instructor Mordecai. They needed to be found—they *deserved* to be found.

I'd set fire to them, I had decided, surprised at my own clarity of thought about what I needed to do. They at least needed someone to say a few words over them.

As I stepped over the soot-blackened door that led into the kitchen—and from there to quarters—my boots crunched on broken glass and dirt tramped or blown in from the training yard. A sense of terrible finality settled into my stomach, as if this really was the end of days. This might be the last time I ever set foot in the Academy.

But we do what we have to do for those we love. I stepped further into the darkness.

My steps echoed down the corridors. I didn't remember the Academy being this foreboding, but I had never been far into the kitchen or the instructor's quarters. We'd had cleaners and servants to deal with this. Smoke choked the air and smashed pottery littered the floor. A number of the rooms that could be easily broken into had been and the contents—from clothes to tapestries to food—had been either dragged out and trampled on or taken. It looked as though the Wildmen had sought to set numerous fires in the rooms but the ancient stone had ultimately defeated them. Some of the rooms were completely blackened, but the fires hadn't spread.

In one room, a couple of old, horned dragon helmets sat on the floor, dented and sad looking.

No bodies.

I let out a breath and crossed to the heavy iron-barred door that led to more instructors' quarters. The door was heavy and difficult to open, and as soon as I did, the foul smell of sulfur had me choking. Like acrid, rotten eggs, it made my eyes run. Putting a scarf over my face, I headed down the hall.

Feeling my way, for I had hardly any light, I walked down the hallway. A few fires gave me enough light not to trip over anything. I stopped and stared at one door that looked as though it had been blown out *against* the far wall, from the inside.

I peered in, finding the room gutted by fire. That foul smell swirled around me, so I hurried on to find the same situation in the next room and the next. These rooms must have been studies.

Had the Wildmen or the raiders set fire to the doors, heedless of what potions or supplies might be held inside?

I stepped forward again.

Out of a bare patch of wall, a large shadow lurched at me. A club with a small spiked iron ball at its head fell toward me.

I just managed to deflect the blow with the shield on my arm. The heavy thud of the mace reverberated through the buckler and up my arm. Had I not been wearing armor, my arm would have been broken. My attacker was much wider and larger than I was, but shorter. He moved fast and whisper-quick as he lashed out again, driving me back up the corridor. He had come out of nowhere and I realized he must have used a secret passage, and I could think of only one person who would know such things.

I blocked his next blow and asked, half panting out the words, "Instructor Mordecai?"

He lowered his mace and stared at me, his chest heaving. He gave a nod. "Ah, Flamma. Late, as usual I see."

CHAPTER 4
NEW ALLIANCES

Danger!

The thought spread through me like a wave and it took me a moment to realize it hadn't been mine, but Kalax's.

What is it? I thought back at her, trying to keep one eye on the king and Ryan, who were arguing about what to do with the now recovered Beris and Syl. Ryan was being polite, but the king didn't want to change his mind. Beris and Syl knelt on hard stone, heads bowed, and I was starting to think that was going to be punishment enough—it didn't look comfortable.

I stood next to Merik in a corner of the room, with one of the king's men-at-arms standing next to us, a wearied look on her face. Merik was nursing the black eye I had pretended to give him, and I had my arms crossed over my chest, trying my best to look as annoyed as possible. In order to distract the king, the only plan that I had been able to come up with was to have a fight with Merik over the fate of Beris and Syl, and now it was looking like we'd all end up under reprimand. Ryan was arguing that the king needed every Dragon Rider he had—and I thought he was starting to convince the king.

Sending my thoughts back to Kalax, I asked, *what danger?*

Smell Wildmen. Enclosure. Academy.

Tensing, I shifted on my feet. The king's guard took notice of my sudden movement—she seemed to think I was about to pounce on Merik once more. Hand dropping to her sword hilt, she glared at me. I glared back at the guard, and told Kalax, *It's going to take me time to get to you.*

"Watch yourself," the guard muttered, standing a little straighter.

I dropped my arms and faced her. "You don't understand. There's trouble at the Academy."

King Justin looked over at me. "Rider Smith? Isn't it enough that you have upset one meeting already?"

"No...I mean, yes, I mean, sire, we have...there are still dangers nearby." He had no real reason to trust me or my affinity. Now I wished Thea had stayed—the king might have listened to her.

Taking too long. Going to hunt. I felt Kalax leap into the air, her muscles rippling as her wings unfurled.

No—you need me!

Ha! Little Seb, dragons never need humans. Liking you joins us together. I could feel her amusement as she shared her thoughts with me.

Every beat of her wings brought with it a rush of excitement. I was certain Kalax was in danger—there were so many wild dragons still near the city. Surely they could smell her. It was then that I realized some of the strange benefits that I could give to our bond.

The Dragon Affinity wasn't just about controlling a dragon—although the Darkening used it that way. It was about sharing the minds and the senses of dragons. As Kalax sped down from the mountain, heading to the Academy and keeping her glide barely above tree height, I sensed her searching the horizon for enemies.

Stretching out my own senses, I could feel, smell and hear things going on at a far distance from the city. Dark shadows in the shape of passing dragons were gliding just a few leagues away. They caught Kalax's scent, but I sent out a suggestion that it was no threat—this was an old smell.

Their interest quickly faded. It was working because Hammal Mountain always smelled of other dragons due to the dragon enclosure.

Kalax was safe, but I began to slip away from this room. Words became distant and ghostly. I was swept up in being with Kalax, skimming the tops of trees, smelling the air and the night —it seemed far more real than anything else.

Careful, Kalax warned. She pushed me back a little. With a blink, I was back in the room with the king and the others. Only a part of me was still with Kalax. I wondered if this was how the Darkening came to be. Had Lord Vincent once been caught up in this need to join minds and then control others?

No! Kalax thundered in my mind, disgusted that I could think such a thing. *Evil comes from hatred...fear and greed. Sharing hearts is good. You have no needs to feed and feed—you have all you want.*

Well—it would be great to be able to fly on my own, I half-joked with her, but I sent her my gratitude for her confidence in me.

And then I sensed her sweeping down on a group of thirty Wildmen heading for the shattered gates of the Dragon Academy.

I gave a gasp, and Merik nudged my shoulder, but I was too caught up in what had happened to the Academy. Through Kalax's eyes, I saw the walls still stood, but scorch marks from fires had blackened the stone and the deep grooves of dragon claws had left scars. The wooden platforms where dragons had once landed hung in splintered tatters over the sides of the wall. The map tower lay in rubble.

"The Academy is gone!" I whispered. My stomach gave a sharp lurch even to say the words out loud.

Stone stands. A cave is a cave still. Good enough to make a home here if we need. Kalax's casual thoughts reassured me. But I still couldn't help but feel regret tugging at me.

When Kalax looked down at the centuries-old Academy, she just saw another human den—one that had lasted for a fraction of time in the whole scheme of things. She did not see the memories or the lost knowledge, the books gone, the flags and armor of past riders. She just saw it as a place we could use for shelter if we wanted it.

I wondered if her view was better or worse than mine, but a flurry of arrows from the Wildmen jarred me from such thoughts.

The arrows clattered off Kalax's scales, but I winced and pulled in a breath.

"What's wrong, Seb?" Merik poked at my ribs.

I shook my head. *Too many!* I thought to tell Kalax, but her anger was rising like a flame in her throat.

She swooped low over the fallen gates, buffeting the first rank of the Wildmen with her wings, sending them sprawling. But the Wildmen—although controlled by Lord Vincent and the Darkening—knew how to fight dragons. A few at the back of the group crouched low and drew back their bows. Others were readying their long spears and nets.

And then a sound reverberated through the night—a low, sad call that I had thought I would never hear again.

The Dragon Horn called out—someone sounded it. I heard the horn in multiple echoes through Kalax's ears as well as my own.

In the room around me, all talk stopped. "The Dragon Horn," King Justin said, breathing out the words with a touch of awe.

The shock and command of hearing that call slammed me back into my body. I slumped against the wall, for it felt odd to be back in my own body and not sharing Kalax's flight.

Pushing off the wall, I said, "The Academy is in danger— there are Dragon Riders still there!"

The king nodded—he was a Dragon Rider, too, and he knew that the summons of the Dragon Horn could not be ignored. He nodded at me and Merik. "Go. And tell the idiot blowing the horn to shut up before they draw down every wild dragon this side of the mountains!"

Too late for that, I thought, feeling the echoing call of the wild dragons that were near the city. Kalax had wheeled and turned and was swooping down for another attack. I turned to Merik.

With a slap against my arm, Merik pointed at the door. "Ferdinania won't mind giving you a lift, I think. Although you'll owe her some fish." Merik grinned. We raced out of the room to rescue our partners.

Before we'd gotten down one flight of steps, a voice called out from behind us. "Wait!"

I turned to see Beris and Syl rushing after us. I tensed, half expecting Beris to throw a punch or point out how stupid I was being. His face still pale, Beris came up to me. "Gaxtal is by the palace gates. We can help. The king has given us leave to prove our loyalty."

I looked at him for the briefest second, still aware through Kalax of the clatter of black arrows and the readying of long spears.

I hope this is the right decision.

With a nod, I said, "Come on."

I kept a sliver of awareness with Kalax as I greeted Ferdinania as properly as I could. Ferdinania was an older dragon— one who had chosen Varla as her rider long before she had accepted Merik. In the pale moonlight, she regarded me coolly, but when Merik relayed to her that Varla was in danger, she hunched down so I could climb up on her back. I was a bit more worried about Gaxtal. The blue dragon that Beris and Syl partnered with still looked a little groggy, for he was slowly blinking his eyes and looking around as if he wasn't sure where he was. Gaxtal, too, must have been under the control of the Memory Stone and the Darkening's enchantment.

Still, this was not the time for wise caution. I swung up into the unfamiliar protector's saddle on the back of Ferdinania, feeling awkward and uncomfortable at riding another dragon.

So you should! Kalax thought at me, laughing as she threw out her claws to destroy two ground lances. The Wildmen had lit fires and held torches high. I saw that a heavy rope net had caught at Kalax's claws, tangling the talons. Kalax flew high into the air and landed on the wall of the Academy with a snarl. She turned her head, and I heard what she had heard—the rush and beat of wild dragon wings.

We'll be there soon! I thought at Kalax.

Ferdinania launched into the air and Merik helped guide her to the Academy—we didn't have far to go. The cold, night air rushed over my face, and I was sorry now I didn't have goggles like Merik or a proper helmet. Glancing down, the pale walls of the Academy loomed up and I saw the assembled forces of the Wildmen below. They turned and glanced up, faces going pale in the firelight when they saw us. Three dragons against thirty trained fighters seemed poor odds, but we were Dragon Riders. We had a reputation of being fearsome—that had to count. The trick would be to get the Wildmen to run before the wild dragons arrived.

There. Through Kalax's eyes I saw three shadowy figures heading along the top of the wall toward her. At first I thought they were Wildmen who had found a way to scale the wall. But the moon rose higher, glinting off Dragon Armor. Thea's red-gold hair shone bright, and I caught a glimpse of Varla's long braid that bobbed as she struggled forward. They held a bulkier, hobbling third person between them, and I thought I knew that limping figure. *Instructor Mordecai.*

The last I had seen of him had been at the king's council in forest, after the battle. He had vanished after that, and I had wondered if he had been sent on some mission for the king or if he had gone off on his own on some errand. How he had managed to survive on his own was a mystery, but it was good we had found him. But now we all needed to escape.

I waved, and Ferdinania swept down, giving Thea, Varla and Mordecai cover as they headed for Kalax. It was too dark to see much more, and I didn't know how Kalax was going to carry three riders in two saddles.

I felt Kalax balk a little at the extra weight, but she launched into the air. Below us, Beris and Syl on Gaxtal distracted the Wildmen with attacks that kept them crouched low. I briefly considered trying to use my Dragon Affinity against the oncoming wild dragons, but I hated how the Darkening had already killed one dragon that refused to obey. I also worried that the effort to use the affinity again so soon might drain me of what little energy I had left today. I would have to rely on good old fighting skills.

We swooped low a few times, Ferdinania and Gaxtal coming at the Wildmen from different directions, drawing their arrow fire away from Kalax so she could escape. She flew up into the sky, disappearing into the stars.

The wild dragons were getting close. I could feel them drawing close and see them as they blotted out the stars. I judged three were near, and two more followed.

"We have to go!" I shouted.

Merik nodded, thumping the side of Ferdinania's neck once in a particular spot just over her collarbone. Ferdinania knew the command, puffed out her chest and roared a rain of fire out onto the Wildmen.

It took a lot out of Ferdinania—or any dragon—to spit fire. Only many days of eating and bulking up on the right foods could replenish a dragon's natural fire. A substance like molten rock fell on the Wildmen, sticking to wood, cloth and flesh, melting metal and everything else it touched in an instant. Ferdinania's scales changed color slightly but she roared a victory cry.

Beneath us, screams could be heard. In the chaos and smoke, we flew up, not following Kalax, but flying over the ridge to ride in different directions before looping back to head into the mountains. From there, we could make our way to our hidden camp, but we had to be certain we weren't being followed.

Exhausted, Ferdinania still kept flying fast.

As the night cleared to reveal stars some hours later, we finally admitted that we had done it. No enemy dragon was following. They had been distracted by the dragon fire, by the smoke that had obscured their sense of smell and sight. Merik and Ferdinania visibly relaxed, turning in a wide, gliding arc to coast back to our hidden camp and relative safety.

I just hoped Kalax and Gaxtal had made it back, too.

Varla pointed to a mark on one of the old scrolls she had managed to find. "Here—that's the place to begin. In the north. And I think…well, that may mean monastery—or it may actually mean tomb. Or even statue."

I let out a long breath.

It was a few days after we had escaped the city, but it felt as though we had only just managed to recover from the flight. We had to keep moving the camp every other day, hiding from the occasional wild dragons that were searching for us, and we had started to train the new recruits and the soldiers who'd never worked with dragons. We barely had time to eat and sleep.

But it was well past time to start the search for the one Dragon Stone that controlled all. However, the king was still talking about attacks and the need to secure his palace.

The one bit of good news was that Varla had managed to get a few scrolls from the Academy—the only ones not lost to fire. She and Merik had been studying them to try and read the old writing, which wasn't always clear.

Thea, however, still seemed torn about the search.

"It's not that I don't believe in it," she said. She stood at my side, leaning against the wooden sapling-pole that held up the small tent we shared. It was morning and she was nursing a bowl of porridge with a few wrinkled berries we'd managed to find. She grimaced at the sour taste of the berries, and I could have almost laughed, had it not been for our predicament.

Varla and Merik had already eaten and sat on the ground,

pouring over the old scrolls. I liked maps, and even I had trouble reading these, but Varla and Merik were certain they could make sense of them. I hoped they were right.

Turning to me, Thea said, "It's just that...I hate to leave Torvald as it is. It's our city. We pledged as Dragon Riders to defend it." She poked at the boiled oats with her spoon.

I gave a shrug. She wasn't wrong, but I could see no other choice. "What have we got? Lord Vincent has control of others, healing for himself and armor. The Darkening now has wild dragons and an army. What do we have?" I waved at the tents scattered through the sparse forest where we camped right now.

We had almost two squadrons of Dragon Riders, a bunch of people who had never fought, and two troops from the King's Army—foot soldiers and men-at-arms who had either fled the city or who had been stationed in watch towers and had found us. They were rough men and women who had been trained, but they had never been in a war. Years of peacetime and having Dragon Riders who could deal with bandits from the Southern Realm had left many of them lazy.

And they didn't know how to work with dragons.

Maybe I was being too harsh, but in my experience, soldiers distrusted dragons. And dragons had to choose their riders. The king had troops that didn't want to work together—so either the dragons had to be used for scouting missions, or the soldiers had to be used for that so they didn't have to accompany a dragon or have anything to do with them at all.

Thea nodded and put down her bowl of porridge. She waved her arm at the men and women just now starting to take up staffs and swords for training. "They are good fighters; they'll learn how to dig in and stand their ground. I can see that in them, I know that. But what I wouldn't give for Reynalt and his Storm Claws right now."

The sorrow in her words told me she wasn't just talking militarily.

Thea's brother hadn't come back to camp yet. He, his squadron of Dragon Riders, and the rest of the Flamma family were still unaccounted for, along with four other Dragon Rider squadrons. No one talked about it, but everyone had to be wondering if Commander Reynalt had as little faith in King Justin as the rest of us.

I glanced at the royal pavilion. It wasn't that I didn't trust King Justin. I was just not sure I liked him. He had been proud and arrogant as a prince, but now he seemed uncertain and more interested in vengeance than anything. Even worse, he kept changing his mind about how he wanted to launch a counterattack. That was a poor trait in any leader.

I was hoping that at least Instructor Mordecai could make the king see sense and sway his plans. Judging from the shouting coming from the king's tent, I wasn't certain that would happen.

Rolling her eyes, Thea muttered under her breath, "That's not going to help." She pushed off the pole. "Sorry, Seb—I have to sort this out." She left, making her way across camp, issuing a few sharp orders to the idlest gawkers and headed inside the king's tent.

Ugh. Politics. It had been much simpler to share a dragon's world.

I headed over to get a second bowl of porridge—it wasn't good, but it was hot and filling. When I came back, I saw Syl and Beris standing over Merik and Varla. I braced myself for some rude comments, but Syl was excitedly pointing to a symbol on one of the scrolls. "I've seen that one before—I know it."

"Where?" Varla asked. "Where did you see it?" She tossed her long, red braid back over her shoulder. She no longer looked the freckled girl I'd first met.

Merik looked up at Syl with unabashed amazement. None of us had thought about Syl much—he was just Beris' navigator. But now it seemed he was a little like Merik—he seemed to have a liking for scrolls and books and little bits of history.

Well, he wouldn't have made navigator if he didn't.

The thought left my stomach a little sour—and then shame washed through me. Truth was I wanted to think I was a better navigator than Syl was. I had the Dragon Affinity, after all. I could commune with dragons.

Ah, green for more—like a dragon, Kalax thought to me with a slight mockery.

I sent her my feelings, letting her know that what bothered me more was just how easily she could read my mind.

What can I say, little Seb, human minds are easy for a dragon to learn. When I tried to answer back, she had put her mind on fishing in a nearby stream.

"It was on an old scroll of Nord-Juhle, I think?" Syl said, bending down for a closer look.

Merik's mouth fell open. He blinked and said, "You found mention of Nord-Juhle? That's the oldest territory ever known.

They didn't have any written records back then. How do you know it wasn't a fake?"

I harbored a secret, nasty little wish that perhaps it *had* been a fake.

Syl straightened and crossed his arms. "No—well, I think not. It was in a book compiled by Brother Rhymer, and that was real because it had his seal."

"Brother Rhymer!" Merik grinned. "That monk is as famous in archivist terms as any of the old monks of the Draconis Order." He turned to Varla. "Rhymer apparently traveled far and wide collecting stories, tales and bits of lore from the three king-doms. He became one of the earliest navigators, maybe even the first."

Beris rolled his eyes and sipped a cup of something steaming hot. Even Varla shook her head as Syl and Merik started to swap navigator stories—who was who and names of great mapmakers that left me wondering how they knew all this. But they were navigators—they were supposed to carry knowledge with them.

Suddenly, I felt like the blacksmith's boy again—barely able to write my name, struggling with my letters, and chosen by a red dragon for reasons known only to her.

Maybe I'm not a real navigator? What if this Dragon Affinity has made me into something else?

I waited for a moment, but Kalax did not rebuke that idea this time. Was she distracted—or was that the truth?

Kalax didn't recognize different roles. To her, humans were humans, dragons were dragons, and castles were just a cave made to use.

She would probably tell me I'm just Seb.

The thought was oddly comforting. Still, a little regret curled up in my chest that I couldn't join in with Seb and Merik. I had to be honest, too—I didn't care that Syl, who had never liked me, had won over Merik's respect. He was supposed to be my friend.

"Seb?" Merik asked, looking up at me from where he sat. His goggles made his dark eyes seem really big.

I straightened. "I was just wondering whether I should go check on the dragons."

Merik cleared his throat and adjusted his special goggles. "Actually, Seb, you know the most about the Dragon Stones. Can you give us your advice on this? It's a story from Brother Rhymer about something he was told. It says one of the old chieftains had a magician from the north fashion a jewel that could make him invincible. He never grew old or sick and a host of other things. Does that sound like you're the king of all Dragon Stone to you?" He tapped the scroll.

I felt a rush of guilty pleasure. They did need me. When I looked at Syl, he offered back a small, nervous smile. I glanced at Beris. He stared back—he wasn't being friendly, but he wasn't being an ass either. He waved at the ground as if giving Syl permission to sit down. Syl did. And I did the same.

We were all Dragon Riders—and we had the king of Dragon Stones to find.

CHAPTER 5
DISSENT IN THE RANKS

Mordecai was in the right to argue caution. But that wasn't something King Justin wanted to hear.

I knew that Seb had little faith in King Justin. To Seb, the king had not proven himself a good or wise leader. I guess I had more trust because I had grown up with Justin. I didn't know him as well as Ryan did, but I expected my brother would be blind to the king's faults—Ryan always wanted to see the best in everyone. So I was the only one in the unenviable position of both knowing how strong and determined the king could be, as well as being able to see when he was acting like a stubborn brat who wanted his own way just because.

Right now, I was worried the latter might be true.

The problem was Instructor Mordecai had instantly assumed he could tell everyone what to do—he was the eldest here, and he had trained more Dragon Riders than anyone. He'd also once trained the prince—and Mordecai couldn't seem to forget that. It wasn't helping that Commander Hegarty still seemed a little foggy from the Memory Stone enchantment that had held him. So was King Justin. But Mordecai seemed fresh as a daisy mentally, although spiky nettle might have been a better comparison for the grumpy old man.

King Justin and Ryan were arguing for hit-and-run raids and creating chaos to free more people from the Memory Stone so they could join our side. And then we could attack Lord Vincent directly. Commander Hegarty stroked his mustache and agreed.

Instructor Mordecai insisted this would be a costly strategy— we would lose riders, dragons and soldiers with these raids. More than we ever gained. He argued we should send an envoy south to enlist their aid. Commander Hegarty stroked his mustache and said this was wise.

But the South had always wanted to keep out of any fight. Yes, they had tame dragons, but they weren't Dragon Riders like we were. Commander Hegarty rallied enough to remember he had been working on finding dragons in the hot South, but he couldn't remember where his map had gone or even if it had made it out of his study at the Academy.

Not a lot of help.

When I even thought about bringing up the search for the one Dragon Stone that might give us a fighting chance, I worried that I would be yet another voice adding to the arguments and doing nothing more. I could see King Justin was growing impatient. His blue eyes had taken on a bright, hard glitter. I had to do something.

Stepping forward, I said, "Can we not decide anything, sire, until we have more trained troops? It would cost little to wait a few days, and then to decide based on what you see as you review those at your command."

The king frowned, but I could see the idea pleased him—those at his command. He would enjoy a troop review. He gave a nod. "A few days. I'll review the troops then and we will decide. See to their training."

It was obvious Mordecai disliked this idea—he left the tent with a huff. The king turned to talk to Commander Hegarty and I bowed out. I needed to work out some of my frustration with a quarterstaff.

Heading into camp, I found some training going on. Mordecai wasn't here, so I grabbed a staff and got the two dozen scruffy citizens paired off to spar. I showed them the basic moves and started them into bouts. Finding one—a tall, dark-skinned woman with some muscle on her—who lacked a partner, I squared off with her.

Her first blow met my quarterstaff. I blocked it and returned a sharp prod against her ribs, forcing her to duck back. She held her staff as if it was a sword.

Striking her staff, I gave a sudden twist and prod, sending the woman's staff sailing through the air to strike a sapling and fall to the ground. "You must always spread your grip on the quarter-staff, spear or lance. Even when using it as a spear to run an enemy through, use a wide stance and a wide grip. It's not a club." It was hard to not be irritable. They would soon be fighting for their lives.

"Okay, wide grip—got it." The woman massaged her wrist. Her mouth pulled down and she seemed annoyed, but I thought it was more with her own lack of skill. Heading over, she picked up her weapon and faced me again.

But a familiar voice called out, "Flamma?"

Turning, I faced Beris.

He and I had sparred and trained, and nine times out of ten I had bested him. It wasn't that he was a bad fighter, but I was better. I gave him a nod. He swept up a staff and headed over to me, motioning to the woman to step back. "Let's show these recruits how it's done."

"Are you sure?" I asked. I was weary of the bad blood between us. Was he trying to prove again that he was of nobler blood than I, or that he was better in all things?

He seemed to notice my hesitation for he said, "I would like the opportunity for a rematch. And I can't stand over there listening to those navigators talk and talk about long-dead scholars and sages. I need to do something." He gave a nod and hefted up his staff.

"Really, Beris?" I shook my head. We didn't need any more dissent in the ranks. It was difficult enough with the king and Mordecai butting heads—what was going to happen if Beris started making trouble?

Beris nodded to the other recruits, who were now starting to watch us. "Show off what you've got, Flamma."

"Fine. Usual rules—surrender, disarmed or knocked down," I said, adding a little more snarl in my voice then was probably necessary. We took a few paces back from each other in the small clearing. I kept my trusty quarterstaff and noticed that Beris kept his.

"Let's make this quick," I said and counted down, "Three, two…one."

Beris narrowed his eyes, kept his grip on the staff, his feet wide and leaned in. I could tell that he was more than ready for this bout.

He struck first and the sound of wood against wood reverberated around our small clearing. Beris was better than I remembered him being—more controlled, assured and no longer prone to losing his temper. I countered his first jab and was pleased to see him wait for me to retaliate. He was trying to size me up and looking for weak spots.

I faked a clumsy swing. He batted it away with ease before striking back as I knew he would.

Reversing my staff, I twirled it and slid my quarterstaff down his staff, toward his hands, meaning to bash his knuckles. It was a simple move, but many experienced fighters forgot about it, trying to overcome their enemy rather than target their hands.

Beris managed to jump back just in time. I saw him lick his lips and nod.

I smiled. *I am not going to go easy on you.*

It seemed he had no intention of going easy either. He spun around and lashed out with his staff in a blisteringly quick maneuver, which I ducked, only to realize that was half of the attack—the next was a sweep to my knees. He had hoped I would be so caught up in the speed of his initial attack I'd forget about the second part. I saw it coming just in time, jumped over the staff and let my momentum swing my staff around my body. Beris had to dodge the out-flung, whirling staff.

I twirled again, using the gathered momentum of the staff to spin me around so I'd be even faster. Jabbing my foot down, I stopped my movement. Sweat stuck my shirt to my back and a wave of dizziness from the spin swirled through me. Ignoring that, I jabbing out with my quarterstaff in a high blow that Beris would have to parry.

He swung up his staff. Using Beris' strength, I let him swing me around. I pushed off from the ground, whirled around and hit the staff solidly against the back of his knee.

Beris pitched forward to one side of me, dropping his staff as he caught himself in the dirt, wincing. I hadn't hit him that hard, but it was hard enough to teach him not to try to show me up again.

Turning, I started walking away. I heard Beris scrabble to his feet. My shoulders itched with the promise of violence. I spun around, certain I would see Beris' furious face as he came after me. Instead, Beris had left his quarterstaff on the ground. He held out an open hand. I stared at him—what kind of trick was this?

"Uh—thank you," Beris said and kept his hand outstretched.

Does he want to shake mine? Like real duelists?

Switching my staff to my other hand, I took his hand.

He nodded as if something had been settled. "I—I don't know how you did that—the spinning around, adding speed. Will you teach me? And then I can show the others."

I had to blink and glance around. Was Beris, my tormenter

who had made my time as a cadet miserable, asking me for advice?

"Uh, well—it's all about balance and timing," I heard myself say, too stunned to stop myself.

Beris made a face and lifted a hand. "I've tried it. I just get dizzy and fall over."

"The trick is in the shoulders and neck." I mimed turning on my feet, but turning my head a fraction later than my body, almost like two different wheels rotating. "You don't really spin. It just looks like you do. Your body and feet turn around, but your head just turns once and pauses, then turns again once and pauses." I demonstrated it for him. It was an old trick I had learned from my dancing instructor that allowed you to spin and glide across a ballroom floor.

"But you go so fast," Beris said, falling in to walk next to me. "Don't you feel sick?"

I smiled and shook my head. "The speed is in the quarter-staff. It's not just a weapon. It is also a prop—you can't do this with swords, they aren't the right shape. But that's why I like short spears—you can use them like that." I was glad to find someone who could enthuse with me about the wonder and elegance of fighting.

"Spears, lances, quarterstaffs—you can do all sorts of things with them that you just can't do with bladed weapons. You can lean on them, use them to climb, pole vault. I just lash out with it as I spin to add speed to my movements. Like a counterbalance, see?"

Beris laughed. "Clever."

It was strange, but I found myself almost liking Beris. Something had changed since he and Syl had been brought back by Seb, Kalax and the others. Had we done something to him? Changed his personality? Could the Dragon Affinity do that? A shiver chased down my back—I didn't want Seb thinking he'd changed others with his Dragon Affinity.

Maybe this has nothing to do with us and everything to do with Beris realizing he needs other riders.

We made our way over to the weapons rack and started stacking weapons and talking with the recruits about their training.

Over the next two days, Beris started to help with the training. He was hard on the recruits, but they needed that.

Everyone had been through a lot—every person here had lost someone and had seen their homes destroyed. I started to think we had all changed. We couldn't afford to be jealous or prideful.

With the city in ruins and almost no Dragon Riders left, I had to wonder. I hadn't heard Beris mention his own family. Had he tried to get to them? Were they lost?

In the afternoon, after we had finished training and while Seb was with Varla, Merik and Syl, I asked Beris, "Your family—how is the House Veer?"

Beris turned away from me.

I put a hand on his shoulder. "If you need to get word to them, then I'm sure King Justin will send a rider or—"

"Don't," Beris said thickly. He kept his gaze averted as he

headed back to the main area of the camp. "I don't want to talk about it."

I didn't know what had happened to Beris' family, and I wondered if he even knew. I felt like such a fool. How would I feel if Beris started asking me where Commander Reynalt and my parents were? And why they weren't here with the king?

I headed after him, hoping to catch up and talk about other things. Before I could, the short, shrill blast of the whistle we were using to send signals around the camp split the air.

I headed over to where Seb stood. I waved him to follow me. All senior Dragon Riders must attend—that included me and Seb. I glanced at Beris and Sly. "You and Syl might as well come. You're as trained as any, and more than most. We needed the Dragon Riders to come together—we're dangerously short on them."

⚜

"Absolutely not!" Instructor Mordecai folded his arms and frowned at us. We sat or stood around the simple collection of rough-hewn camp tables in the king's pavilion.

King Justin sat at the head of the table, a pitcher of water to one side of him and a large display of maps and charts held out in front of him. He had reviewed the troops this morning, and now we were to make a decision about action.

At the king's far side sat Ryan, glaring at Instructor Mordecai. Commander Hegarty sat on the other side of the king, staring at the charts, a frown pulling his bushy eyebrows down low. Seb sat on the left of Hegarty, and he kept shooting Hegarty sideways looks. We both wanted the old Commander Hegarty back—the man who could influence a king.

Beris, Syl, Merik, Varla and a few captains of the foot soldiers stood near Instructor Mordecai. I had put myself between Syl and Merik. We had to look a rough, untidy bunch— patched uniforms that had been sponge washed, mismatched armor we had scavenged from others or made from what we could find. All of us were hungry—meals were small in camp. My mother would have fainted to see me like this, and Father would have barked out orders and slapped our disorganized group into better shape.

But everyone here looked more like they were ready for a tavern brawl and not a council meeting. We were also back to the same arguments as the other day—attack or seek help.

"Do we sit and train and allow the enemy to grow ever stronger?" Ryan growled at Mordecai.

Even though I was siding with Mordecai on this one, I was impressed by how Ryan was standing his ground against Mordecai—the instructor had once struck fear and terror into the hearts of every Dragon Rider recruit.

"If you open your eyes, boy, you'll see we do not have the forces needed for even a small victory," Mordecai said, his tone weary and his shoulders slumping. "Yes, we can raid and hit and run, but what does it matter if we become a minor irritation? We do not have the army or riders or dragons enough to defeat Lord

Vincent. If we wish an end to this conflict, it seems clear, we have is to find the Southern dragons and their riders and entreat them for aid."

"That could take months," King Justin said. He didn't sound angry, but he looked tired as any of us. We had all been in this meeting for the last two hours with opinions and going back and forth. I doubted anything could be decided before nightfall.

Mordecai straightened. "Then we take months! By the First Dragon, our forces could do with the rest. And we have maps for the hunting, after all; the commander was doing all the hard work to find the Southern dragons."

Commander Hegarty looked up and then glanced at the king. He frowned. To my dismay, he also looked at Seb as if the commander was unsure who was being referred to. When he had ascertained that there was no other commander present—Reynalt, to my shame, had still not rejoined the king—Hegarty coughed and stood, slowly rising from his seat.

I saw Seb's face tighten with worry and his brown eyes darkened—we were both worried about Commander Hegarty. It seemed as if new gray hairs appeared in his hair and mustache every day and new lines marked his face, leaving him looking old and worn.

"Uh—yes, Prince, *um,* King Justin," Hegarty said. "As you know, your father, the old king, tasked me with finding out all that I could about what lineages and breeds of dragons the Southern Realm had—orange tails, double tooth, sunglares and the like. There are several great enclosures for their dragons, and the messengers and travelers I questioned told me where they might be found." His shoulders slumped. "But I have lost the maps." He sat down, muttering, "Marvelous breeds. The double tooth is as fierce as our greens."

"Yes, thank you, Commander Hegarty," King Justin said, sounding even more exhausted than before. The implication was obvious—the king did not think the commander would recover sufficiently in time to lead us. We might spend the next few months following his absent-minded guesses.

To be honest, I rather agreed with the king on that.

Ryan cleared his throat and said, "We have our own Dragon Riders that we need to find—and more still who are under the spell of Lord Vincent. If we free them, we can add them to our numbers and then we stand a chance."

The king waved a hand. "Perhaps we should take a brief break while I consider our options." He stood up, followed by the shuffling of the entire room as everyone stood to salute or bow to him. The king turned to the back of the pavilion, sweeping aside the heavy canvas tent flap and striding outside. His guards started to follow him, but he waved them off. Not even Ryan was allowed to go with the king—he truly wanted to be alone, and for the first time I saw how the decisions were weighing hard on him. Thousands of lives—and the fate of the kingdom—depended on him making the right choices.

Inside the tent, a moment of quiet held before grumbled conversation broke out again, and Beris said, his voice loud, "We all seem to agree that we need to find more men and dragons. If we have to go all the way to the Southern Realm to do it, then that is just what we'll have to do!"

I nodded, but I was still torn. My family was out there some-where in the wilds—if we left Torvald to fly south we would effectively be leaving them to fend for themselves.

"At last, someone sees sense," Mordecai muttered loudly.

"We can take 'em on. My marchers have taken down two of 'em wild dragons 'afore." One of the captains—a tall man with long, slate-gray hair and an eye patch, shifted in his chair and nodded. He was from one of the border outposts.

Another captain shook his head. "You didn't see the monster Lord Vincent rode. There's talk of all sorts of things now—dragons with two heads or four wings or that breathe cold…"

"Children's stories. Rubbish." The first captain shook his head.

"Not so, actually." Commander Hegarty sat up. "If you study the lore, it was once common for there to be many different kinds of dragons. Depending upon how exposed they have been to wild magic, it was said some could grow to monstrous size and others had multiple tails, heads or could even bring storms."

I heard one of the captains mutter that the commander had lost his wits, but Mordecai was nodding. "Yes, so then let us hope there is little wild magic left in the world—and that the Southern Realm has so far been spared."

From the Darkening?

I looked to where Seb sat. He had scrubbed a hand through his brown hair and it was standing on end. His mouth pulled down. He seemed to sense my stare for he looked at me and muttered, "We need to find the Dragon Stone. That is what is going to save us—not hoping to bump into a few more Dragon Riders or fleeing for the South!"

"We wouldn't be fleeing," Beris said, a shadow of his old grumpiness back in his tone. "We would send scouts and riders ahead to entreat with our allies."

"What allies?" Syl stood and waved an arm around the group. "Who here has ever talked to a Southerner before? When was the last time that anyone saw a Southern Realm lord at the palace? And what of the South Raiders who have joined with the Darkening? Why do we think the Southern Realm will be spared in this war? I think Seb is right. We have to find the Dragon Stone—the one that controls them all."

Mutters lifted up—some against, some for. Mordecai sat in his chair, shaking his head. Seb hated talking in public, but he turned to me and pinned me with a look that left me squirming. I knew he wanted me to back him, but I wasn't certain he was right. The other stones we found had brought more dangerous magic to Lord Vincent—not to us.

Next to me, Beris shook his head. "What do we have but scraps of parchment written down by someone long since turned to dust who might have been making it all up for all we know?"

Syl glowered at his partner, and I could tell this was an argument the two of them had been having for some time. "We have evidence, Beris. Cross-referencing, multiple sources, common descriptions even."

"But do you know where this Dragon Stone can be found?"

Syl didn't answer. And that was the problem. We had looked before this for the one Dragon Stone that controlled them all.

And in our search for the Armor Stone, we'd only found that through sheer luck. Or maybe we'd found it because the stone had wanted to be found. But I didn't want to put more powerful magic into Lord Vincent's hands. However, I wasn't sure that flying south would get us anything, either. Glancing around, I said, "We should think about saving our people first—and that means getting help from the Southern Realm. That could be our best chance." Beris nodded, and Syl pressed his lips tight, but he didn't argue.

"Thea?" Seb whispered, his voice full of disappointment.

"Seb, the king needs us. The *rightful* king," I said pointedly, trying to make sure he knew what I meant.

I was certain Beris hadn't been the only person sent out by Lord Vincent to start rumors that Lord Vincent was the true king. And, with my brother out there plotting his own rise to power, King Justin's position seemed tenuous at best. We couldn't let him down. We had sworn to uphold the throne. And we needed to protect our people.

The arguments started up again, but one word cut across them.

"Enough!"

We all looked up to see that King Justin had returned. He stood just inside the door flap. I wondered how long he'd been standing there—and how much he had heard. His stare swept over the crowded tent. It seemed as if he had made up his mind about something. He looked more composed, less tired. He straightened and something of a regal air settled onto him, like a handsome cloak. Perhaps walking alone through the makeshift tents and camp kitchens of his shattered people had made him realize they needed a true leader.

We all stood to attention, and I think it was more from a response to his kingly air than to any courtly expectations.

"I have decided what it is we are to do and where I will be leading you." The faintest waver caught my attention.

Is he still just a little bit undecided?

I bit my lower lip, hoping for his sake that he would do well in this critical moment.

"It seems to me that although our arguments are heated, there really is very little difference in what we want—we want our kingdom back, and we want to be revenged against those who took it from us."

A few muttered 'ayes' sounded in the tent. I resisted looking at Seb, but I could feel his unhappiness with King Justin's speech.

The king glanced around the tent. "To do that, I have decided Instructor Mordecai is right—at least a little. We do need more forces—more dragons and riders. But I will not abandon my people to their fate! And neither will I stand idly by while Lord Vincent and his thieves seek to occupy the royal palace."

Frowning, I wondered how he intended to hold the palace against any concerted attack by our foes. The city had fallen once already—it would fall again if we tried to occupy it.

The king didn't explain, but said, "A small delegation will travel south. The rest of the army will stay close to Torvald, to the west and south of the city. We will use our foot soldiers to harass the enemy, and let our people know that all hope is not lost. Given a few successful attacks, we will find and free other Dragon Riders. More will rally to our banner. Those who have fled to the wilderness will return. And once our forces are gathered, we will strike at Lord Vincent."

I could swear the king flashed a brief look at me and then at Ryan as he said *those who have fled*. Was the king banking on the possibility that Reynalt and his Storm Claw and the other squadrons would return? I rather doubted that was even a possibility. The Flammas were a stubborn lot, and if Father had convinced Reynalt that King Justin was a lost cause, then Reynalt would be done with taking any orders from the king.

But the king had come to a balanced decision. We had to be here for our people, and we had to seek aid where we might be able to find it. I noticed the king had not mentioned the Dragon Stone—I knew it was not because he didn't believe in it. We had all had too much contact with the stones to doubt them. But I thought he must feel as I did—we could not afford to find more magic that Lord Vincent would take from us.

I couldn't help myself, I was proud for my childhood friend —he was becoming a true king. Someone started the cry, *"All hail the king!"* I took it up and echoed the words. But I didn't hear Seb's deep voice shouting those words.

Casting a look over to where Seb was still sitting, I saw he looked pale and worried. I wondered if that had to do with the fact that Commander Hegarty had left the tent, or because the king had not mentioned trying to find the one Dragon Stone that controlled them all.

King Justin held up a hand and urged us to get what food that we could and to rest. "Tomorrow will be a long, hard day."

Standing, Seb made for the exit flap and slipped out without waiting to speak to me. A knot tightened in my stomach. Had I let him down? Was he expecting something more from me? But he had to see that this was the right course of action, surely.

Surely?

CHAPTER 6
DIVISIONS

I couldn't believe Thea hadn't argued for finding the Dragon Stone. What was wrong with her? Did she not remember how Lord Vincent had used the Memory Stone on all of us and almost destroyed the entire kingdom with his powers? And Commander Hegarty had once mended a fatal wound Lord Vincent had given Thea with the Healing Stone—she had to know their powers.

But now Thea was siding with Beris—two noble-house protectors backing the king.

A surge of anger choked me. I knew it was mean and selfish, but I couldn't help it. I had felt so helpless when she had been hurt, and now I was almost as helpless again.

It had taken me a long time to realize I was good at something, and that something happened to be as a Dragon Rider. It had taken my friendship with Kalax to find that in myself—and it

stirred the fog. Clouds had gathered, blotting out the stars and moon, leaving the sky dark. The splash from the river mixed with the dragon's breath, and the scrabble of night animals and calls of night birds. The woods thinned. The tall trees did not allow enough light for saplings. In the trees, a shadow moved, and I stiffened. I'd come out without a sword or even as much as a knife. I glanced back at the clearing, at the flutter of dark tents and the faint glow of lanterns, and then looked back to that shadow.

The shadow came toward me, taking on the shape of a man. His dark cloak flapped around his boots, and he hummed a low, tuneless melody as he headed toward me. A faint light from the camp glinted off the sword that hung from his belt. My throat tightened and my heart thudded hard.

Ridiculous. It's just a rider, checking on his dragon or one of the foot soldiers out on patrol.

I suddenly recognized the short and stocky silhouette as that of Commander Hegarty.

He came up to me, stopped humming and clapped a hand on my shoulder. "Rider Smith, nice to see you again, boy. Did I tell you I knew Monger's Lane a long time ago? Different place now though. So different…" His words trailed off.

I wondered if he was speaking of the difference between his years there and mine, or how different it was now it had been burned to the ground. I started to ask what the commander was doing out here—was he as unhappy as I was with the king's orders?

But Kalax thought to me, *I called him.*

You can speak to the commander?

I wondered if Kalax picked up on my astonishment. Exactly how many other things could Kalax do that I wasn't aware of? I had thought a dragon only shared their thoughts with their riders and with other dragons. But I knew anyone with the Dragon Affinity could talk to any dragon.

Yes, Kalax agreed. *He has some affinity. A touch of the old magic.*

That made sense. The commander's half-brother, Jodreth, had been something of a wizard—but even his power hadn't been enough to defeat the Darkening.

Before I could ask why Kalax had called the commander, she thought to me, *He is fogged. You need him. You need a friend, as does he.* She settled back into a light sleep, ending the communication between us. I was left feeling grateful and staggered at how wise she was.

Commander Hegarty leaned forward to stare at me for a moment, and then his eyes seemed to focus on me as if he was really seeing me for the first time in days. I realized Kalax had called him to help clear his mind with the Dragon Affinity.

"Ah, Seb." His words came out clipped and sharp, more like the Commander Hegarty of old. A rush of hope lifted in my chest —we at last had the old commander of the Dragon Academy back with us.

In the dark night, he let out a long breath. Sadness deepened his voice. "I remember when my dragon used to talk to me." He shifted on his feet, the leather of his jerkin creaking in the night. "But never mind that. You know what is at stake—Torvald. We must …" His words stuttered off, just as they had been doing over the past few weeks. He glanced around us as if unaware where he was or why he was here.

No! I thought, reaching out to him with my hands, heart and mind.

I seized his shoulders to shake some sense into him. A charge like lightning jolted through me, searing my skin, but I reached out with my mind, with the part of me that was always connected with Kalax. I could sense the commander with the dragon's senses, but this time something more came into my thoughts.

I sensed the commander's Dragon Affinity—his link to dragons was like a shining thread, and I knew it was not natural born to him but had grown over decades of living with dragons.

I couldn't connect with him the way I could with Thea or a dragon, but I could see now the fog that had been placed on him by Lord Vincent's Memory Stone. It was there in dark shadows, lurking and rising again. I saw how black lines like the tendrils of a vine clung to his mind, waiting for him to think anything about defense or fighting. No wonder his mind kept wandering—Lord Vincent had woven in a dozen ways to keep tripping up Commander Hegarty. The Darkening hadn't just sent Hegarty back to us as useless—it had left the commander a danger to all those he commanded.

A growl of reptilian anger stirred in my mind as Kalax woke and sensed my connection to the commander. She added her own courage and determination to my efforts. For a moment, we struggled with the tangle of darkness in the commander's mind. Every vine I cut shrank back, but then another sprouted. Kalax gave a roar and light blasted through my mind, brilliant as the sun and hot as dragon fire.

A stabbing pain shot through my eye. My head throbbed and I could see only blinding light. I slapped a hand over my eyes and staggered back.

"Easy there, Seb." Now Commander Hegarty had his hands on my shoulders, holding me up. He leaned against the nearest tree. He looked pale and his features gaunt, as if he had run a race, but his eyes were clear. I reached out with my affinity and this time could see no darkness in his thoughts.

"Commander," I gasped, rubbing my temples.

"Take your time, Smith. The pain eases in a short time." Hegarty patted my shoulder. The commander let out a low chuckle. "Jodreth taught me much about the affinity, and a few things of the old lore. But knowledge alone didn't save me. I thank you."

Swallowing hard, I nodded. Jodreth had given his life to save me, Thea and Kalax. His house on the mountain was now rubble, destroyed by Lord Vincent, and I doubted the sorcerer could have made it out alive from the rocks heaped down on the hut.

Hegarty took a deep breath and turned toward the camp and their low fires, which were now being put out, one by one. "Although fogged, I remember what happened at the council meeting. You are in the right, Seb. We must find the stone of legend—the Dragon Stone of the king, the First Rider. It is the only way to stop the Darkening, and we must stop it forever this time."

"What of the Southern dragons? You said in council we needed their help. I'm…. confused."

"You know as do I, Seb, there is no real sign they will come to our aid. And if we could not defeat Lord Vincent and his forces, what hope do they have? He has the stones of power. He will use them on any who oppose him." Slapping my shoulder, he said, "Walk with me, young rider."

I fell into step with him and he slowly started back to the camp. Voice deep and soft, Hegarty said. "I've a clear mind now, and I know why Kalax brought me here. It wasn't just to clear my thoughts. Whatever happens next, whatever the king announces or orders, you must leave and search for the one Dragon Stone that controls them all. You, more than anyone, Seb, know the danger in the Darkening." He looked at me pointedly.

Panic tightened in my chest. "So—so you agree with the old stories? The Dragon Affinity is more of a curse than a blessing? That it will lead to me becoming like the Darkening…to becoming one with it?"

"No!" Hegarty sliced the air with one hand. His cloak fluttered around him. "The Darkening—it's wild magic. It's twisted beyond all measure. For it to take hold it needs corners to hide in and evil it can bleed into. That old story—the one of the middle son, the prince who wanted power over everything. Over everyone. It wasn't the Darkening that called him—he called to it. Did you know that the Wildmen even have a name for that ancient prince? They call the Darkening and the prince who called it into our kingdoms the *Ghoul*. The tribes I once treated with in my youth feared and hate that old, black power. They kept the old stories alive and told them around their campfires. The Ghoul became over the long decades a tale to frighten their young with —until it came back again at Lord Vincent's hands."

"Even the Wildmen want to be free of the Darkening?" Remembering their savage faces as they raced into battle, I hunched a shoulder.

"Not all of those who are different from us are our enemies, Sebastian. You should know that. And now, I have already spent too long asleep—both in mind and in action. I need you to continue this quest, Seb, no matter what happens next."

I kicked at a stone in our path. "I'm not sure I can. Thea—"

"Seb, you must find a way. We cannot rely only on the one Dragon Stone. We will have to fight our way to where it can be used against Lord Vincent, and that means we need troops. I know the way to the south. I mapped the locations of the Southern dragons. I will go."

I opened my mouth to protest, but the commander straightened and said, his voice clipped, "You have your orders, Rider Smith."

"Aye, Commander." I gave a nod. I wasn't sure the commander was in a fit state to be traveling for weeks across difficult terrain. He looked thinner than he had once been, and in the light of the last fire burning in the camp, his face seemed pale. But what could I say? He was still my commander.

As if sensing my thoughts, Commander Hegarty gave me a crooked smile. "Chin up, Seb. The end isn't here yet. And we have much work to do before any of us can rest. I thank you,

Rider Smith and Kalax, for aiding me. Now see to your dragon and recruit your protector to your task at hand." Wrapping his cloak around him, he headed for the king's tent.

Arms crossed against the chill of the night, a small bubble of happiness rose in me to see his stride firm and strong again. But my stomach churned at the thought of what I had to do next—convince Thea she had to help me find the one Dragon Stone of legend.

༺༻

The Wildmen fear and hate the Darkening...Only the one Dragon Stone can defeat the Darkening. We need an army to get close enough to Lord Vincent to use the power of the one stone against him.

Lying on the hard ground, I turned over, my blanket doing nothing to keep the cold away. I turned again, thoughts going around and around like a dragon falling from the sky. I had my arm for a pillow and the wind tugged at the flaps of my tent. It was useless. Getting up, I headed to where Kalax lay and huddled against her, under a flap of her wing. She tucked her snout up close and with her warm breath on me, I felt safe and fell asleep.

I woke warm and rested. Her scales, while strong, were surprisingly supple and made a much better pillow.

Rising, I stretched and saw Thea heading toward us, picking her way through the trees. Pine needles crunched under her boots. I could tell from her purposeful stride and the way that her head was bent, her red-gold braid swinging as she walked, that she was thinking about something.

"Thea, come have breakfast with me," I said. Behind me, Kalax settled back to sleep.

Looking up, Thea shook her head. "No time, Seb. Commander Hegarty has left for the South. Last night he marched into the king's pavilion as if he had never been ill, demanded a horse and two riders to go with him and told the king that he would be the scout to the Southern Realm." Thea sighed, as if it was a terrible idea. She hunched a shoulder and crossed her arms. She wasn't wearing a cloak, just her leather jerkin over a tunic, and her leather breeches and boots—she was dressed for flying.

With a frown, I blew on my hands. The morning air was chill, and I was wishing for a warm drink. "Wasn't that exactly what you said you wanted to happen?" A little touch of sorrow wove its way into me—I'd wanted a chance to see him off before he went.

Thea nodded, but then she pulled a sour face. "He went last night—no rest, no planning, nothing. He didn't even wait for the king to agree with him, just demanded the provisions, strong armed the king into agreeing and left." She scowled. "I mean, it is good that he stepped forward like that, but the way that he spoke to the king in front of the senior captains was as if Justin was a rider under Hegarty's command." Thea grimaced.

"It's something that he had to do, whether or not anyone else liked it. And isn't it good to have the commander back?"

She stared at me. "Back? He's gone. I volunteered us to go

with him, and he told me that we had other duties." She turned and glared at the camp.

Ah, that's it.

She hated when people told her what to do or acted as if she couldn't do her job. She had to be thinking the commander turned her down because he didn't have enough faith in her.

"Commander Hegarty—I saw him last night." I blurted.

Thea turned to face me.

"He told me that years ago he'd had to deal with the Wildmen, and that they fear the Darkening. They call it the Ghoul, which sounds like a good name for Lord Vincent to me."

Her face tightened, and her blue eyes seemed to darken. "So the Wildmen are just as scared as everyone else. What good does that do us as long as they are being controlled by the Memory Stone?"

"If we break the hold that Lord Vincent has on their minds, the Wildmen will probably flee on their own." I waved my arms wide.

Head tipped to one side, Thea asked, "And how are we going to do that? With your affinity? Don't you remember what it cost you to just help the dragons and some riders get free of the Memory Stone? Your head almost burst. Not to mention, it only worked with some dragons and some riders."

"Why are you being like this? We need ideas. And what if we have the one Dragon Stone to make us stronger? What if—"

"Wait!" Thea interrupted, her voice sharp. "You said you saw Hegarty last night before he decided to leave? And you didn't try to talk him out of going?"

Anger warmed my face. "The commander—he's thinking clear now."

"Is he? He took Mordecai with him, Seb," Thea snapped. "That's two of our most experienced leaders gone. The king has Ryan to help him and a few captains. No Commander like Reynalt for the few squadrons we do have. No other generals. We needed at least one commander here to lead the Dragon Riders against Lord Vincent. Who is going to do that now?"

Hunching a shoulder, I told her, "Hegarty knows what he's doing—he…Kalax and I cleared the fog from his mind. And that wasn't all he had to say—he told me that *we* had to find the one Dragon Stone that controls the others. That without it, we have no hope of defeating the Darkening!"

Thea stepped up and put her face close to mine. Behind me, Kalax woke and gave a hiss. She was clearly upset at our arguing.

Eyes narrowing, Thea said, "So we're supposed to find more magic that Lord Vincent can take from us? It's not enough that he took the Healing Stone from Commander Hegarty. Or that he stole the Armor Stone after we found it. Or that he got the Memory Stone from the old king, even though it was supposed to be secure in the palace. Don't you see a pattern here? How we keep finding the stones for him. What if Commander Hegarty is really still acting under Lord Vincent's control? What if this is all a trap?"

I shook my head. "I saw into the commander's mind."

"With the affinity," she said, her voice cold. "The same affinity that Lord Vincent used to summon the Darkening. The same affinity he uses now to control the wild dragons and the Wildmen. Don't you see, Seb, magic is our enemy, too."

My face went from hot to cold. So she thought the affinity was dangerous—I was dangerous. Staring at her, I could see now how she was afraid of the stones. And I couldn't blame her.

She'd been healed by one of the stones, and it had left her able to sense them. It had left her a little different, and she was worried about that. I could see that in her eyes, in the white lines around her mouth, in the tension that held her still right now.

The Darkening was real. It was some sort of elemental power like a huge storm that Lord Vincent had harnessed and channeled. And she was right to fear that if Lord Vincent ever got the one stone that controlled all the powers, he could spread the Darkening over all three kingdoms.

But we could stop that.

Hand spread wide, I lowered my voice. "Thea, we have no other choice. All the old stories say that there was one stone that brought all the powers together. How else are we really going to defeat Lord Vincent?"

She shook her head and turned away. "Half of the old stories have been wrong, Seb. And where has chasing after these powers got us? We've lost Torvald, I've lost my family, and now we're about to lose the kingdom. All because we found the stones and Lord Vincent took them from us." She glanced over her shoulder at me, her voice low now. "I need you, Seb. I need you at my side." For a moment, I got a glimpse of the desperation she was feeling. It was in her eyes and in her voice as she pleaded with me.

I stepped around so I could face her. "Thea, you've said we need an army. The commander said it, too. Even if we had the one stone, we still will have to fight a battle to get to Lord Vincent. Well, the Wildmen have just as much to lose as us. And you saw how Lord Vincent doesn't care if his wild dragons live or die. They could help us."

Thea searched my face, her eyes wide and her face pale enough that I could see a couple of freckles on her cheeks. "You want help from the wild dragons and Wildmen who attacked Torvald?"

"Lord Vincent and the Darkening can't be controlling every single wild dragon or Wildman. We've seen how even the Memory Stone has limits. He's got to be stretching his powers too thin. I can use the Dragon Affinity to promise them free-dom…to get us some help."

Thea started to shake her head. "Seb—that's madness. The wild dragons…you saw what they were like in the city. They're dangerous, unpredictable and—"

"And you don't think I can do it?" I stepped back from her. "You don't want to look for the one Dragon Stone. You don't want to come with me to get help."

Above us, Kalax lifted her head and gave a rumble deep in her throat. Her worry was rattling through my head, but I wouldn't look at her. I kept my stare on Thea. My heart was beating hard and fast in my throat and my stomach was churning. "I'm flying to the north. I'm going to search for the one Dragon Stone in every monastery or ruin I can find, and I'm going to bring back an army of wild dragons and Wildmen. You can say here and try to fight Lord Vincent—and you can watch as riders and others keep dying."

Thea's eyes blazed hot. "Varla's right. The affinity is a curse and it's changing you. It's giving you crazy ideas and you're going to end up taken by the Darkening. You go. I won't stop you, Seb." She turned and stalked back to the camp, her strides long.

My stomach was still churning. I'd clenched my hands into fists. I wanted to hit something, but there was nothing to strike at. Letting out a breath, I turned away and scrubbed a hand though my hair.

What have I done?

I was so awash with feelings I wasn't sure if that thought was mine or Kalax's. But a sense of rightness had settled into my chest. This was the right thing to do. We had to find the Dragon Stone that could help us, and everything that Varla, Merik and Syl had uncovered said to go north in the search.

"If I have to do it alone, I will go," I said. But I was hollow inside at that thought.

Go together. Much better, said Kalax in the back of my mind. I could sense her worry and hurt—and how she did not approve. *You, Kalax and Thea are one. Thea is safe with other dragons. Ferdinania and Gaxtal look after her. I protect you even if you act a sheep with all this bleating at each other.*

With a huff, Kalax closed her mind to me, leaving me feeling horribly alone.

CHAPTER 7
DECISIONS

Throwing myself into training to forget about the argument with Seb wasn't hard to do. We had foot soldiers to train to work with dragons and civilians to train to fight, and riders who needed to brush up their skills and who were still shaking off the effects of the Memory Stone. I also had to attend the king, and we had tents to take down, routes to map, and plans to make for where we might strike at Lord Vincent. I found myself busy from first light to midday, not once stopping for so much as a mug of water.

But I felt as if I had lost some essential part of myself. In the middle of a bout, I would turn, certain someone was there who wasn't. I got smacked with a quarterstaff twice for that. Or I'd be walking through camp and have a feeling I needed to be some-place else. By midday I was annoyed with myself and snapping at almost everyone.

It wasn't until I saw Beris with Syl that I realized they were one of the few pairs of complete Dragon Riders left with the king. Merik and Varla had followed Seb, while the other Dragon Riders were out scouting for a new camp for us.

For the first time, I just watched them.

Beris and Syl moved and joked together as one. I wondered if that was what Seb and I looked like. And I was missing Kalax—a lot. Was this what Seb had been trying to tell me all along by insisting the affinity could be learned? Were Beris and Syl even developing some affinity?

I noticed how even when doing completely different tasks—like Beris would be checking on weapons and Syl would be helping ready tents for us to move camp— Syl would naturally end up his task or find a pause at about the same time Beris would call for help or finish up his work. It was like they were in synch without even knowing it. The strength of their bond became even more obvious during the noon meal when I noticed the way that they would finish each other's sentences.

I saw now why Ryan was so protective and loyal to the king —over and above any loyalty to family. Ryan was the king's navigator—they were paired in a way.

And it is why I feel like I have lost one of my legs or an arm.

The thought was a glum one. I didn't want to be that tightly tied to anyone. It left me even grumpier because Seb wasn't here so I could yell at him, and Kalax wasn't here to put in some sly comment.

Some part of our minds had bonded, and I could see that just like Beris and Syl, Seb and I were also becoming more alike. Seb was becoming more courageous and—I hate to admit it—stubborn and I seemed to be developing a practical side.

I left my bowl of stew and headed out of camp to walk to the river, my head down and my cloak pulled tight around me even though the sun was up. It suddenly felt wrong to me that we would become more and more alike as we aged. What sort of life was that? I was Agathea Flamma of the House of Flamma, a noble of the Court of Torvald. I was no smith's boy, and I was no dragon!

My mind spun around the idea over and over, and a hard knot settled in my chest. Why had no one else ever seen this connection? Or did they know of it and just not tell young riders? Why weren't any of the instructors here to counsel me when I really needed them?

My cheeks heated as I thought about it. I felt silly for fretting about such things—we had far bigger worries just now.

Like finding more Dragon Riders.

With a sigh, I started back to camp. The last of our six wagons had been packed with the tents. The Dragon Riders we had were already in the sky, acting as guards and lookouts. They'd found us a new campsite, higher in the hills and a little to the south. The plan was to try and pick up some more riders if we could find them, or more soldiers, or anyone who could fight. And then to pick a few targets that we could hit to start harassing Lord Vincent's forces. I almost wished that we were heading south and following the tracks of Commander Hegarty and Instructor Mordecai.

Or flying north.

I cut off that thought.

King Justin was adamant about his plan. The king wanted to strike back at Lord Vincent and show there was still some fight in Torvald. He seemed to be ignoring the fact that Seb and Kalax had left, and so had a couple of other Dragon Riders, including Merik, Varla and Ferdinania, but he hadn't looked happy this morning. Neither had Ryan, for he had sent me a dark look and then kept close to the king's side. I could just imagine that they were both wondering why I let Seb and Kalax leave—or maybe they knew Seb had gone after the one Dragon Stone. Maybe they were even harboring a little hope that Seb and the others would find more help for our upcoming battles.

The truth was if I thought Seb's plan would turn out better, I would be out there with him and Kalax. But the other stones had proven to be more dangerous than they were helpful—I could see why they had been hidden away. The old Dragon Riders had been right to try and keep them from ever being used. And I would put my faith in the king's plan.

So why didn't I feel better about that?

The king and Ryan mounted the king's green drake—Naxtal —and the order went out to start.

I had a pony to ride, but it wasn't like being on Kalax's back. The pace seemed impossibly slow, and I kept watching the skies, but I only saw our own dragons above.

We marched slowly southward, taking the least used byways, the herders' and drovers' paths wherever possible, and skirted any village. Several times a flag went up from the riders keeping watch and we had to halt, weapons drawn as we waited for the sign that all was clear again. The civilians had trouble keeping up, and that slowed us. But they helped to make it look like we were nothing more than refugees fleeing the city and the war.

By the time the king and Ryan landed Naxtal at our new camp site beside a dried up riverbed and higher in the mountains, I was starting to worry that we hadn't seen any of Lord Vincent's forces. No black dragons. No Wildmen. Not even a group of raiders from the Southern Realm. It seemed suspicious.

What if Lord Vincent knows exactly where we are and he is only waiting for his moment to attack? Or maybe Lord Vincent figured we were running south with our tail between our legs?

I had to remind myself we were going to bring the battle back to Lord Vincent. We would harass his forces. Commander Hegarty and Mordecai would return with ferocious Southern dragons and more riders. The forces of the Middle Kingdom would strike back with new strength, power and purpose.

The thoughts didn't warm me.

That night I dined on traveler's biscuits and dried winter fruits. It was no great meal, and more than once I wished that I could be out there hunting fish with Kalax. Or just with Kalax and Seb.

⚔

The next day, the king was proven right, for our numbers rose. The Dragon Riders came back with a few more souls who had fled the ruins of Torvald. Some of them were even useful—three blacksmiths, but none knew Seb or his father, ten guards who had survived the palace attack, and a half dozen archers and arrow makers. But most were just ordinary people who would do better far behind any fighting.

A dozen old women arrived and three old men, two of whom were injured. A half dozen children came with them and one pregnant woman. I thought we were starting to look less a traveling army and more like a true group of refugees. I could see that Ryan was worried about this. He eyed the untrained people with a dark frown, but the king gave a speech to everyone and they cheered. I kept thinking this would slow us—and how were we to train any of these people?

That evening, outside the king's pavilion, I raised these concerns with Ryan, who nodded and told me that he would take them to the king.

"Perhaps we could have two marches—one for civilians and another for the army?" I suggested, pulling my cloak tighter about me. The evening wind had picked up and this high in the mountains it would be cold tonight.

Ryan shook his head. The wind was tugging on his hair, and he hadn't bothered with a cloak. His face looked dusty still from having been on his dragon all day. "We have to stay with the people. It is the least we can do for their protection. And…well, we may be able to train a few."

I let out a breath. *We* meant me and Beris and Syl—training duties had fallen to us.

We sorted out a few new recruits, and Beris and Syl started working with them with quarterstaffs. Two showed promise. I toured the rest of the camp, making sure tents were pitched, but to tell the truth, I had little to do. The civilians and the soldiers might not know what to do with dragons, but they were getting very skilled at making camp. Small fires sprang up in rock circles, but there wasn't much dry wood to burn. The smell of bacon frying or stews cooking soon warmed the air. And I listened to the gossip floating around the fires.

The news was mixed. Wildmen and wild dragons still roamed through Torvald and the nearby villages, terrorizing any they found. But the raiders from the Southern Realm had gone else-where. Those who had joined us spoke of how other citizens of Torvald had taken to the deep woods—and some had gone to join them. I wondered if that would be where my parents and Reynalt had gone. A few spoke of how the wild dragons seemed to be searching, always passing overhead.

That put a shiver down my back. Was Lord Vincent searching for King Justin? We had heard Beris and Syl state Lord Vincent's claim to the throne, but if King Justin died, Lord Vincent would be the only one left who was strong enough to make himself king of both the Northern Realm and the Middle Kingdom.

Apart from Reynalt.

My mouth dried, and I moved on to the next campfire, avoiding meeting anyone's stare.

I hadn't spoken to Ryan about what the rest of our family was doing or about the other missing nobles. But I didn't need to. Ryan looked as pale and worried as I felt—of course that could be just a hard day.

But why hadn't my family declared themselves against Lord Vincent yet? Were they even still alive?

With our numbers growing, even as slowly as they were, King Justin might soon have enough of an army to even present a sizable threat to Lord Vincent's forces. At least we might take back Torvald.

Looking down the mountainside and toward the hills below us, I could see columns of smoke. Burning villages and towns, no doubt. The smallest hamlets might hope to escape the war unscathed—apart from having their flocks scattered since dragons had a taste for fat sheep. But how many other cities were now in ruins?

I also wondered how many bridges might have been burned down or torn apart, making the rivers nigh impassable. How many watchtowers were now just scattered stones? The thought of such waste left me angry, but I didn't voice my fears to my brother, to the king, or even to Beris and Syl. However, I did wonder if Lord Vincent was playing a game with us. Were we being hunted, *driven* to our doom?

⚜

Two days later, we moved to another camp, this one deeper in the woods and now on the south side of Torvald. I'd taken lead on a mountain pony, going ahead of the wagons. I still had the feeling we were being tracked, even though we had seen no black dragons in the sky.

We'd found one of the old roads, long ago abandoned. It was grown over, which made for good cover for us, and it wasn't as hard to travel as the rough ground around us. We'd passed two villages that had been destroyed, and a few who had survived had joined us. More mouths to feed and still not as many fighters.

I was thinking about that as I saw two brightly colored caravans heading our way—north on this road. That was odd, I thought, and then I recognized the long, black hair and mustache of the man driving the nearer caravan.

Pulling my mount to a halt, I called out, "Arkady Bismollah Shaar, is that really you?"

The big man pulled his pair of horses to a halt and shaded his eyes with one hand, staring my way. I feared he wouldn't recognize me—it had been a long time since Seb and I had last seen the Gypsies of Distant Shaar. But then his face split into a wide grin. "Thea?" His thick Southern accent made the word long and slow, but he threw one hand out and slapped the reins on his horses. He pulled the horses to a halt with his caravan close to me. "By all, it's good to see the face of a friend. We've seen nothing but fires and trouble."

Before I could say anything else, a dragon's shadow flew overhead. I glanced up and saw the king on Naxtal. But if the king was on the dragon, where was…?

"Rider Flamma!" Ryan shouted from behind. I turned to see him striding toward me. He must have dismounted from his dragon, for he still wore his riding leathers and his dragon armor.

Turning in my saddle, I called out, "Ryan, this is Arkady Bismollah Shaar. He and his wife, Sansha, once looked after me." My horse gave a snort and stomped as if even he knew the Gypsies were friendly enough.

Ryan came up to my side and put a hand on the hilt of my sword. He glanced once at me and said, his voice soft, "You will address me as Commander Flamma. The king has charged me with military defense as well as his own protection."

Hurt welled in my chest. Ryan seemed more distant right now than Reynalt ever had. I tried to tell myself it was just the worry—if the king thought he needed more protection, then even he was starting to feel as if we were being hunted and invisibly tracked.

I gave a nod and waved a hand at Arkady's caravan. "Of course, Commander Flamma. As you say, Commander Flamma. Now, might I visit with my friends, Commander Flamma?"

Ryan shot me another hard look, then turned to Arkady. "You come from the Southern Realm? What is your business here?"

I rolled my eyes. "Ryan…I mean, Commander Flamma, I can vouch for these people. They are no threat, and they might bring us valuable news."

Ryan seemed to at least be thinking about that.

Roluz, Arkady's son, poked his head out from the back of the caravan and waved at me, looking skinny but so much taller than when I'd last seen him. I waved back before giving Ryan a shrug. Arkady was smoothing his mustache and trying to dust off his vest as if that would make him look respectable. The Gypsies were probably used to poor receptions from many—they were often thought to be thieves and liars. But I had always found them to be good folks.

I started to tell Ryan that, but he cut me off with a wave of his hand and said, "Report to the supply wagons. I will deal with this."

Opening my mouth, I was going to tell Ryan what he could do with his orders and his arrogance. But I could hear the clatter of foot soldiers behind us. I glanced back to see the troops had caught up to me. Behind them a good distance were the wagons. Well, if Ryan wanted to talk to Arkady, he could. I gave Arkady another wave and turned my mount around, grumbling as I trotted to the wagons.

Who does he think he is?

Yes, Ryan was now confidante to the king, and he was my senior. But I had combat experience—maybe as much as he did. And I knew I was better with a sword or a bow. I had also helped find the Memory Stone—before Lord Vincent took it. And I helped find the Armor Stone—before Lord Vincent took it.

In fact, it wasn't so long ago that old King Durance was looking on me as a suitable candidate to wed his son. I might have become queen of the Middle Kingdom.

Not that I wanted that, of course.

But now I was beginning to see that Ryan still regarded me as his little sister. He probably blamed me for not keeping Seb here. And the king—well, he didn't have time to think about anything except planning his attack on Lord Vincent.

My skin heated and I squinted at the dust stirred up by the wagons. Maybe Seb had been right. He'd acted like a true Dragon Rider, taking on the orders of Commander Hegarty. I should be up there flying, attacking and protecting as only a Dragon Rider can. Instead, I was stuck on the ground.

With the supply wagons.

࿊

By late evening, we had made camp in the forest, and Ryan had released Arkady and his family. I heard Ryan tell Arkady to camp with us, and I was pretty sure that meant Ryan still didn't trust the Gypsies not to go running off to tell Lord Vincent where we were. As if the Gypsies had any love of the Darkening.

The sun had already set by the time I was able to head over to Arkady's camp. My stomach grumbled when I remembered the fine meal Sansha had once cooked. I made sure that I arrived at the Gypsies' two caravans with a brace of fish I'd caught in the nearby river.

Sansha beamed with a wide smile when she saw the fish. She still had dark hair and wore a black dress and skirt. She started to order Afiyah—who now looked so much like her mother—to get out the iron skillet. Roluz, who was trying to grow a mustache and had grown a foot taller, sat with Arkady's brother Turri by the fire. Roluz was playing a violin while Turri played a flute. They nodded to me, and Arkady waved me to sit next to him by the fire where he was smoking a pipe. "It seems your new king is suspicious of everyone and has lots of questions!" Arkady laughed as if that was a great joke.

I nodded, saying nothing, and held my hands to the small fire.

The Gypsies had set up camp a little ways distant from everyone else, under a stand of tall pines. Arkady seemed very much as I remembered, a cheerful soul, and he started into stories of how they were trying to make their way to the coast, for they had heard it was safer there.

I shook my head. "Is anywhere safe?"

Arkady nodded. "There is truth in that."

Sansha and Afiyah had brought out iron pans to fry the broad river fish. Pausing with her hands on her hips, Sansha raised her eyebrows and stared at me. "No Seb?" she asked.

Behind her, Arkady cleared his throat. "We should not ask if we do not want the answer."

"No—it's not what you think. Seb is fine. At least, I think he is…or he was the last I saw. The fact is…" A knot tightened in my throat as if there was something trapped there. I blinked hard and said, "He's as safe as anyone can be these days."

Arkady swapped a look with his brother, Turri, who nodded and started to play a sad song.

"Oh, shush." Sansha waved a hand and then told Afiyah, "Get out the salt and the wine." She looked at me. "Don't tell me you and your Seb had an argument? And what of that dragon of yours? You and your Seb were as alike as peas in a pod."

I gave a shrug, and Arkady waved at her. "Food first, then talk."

Sansha grumbled, but soon had the fish sizzling. Afiyah brought out a bottle of something tangy that went down with surprising speed. Crusty bread came out, and I had the best meal I'd known in what seemed forever.

The Gypsies managed to ignore the soldiers that kept wandering past. Guards, I thought, posted by my too-cautious brother. I had the feeling this might not be the first time the Gypsies had seen an army camp.

Sansha confirmed that, bustling around the fire to gather up the plates. "Your king isn't the only lord to go a-marching. The Southern Realm…" She let the words drift and made a tutting noise. "We daren't go north now, and we daren't go back south. East is the mountains and west is the sea. We will run out of land soon." She threw one hand in the air.

"It's bad in the South, as well?" I asked, worried now for the commander and Mordecai. "How bad?"

Arkady took out his pipe again and tapped it on his palm. "The Southern Realm has a vile disease and it is called sudden patriotism." He spat on the ground. It was the first time I had seen him speak so frankly and harshly.

"Patriotism? But…that's a good thing."

"Not when aimed at Lord Vincent and the Darkening. To go against him is death." Arkady shook his head and stroked his mustache.

"Wait—Lord Vincent's in the Southern Realm?" My mouth dried. If Lord Vincent was there, then Commander Hegarty and Instructor Mordecai were in great danger. And what of the dragons there? Were they fighting the Darkening even now?

Arkady shook his head and took his pipe from his mouth. "You should come away with us. We go west as far as we can, and then we will take boats to return to Shaar, if all goes well. You will be safe with my people. At least, I think you will."

Reaching down, I grabbed a log and tossed it into the fire. "I doubt any spot is safe. Lord Vincent holds the North—or so we hear. Torvald has fallen. The Middle Kingdom is ready to fall. And now you say the Southern Realm…that not all is well?"

He let out a breath and leaned his elbows on his thighs. "The stories I hear told is that Lord Vincent came to the Southern Realm, making friends first with one prince and then another. He made himself very useful, had many trade contacts that reached to the far north."

"That sounds like him—the snake!"

"Then the stories change. People started to forget things, such as the names of their lords. Whole settlements seemed to vanish as if they never were. When the Golden Eyre was lost—that is the home to all of the dragons of Vyr—well, the talk turned back to the last time that happened…the time of the Darkening. Lord Vincent swept in with an army of black dragons, saying he would protect the Southern Realm. Instead, he has spread war and fire, and now everyone lives in fear of the raiders who roam the land, taking what they want all in the name of Lord Vincent." Arkady shook his head. He glanced down at his pipe as if he had forgotten it and tucked it away.

Turri had taken up his flute and was playing it, and Sansha sent Afiyah and Roluz to the river to bring back water.

Glancing at me, Arkady said, "The land did not get better under Lord Vincent's rule. There are more raiders. Gypsies like us were not encouraged to stay. There were battles, we heard. And now it is nothing but fighting and more fighting."

"Which is why you are heading back to your homeland?"

"Yes." Sansha smiled, but her eyes still seemed sad. "We

would rather stay, but what can we do? We know nothing of war and this looks to be a terrible one."

"Your dragon, is she well?" Arkady asked.

"Kalax? She's with Seb. They traveled north."

Frowning, he asked, "And why aren't you with them?"

"I—uh…it's complicated."

Arkady straightened and slapped the side of my thigh. "Come with us. You can come find a new life. Leave word for your Seb and your dragon to follow you."

I shook my head. I didn't quite know what to say. The offer was said so lightly, I couldn't feel like he was being serious, but when I looked into his eyes I could see he really did see me as family.

More so than even Ryan does right now.

It had been a long time since I'd last seen Arkady and his family, but the few nights here and there had somehow formed a tie between us. They might be outsiders, but they were also generous and kind. This was a family I felt pulled toward.

Afiyah and Roluz came back from the river with buckets of water. Afiyah sat next to her father on the ground, demanding a story. Roluz groaned and rolled his eyes, looking more like a young man, but he, too, sat and leaned forward, eager for a tale. Sansha poured more wine for all of us and even Turri tucked away his flute and waited for Arkady to start talking.

After smoothing his mustache, Arkady said, "Well, because we travel the three kingdoms and war has come again, the story must be of war and the kingdoms. And the story will be of the First Rider and the First Dragon."

I settled back, leaning my palms on the ground. It was warm next to Arkady's fire and I could do with a story.

Leaning forward, Arkady's voice dropped to a deep, soft tone, so I had to strain to hear him. "Long ago, or so the monks always used to say, there was indeed a dragon who became a First Dragon, and he was called so because one great king dared to ride that dragon—and he became the First Rider. But this king, he did not start a king. No, he began as a boy who swept out the monastery. It was said he grew up an orphan. The monks who took him in lived near Mount Hammal, in the shadow of the dragons. For many years, the monks had fed sheep to the dragons, hoping if they did so the dragons would not eat them. But the boy thought this a silly idea. He thought the dragons were kind. So one day he went to where the dragons lived, into their caves."

"What happened next?" Afiyah asked. She had her chin propped on her hand.

Roluz gave a snort. "You know this tale already."

"Well, I don't," I told him. And it was true. I had heard stories of the First Rider—but only those stories of the First Rider and his dragon and how he took up his friend to be his navigator. I'd grown up on stories of battles and war—but I'd never heard a story of the time before the First Rider had learned to ride a dragon.

Arkady smiled and smoothed his mustache. "Well, the boy went to the dragons. The monks followed him and tried to stop him, but the boy was determined. Gradually, the monks fell back, for they feared the dragons. But the boy didn't. By some luck or magic, the boy came first upon a dragon egg—not a dragon. He put his hand on the egg, and right then it cracked open. The dragon looked at the boy and the boy looked at the dragon and the two knew at once they would be forever friends. That dragon became Jalax—the First Dragon. But it took years for the boy to grow tall and the dragon to grow strong."

"Was he a red?" I asked, thinking of Kalax's crimson red scales.

"Ah, yes, she was," Arkady said. He winked at me, and I wondered if he was making up this part of the story. "The boy spent years with the dragon, and one day he worked up his courage and climbed up on the dragon's back, sitting just in front of the wings. And the two took to the sky, forever paired as rider and dragon…" Arkady's voice trailed off.

I let out a sigh. I missed Kalax—I missed Seb. They were my real family.

Now I saw I'd been afraid—afraid to find the one Dragon Stone that controlled them all. I was still afraid.

A memory of cold steel stealing my breath as Lord Vincent's sword pierced my back rose in my mind. I tried to shut it off, but it came back again and again. But I was a Dragon Rider—I had to have as much courage as that first rider had. It was time I faced my fears.

I glanced from Arkady and Sansha, then to silent Turri, and pretty Afiyah and young Roluz. These were the faces of so many who were fleeing the war. But what hope did they have? What hope did any of us have? Would there be more battles, more fighting, until Lord Vincent held all the lands? If he held the

Southern Realm, the North and the Middle Kingdom, then we needed far more than a few more dragons.

Seb had been right—and I'd been too stubborn to listen. Too afraid.

I shivered, thinking again of Lord Vincent's blade piercing me. But I stood, the firelight warm on my face. "Sansha, Arkady, Turri, I am sorry, but I must go. Your hospitality has been, as always, better than any king's." I nodded to each, smiling at Afiya and Roulez.

Sansha came over and gave me a hug. "You stay safe out there."

"And come find us someday. Come find us as west as west, and as south as south can go," Arkady said. "But bring Seb and your dragon next time."

With a nod, I turned and headed to my own small tent. I'd pitched it beside one of the wagons. It took no time to bundle my few belongings into a small pack. I wanted to travel light, with only the bare minimum of equipment and weapons.

When I stepped out, Beris poked his head out from under the wagon where he had spread his blankets.

Crouching down beside his pale, moon-like face, I said, "Take this to Commander Ryan at first light. Tell him you found it by your bed roll which, in a way, is true."

"Agathea? Wait?" Beris wiped his face and struggled to sit up. I pressed the folded note into his chest. I hadn't even bothered to seal the hastily scribbled scrawl. I didn't care if he read it or not. In fact, I was rather hoping he would.

It was short and simply told Ryan that I was sorry—but a

Flamma was never far from their dragon. I left the camp, heading over the hills, back the way we had come until I found a narrow path that cut through the highlands. I followed an old sheep trail, my heart beating faster with exhilaration and effort. Behind me, there was no sound of hue and cry, no one following me.

For the first time in what seemed days, I felt as if I was doing the right thing. I wasn't afraid.

By noon that day, a shadow fell over me. I looked up, braced to see a black dragon. I had my bow and six arrows with me. But it was Gaxtal who circled once. I knew that blue anywhere. Gaxtal landed in the clearing ahead of me, and I headed for Beris. "I thought I said—"

"We were sent to find you," Beris said.

Syl grinned.

Hand falling to my sword hilt, I backed up a step. "I'm not going back. I'm going to help Seb, and Varla and Merik."

Beris shook his head and glanced at Syl. "Well, we found her."

Syl nodded. "Yes, we did."

I glanced from one to the other. "You're not taking me back."

Beris shrugged. "We could say you overpowered us. But I think we'd rather not go back until we get you to where you need to go to."

Looking at Gaxtal, I asked, "Can you find Kalax?"

Gaxtal snorted as if I'd asked a stupid question. I was starting to think the Dragon Affinity really did rub off on you.

Beris held out a hand to me. "It's going to be tight, sharing a saddle."

I laughed. "Just don't crowd me."

With a grin, Syl gave Gaxtal his head and the blue leapt into the sky. It was better than wonderful to be flying again. I closed my eyes and put my face into the wind. And in the back of my mind, I felt a pleased rumbling that sounded like Kalax.

Together, we are strong.

CHAPTER 8
PUT TO THE TEST

The scent of wild dragon was heavy in my nose when I woke. But Kalax would have warned me if black dragons were near. She'd known hours before Gaxtal had showed up.

Two days ago, it had seemed perfectly normal—and wonderful—to see Thea. But it was odd to have her arrive riding with Beris and Syl, on their sinuous blue dragon.

I still felt wary around them, but Thea's delight at seeing Kalax—and Kalax's pleased thoughts—made it hard for me to be as jealous as I'd once been of Beris. Varla and Merik seemed relieved, too, to have more help.

That first night, we'd sat in a circle, our dragons warming our backs, and had talked about the search we'd started. We'd pledged to find the one Dragon Stone or die trying. The King's Dragon Stone, Thea had called it. The name stuck.

And Beris and Syl seemed to realize more than any of the rest of us how important the King's Dragon Stone was. I was sure the power they had felt from the Memory Stone made them aware that we had to find strong magic to fight magic.

Scrubbing a hand over my face, I sat up. Sharp, winter air made me shiver. Just what was that scent like?

Something like water on rock? Or the smell after a storm?

I didn't know. And then I remembered that last night I had shared my dreams with Kalax. I reached out for her now, for she was no longer keeping me and Thea warm.

A flash of red over blue lake came to me. She must have left before first light to hunt for lake fish—her favorite. I stiffened as I realized she had sensed the wild dragons. But why was she so quiet?

Kalax, are you hurt?

Seb. Keep your mind small. She answered me with a thought like a whisper and so fast that it was there and gone. I knew she was worried that my much clumsier use of the Dragon Affinity would betray her position and mine to the wild dragons.

Throwing off my blanket, I rose. A rustle announced Thea was awake. "You felt it, too?" I asked.

She nodded. She was as connected to Kalax as I was, a bond stronger than any friendship. Thea looked a little paler than usual, but we were all sleeping in our jerkins with our armor close by. There was a new calmness to her, a return of her old confidence—I'd missed that.

"Are you ready?" Thea finished buckling on her breastplate and taking up her bow. I nodded, strapping on my boots.

Not far from us, Merik raised his head. "What?" he mumbled.

"Shh. Try not to wake the others yet," Thea said to him. Her tone sharpened with command. It wasn't like an order from King Justin—he snapped at people, Mordecai yelled, and even Commander Hegarty liked to bark orders. For Thea, leading people was as natural as shooting an arrow or swinging a sword. She had a knack for seeing what needed to be done.

Merik's eyes widened. "Trouble?"

"Don't know yet," I said. "It's Kalax."

"And Lord Vincent?" Merik slipped on his optics and reached for his boots.

"Don't think so," I said. "Wild dragons maybe. We're going to go see if there is anything we can do."

"We'll be ready for whatever you bring with you," Merik said. He gave a nod, and I knew that he was telling the truth. I imagined him packing up the camp, waking others with an easy nudge and a finger over his lips, and urging everyone to have their weapons ready in case we came back with either a wounded dragon or being chased by one.

Of course, there is always the third alternative—we might win over a wild dragon.

That was the idea I had shared with Thea some nights ago. Hope quivered inside me—but I knew Thea had been astounded by the apparent stupidity of the idea.

But we might do it.

Commander Hegarty had even said the others were right in that we needed more troops. Even with the King's Dragon Stone, we would still be facing a battle to get to him.

"You really think that this is going to work?" Thea asked.

We headed up one of the deer paths to the wooded hills behind us. On the other side of the rise, across a meadow surrounded by birch copses, a mountain lake sparkled in the morning sunlight. Kalax now hid in the trees, watching the wild dragons eat her fish.

I mentally thanked her for being so patient without actually reaching out to her. It wasn't in a dragon's nature to give up their territory or kills. Food in particular was the number one cause of dragon on dragon violence in the enclosure at the Academy. That thought had me remembering how I had last seen the Academy. I shut out the image of the tumbled-down tower.

Thank me in fish.

Kalax's thought carried annoyance at what she was having to put up with for her human riders. She added another thought. *Two dragons. No humans.*

Large, small? Fierce? Any problem?

Kalax snorted at my stupidity. *All dragons problems. Made to be so for humans.*

I heard the warning chirrup of the wild dragons.

May have to kill them now, Kalax said.

Kalax—no! I urged her, knowing that I was probably radiating worry.

Easy, Seb. Dragons joke. They too busy with fish to hunt me. I stay close. You see their minds.

Kalax abruptly shut off contact, leaving me gasping with the sudden sensation of being alone in my own mind.

"Seb?" Thea glanced back. She was crossing the top of the hill.

I pointed ahead. "Two wild dragons. No humans."

Thea frowned, as if she was sad not to have a good fight ahead.

She gave a nod, pointed me in one direction, so I would come in from the more north. She headed straight toward the wild dragons. She held up her hand, three fingers in the air, then lightly tapped her own chest.

I nodded, a sign for waiting three breaths, and then crept forward.

This early the air was still, with only the faintest breeze rustling the trees. It was impossible not to think that the dragons couldn't hear me as my boots crunched against pine needles.

I can hear you.

Kalax needled her thought at me like an arrow, giving me the image of a path to follow so I could find the black dragons. Kalax crouched just ahead of me, managing to hide her bulk and her deep russet-red color behind a thicket of brambles. Her tail flicked lazily in the undergrowth, directing me toward the lake.

The mountain lake was vaguely diamond shaped, formed out of gorges and river hollows. We came on it at the wider, teardrop-shaped end where the two dragons were splashing in the shallows.

A sudden plume of water lifted from the lake surface and a large scaled head with a stubby jaw followed it. The dragon croaked to another black dragon on the shore. Both were wild dragons all right, with sleek scales.

The dragon that stood at the edge of the lake seemed larger than the one in the water and sported a mane of spikes around its ears and jaw. It snuffled the air, and I was sure it could smell me. I worried for Thea, wherever she was. But the dragon bent its long neck once and lapped at the lake water.

Here your dragons, what to? Fish? Or the glory of King Justin's thanks?

I couldn't help but hear the sarcasm in Kalax's voice. She, like Thea, didn't think much of my plans to win over some wild dragons.

Looking at the two dragons as they fished, I thought they were healthy and strong. Not the biggest by any stretch, but they didn't seem worried about being chased away from here.

Now that Torvald had fallen, it seemed the wild dragons were spreading much further into the Middle Kingdom. I had to hope these two weren't controlled by the Darkening. Reaching out with a ghostly thread of awareness, I could detect no dark shadow in their minds.

Maybe even the Darkening and Lord Vincent have limits, as do I.

I remembered how Lord Vincent had barely been able to keep control over all those in King's Village.

Careful.

Kalax's warning came as the wild dragon on the lake's edge lifted its head and flared its spines. It had felt my presence. I wasn't sure what idea was worse—the thought we might have to fight these two dragons or that they might fly away.

I won't control them, not as the Darkening does.

The wild dragons seemed almost perfect, not as perfect as Kalax, of course, but no other dragon could ever be her. The black dragons were beautiful hunters. To control such a wild thing seemed almost a sin. It meant controlling every instinct that made them what they were.

Water splashed, and the dragon by the lake hissed—not in my direction or the direction of its mate. The splash had come from a point where the trees overshadowed the south edge of the lake.

Thea.

I pulled in a breath and tried to concentrate.

Something small hit the water and skipped the surface three times before vanishing with a watery sound into the lake. The head of the half-submerged dragon followed the stone down while the dragon on the shore tipped its head to one side. They appeared like cats, fascinated by anything that moved.

That had to be Thea. Who else would be hiding out there, skipping stones.

Another stone skimmed the surface of the lake. Like before, the dragons followed the stone. The dragon on the shore tensed, muscles trembling. Thea was holding their attention so I could use my Dragon Affinity.

I wrapped my awareness around the black dragons. Thea threw another stone. I just wanted to *feel* their minds—and in my mind I saw they were both coiled tight. Springs, ready to pounce or flee.

Excitement. Interest. Hunger.

A part of me wondered how Kalax and the other dragons withstood such huge appetites and instincts. It was as if the biggest summer storm ever was trapped in their forms.

Seb, concentrate! Kalax barked in my mind.

The next stone traveled further than Thea must have been expecting. The swimming dragon watched the stone skip over the lake surface, its head bobbing as it matched the movement. The stone stopped and sank, splashing the dragon's stubby nose.

Attack! Defend! Claws!

The wave of anger from the dragon had me stumbling backward. The dragon plunged its nose into the spot where the stone had disappeared, seizing nothing but water in its jaws.

Sitting down on the ground, I wondered how we were going to succeed in taming them. The feelings of a wild dragon seemed impossible to sooth.

Kalax purred against my mind. *Stick with your dragon. No need for these.* She was jealous. I could have laughed if I wasn't still feeling the hot ebb of anger from the dragons beyond. *No, I said. The First Rider did this. I can. We can understand each other.*

I threw my awareness out again at the dragons, this time feeling a curiosity replacing the anger. The dragon in the lake swam forward slowly, stealthy and slinky, heading to where the rocks had been coming from. Where Thea hid. The other dragon was starting to puff up the spikes around its neck.

Feelings from the dragons started to become words, but a pounding in my head left me gasping.

The dragon on the shore swiveled its head to look straight at me.

Seb!

Kalax pushed her nose through the undergrowth. I held my

throbbing skull. It was too much—I couldn't hold this. Too much of everything.

Enemy? Come for food? My thoughts were still latched onto the swimming dragon, which had stopped and raised its head out of the water to also look in my direction.

Our direction.

Kalax wrapped her tail around me. The world spun. I almost couldn't think because of the pounding in my head. The part of me that was always with Kalax could sense the part of me that was with the swimming dragon. Echoes of the black dragon's hatred swirled around me.

Attack! The swimming black dragon surged out of the lake. The dragon on the shore seemed more confused...as if it was aware of the Dragon Affinity.

I threw my thoughts at it. *Clutch friend. We mean no harm!*

The black dragon in the lake let out a long, ululating roar.

I groaned, and Kalax took matters into her own claws.

Stop. Human mine! she roared and burst out of the foliage, flinging her wings wide. The mountains echoed her fury and the wild dragons quailed. She dwarfed them. The rare crimson reds like Kalax were the largest of dragons.

My meat. My fish. All mine!

Waves of hatred poured off both black dragons.

Minds like sheep, Kalax thought at me, pawing the ground, ready for a fight.

Thea stepped out of her hiding place behind the trees. I sensed her as a dragon would—small, weak and possible prey.

And then she threw her last stone.

The wild dragons focused their rage against the strange moving target and roared at it.

It was a good throw, I had to give Thea credit for that. She had bought us a second.

I threw my affinity at both of the dragons—this time not using just my awareness, my senses, or my thoughts, but putting all my emotions into it.

Kalax was right, that was the language they understood. I threw my pride at being selected by Kalax as her rider, my confidence when I first put on the Dragon Rider uniform, and the thrill of flying with Kalax.

The dragons' thoughts faltered.

Using old anger at my father for his drunken rages, and the pain of the loss of Jodreth and the loss of Torvald, I let loose my own fury.

The black dragons shrank back.

Big enemy?

My head throbbed, but I used the pain to add to everything else I was throwing at the black dragons. *Yes. Much bigger. But we share meat, share hunt, share fish.*

Meat share? Fish?

The black dragons hissed, heads low. They turned on each other to vent their anger in any direction they could. But Kalax roared again.

I climbed to my feet. I would make them think I was somehow bigger…more powerful. I would settle territory rights over them.

And I was bringing them food and offering to share everything in the lake. If they did accept that, they had to accept they belonged to me.

Meat to share, I repeated at them. *Fly with us. You mine.*

I would much rather be able to reason and treat with them as I could with Kalax, even arguing our cases, not that Kalax ever listened much to me anyway. But Kalax's thoughts hit me hard.

You—mine!

She was right. These dragons needed an alpha to follow. They really needed to belong to her.

The swimming dragon looked from Kalax to me, and then glanced at Thea, one dragon twisting and cocking its head to one side. Slowly, it ducked its head into the water and came up with a fish, which it gulped down, never taking its eyes from Kalax.

Behind it, the other dragon gave a growl of resentment. They were accepting food from Kalax's territory. The black dragons ducked their heads low. Neither one was happy, but both were now Kalax's to command.

Or that's what I hoped. Now we'd see if they could learn to listen to a human, too.

CHAPTER 9
SHRINE OF THE FIRST RIDER

S eb was looking… ill.

If I'd been kinder about it, I might have put it as just tired, but a few nights of rough sleeping hadn't put those deep shadows under his eyes. Sitting by the evening fire, he looked like a creature from one of the ghost stories Merik and Varla loved to tell. Red and orange reflected in his eyes from the fire and made the sunken hollows of his cheeks seem even deeper. I didn't want to talk about it in front of the others, but they could see just as much as I that Seb was looking terrible. Even his hair seemed to stick up more than usual and it had seemed to dull over the past two days.

That was how long it had been since Seb had 'captured' the two wild dragons. But wasn't really the right word for what he'd done. The black dragons were hanging around, but they didn't really obey anyone—not Seb, not Kalax, and not even each other as far as I could tell.

At least they are not attacking us.

I sipped the soup Merik had made from the edible plants Varla had foraged. One of the many interests Merik had that Varla shared was cooking. It seemed that Merik had done more than spend all this time looking at maps. He'd studied the names and classifications of flora and fauna from the large bestiaries and herbariums that had once existed. And Varla loved learning about everything.

As soon as we made camp, Merik would start scouting, often pulling Varla with him and we'd hear shouts of "Marsh-Clover!" or "Lyeni's Root!"

Beris and Syl would both roll their eyes—they didn't think cooking was a skill any Dragon Rider needed, and I had to agree with them.

But I couldn't deny that Merik's soup was surprisingly tasty. It had a touch of garlic and a nutty flavor, mixed with a good dollop of sweet-sour. But I was starting to think we needed to go fishing more and not let the dragons have all the fun.

Not far from our campfire, the wild dragons kept nipping at each other, hissing at each other in the twilight and flaring their spiked manes if anyone even looked at them. They were putting all of us on edge.

They didn't look like they were our allies, despite the fact that they trailed after us, taking to the air when we did, landing with us, watching Kalax. They kind of ignored Ferdinania— she'd slapped both of them across the snout with her tail. And Gaxtal eyed the blacks as if he was thinking about how he wanted to take a bite out of them. I was starting to think maybe he made the black dragons nervous.

Right now, I could hear their soft chirrups from the woods behind us as they bickered with each other. Arguing seemed to be another form of affection for them—a way that they communicated. Gaxtal had settled down on the opposite side of camp from the wild dragons, along with Ferdinania.

As for Kalax, she was keeping to herself tonight. But she went with Seb whenever he went to check on the black dragons. It seemed to me she was more than a little bit jealous of the attention that Seb was giving the wild dragons. Seb was her human after all, as I was.

Coming back to the camp and sitting down on one of the logs by the fire, Seb said, "It won't be long now."

Merik glanced over at him. Syl had already settled in next to Gaxtal to sleep, leaving Varla, Beris and me still sitting around the fire.

"Won't be long before what?" Beris asked, his face pinched with worry. He glanced over to the woods where the wild dragons had settled, hunched a shoulder and turned away from them.

How many of us were actually sleeping at night, or was everyone else like me—waking up to every crack and rumble, worried the wild dragons might have decided on a midnight snack of us.

"Before we try to saddle them." Seb gave Beris a crooked smile. He took a wooden bowl of soup from Merik. To me, Seb's smile looked weak. Varla glanced at Seb and winced, as if she thought Seb was being too optimistic.

A frown pulling his eyebrows flat, Beris stared at Seb. "Are you seriously suggesting we ride those things?"

"They're not things," Seb growled. I could tell from the tone in Seb's voice just how much Beris had managed to offend him. Even though they were wild dragons, Seb still had the greatest respect for them. He wasn't like the rest of us who just saw dangerous dragons—his Dragon Affinity really did set him apart.

"Just who is going to ride one of them?" Beris asked, his words clipped. He didn't seem to see Seb's mouth tighten or how Seb's eyes narrowed. "It's not just the fact that they'll turn around and eat you as soon as look at you—it's also a question of regular riders. Who are you going train to be a Dragon Rider in just a few days? Or are you suggesting we split the teams we already have? One rider to every dragon?"

"If we have to, I'll ride one." Seb glanced at me, his eyebrows lifted.

Our eyes met, I knew what he meant.

One of the effects of Seb's affinity was that it made such a strong connection between the three of us—him, Kalax and me. I could fly Kalax on my own and still be in close communication with Seb, and Seb would also know what Kalax was doing and thinking. But could any of the other riders split up and still be able to both fly and fight? There was a reason why it took a team of riders to manage dragon riding.

Luckily, however, I didn't have to say anything about what I was thinking.

Varla put down her soup bowl with a clatter and announced, "I've been thinking about the story Seb told us—the one that Thea got from the Gypsies about the First Rider. It fits with a few things Merik and I have read in some of the oldest scrolls."

We all stared at her. Face pink, she folded her hands in her lap as if she was in the classroom back at the Academy and had given the wrong answer.

I waved a hand at her. "Well...go on."

She glanced at Merik. He gave her a nod as well and an encouraging smile.

She stood and spread her feet wide like she was about to give a lecture. "We all know that back in the earliest days, dragons lived in the mountains—like wild dragons do now. But the dragons of the Middle Kingdom were always the largest. All accounts have it, too, that the Middle Kingdom dragons are also slightly different from the Southern dragons. Now if the First Rider was raised by monks—like in the story the Gypsies told—then he must have been raised by, or maybe he even started, the Draconis Order of monks and sorcerers. That makes sense—right? So they must be the ones who made the Dragon Stones—they knew magic, after all. We also know there is a story that the King's Dragon Stone defeated the Darkening. Which means that...well, uhm...I think we need to look for the First Rider."

I blinked a few times and asked, "You mean you think the First Rider is still alive?" I was hoping she was wrong about that. It was bad enough trying to figure out if Lord Vincent was really an ancient prince who had become immortal due to magic and the Darkening. I shivered. I didn't like this idea of immortals—that meant trouble that stayed around forever.

Varla huffed out a breath. "Of course not. But haven't we all heard about the tomb of the First Rider? How the First Rider was buried and mourned by the First Dragon?"

I glanced at Seb, then at Merik. They were nodding, so they had heard those old stories, too. Looking at Varla, I said, "You think the First Rider had the King's Dragon Stone?"

Varla nodded and her voice picked up speed. "Think of the Gypsy story. He said the First Rider was a king, but then that Gypsy took the story back to a time before the First Rider became king. Have any of you ever heard that the First Rider was a king? Probably the first king of Torvald? That means the First Rider had to be King Torvald!" Varla put her hands on her hips and grinned. The firelight made her red hair look even redder, and the way she was grinning left her looking almost too young to be a Dragon Rider.

I shook my head. It seemed to me that Varla was reaching more than a little to make this idea work, but it was also at least something we could use to narrow our search from looking at every single ruin of a monastery to maybe just looking for anything connected to the First Rider. This was also a reason I could use to distract Seb from getting too obsessed with the black dragons he was so intent on taming.

Turning to Seb, I said, "We should wait to saddle the wilds until they're able to fly in formation with us. We should listen to Varla."

Varla sat down, smiling as if I'd just told her she was the best

Dragon Rider ever. Merik leaned over and patted her shoulder. Beris just let out a breath as if maybe he thought we were all crazy. I shot him a look—he was the one who'd come to join us.

Seb cleared his throat, glancing from Varla to me and back again. At last, he gave a reluctant nod. "Okay, I guess that you're right. They need more practice flying with us and not being so noisy."

"Thank the First Rider for that," Beris muttered, still loud enough for all to hear. I shot him another frown, but he stood and headed to where Gaxtal and Syl were snoring.

Varla yawned, stood and stretched. "I've got more reading to do before I sleep." She headed off to sit by Ferdinania.

I used the time to try and get Seb to eat more soup, and Merik —bless him—pulled out a flagon of wine that he got Seb to drink, which at least put a little color in Seb's cheeks.

A half hour later, Varla almost ran back to us, a scroll in one hand and her braid loose so her hair frizzed out around her head. "I've got where we start. There's a shrine to the First Rider not far from here—a couple of days' ride on horse maybe."

"Half a day by dragon." Seb said.

Varla nodded, her grin wide. "That's about what I thought." She held up the scroll. "But this doesn't say anything about King Torvald or the First Dragon."

Merik shrugged and pushed his optics up on his nose. "Let's go anyway. It would stupid to miss something just because we decided to be lazy."

Varla shot a quick look at me that I almost missed in the flickering firelight. Something was bothering her. "Yeah—about that," she said, looking between me and Seb. "This does say some not very nice things about the King's Dragon Stone. At first I just thought it was sour grapes—most of comes from the Runes of Hroth."

Seb threw a twig into the fire. "I have no idea who Hroth is."

I was glad he'd said it, since I'd been thinking the same thing.

Varla waved the scroll. "Hroth was a shaman from the north tribes. He did a lot of traveling and actually wrote down the lore he heard."

Merik nodded and leaned forward. Light glinted off his optics and his dark skin. "Unfortunately, he used his own system of runes so there's still a lot of argument about the exact meaning of each symbol." He drew what looked like a triangle in the dirt. "That could mean horse or it could mean house."

I rubbed the knot between my eyes. "How is any of this a problem?"

Varla shrugged. "He probably had a biased opinion, but he claimed the King's Dragon Stone is evil." She glanced at Seb and looked away. "That it's like the Dragon Affinity and that no one should ever use it."

I clenched my back teeth. This was exactly what I had feared.

Seb gave a snort. "Same old stuff. Everyone hated the Dragon Affinity back then and still do. They fear what they don't understand."

Varla nodded. "Yeah. You're probably right, Seb. And maybe I've got the translation wrong."

Merik stood and dusted off his breeches. "Why don't I come

help you with that scroll?" They headed into the darkness, talking softly between them, making for where Ferdinania lay, a large and silent shadow tucked up against the rocks.

The fire had burnt low and the shadows it cast in the trees overhead flickered and danced.

"I should check on the wild dragons," Seb said and started to stand.

I beat him up and put a hand on his arm. "They'll be fine. And you're too tired to do anything if they're not. Get some sleep. You'll be able to do a better job tomorrow."

A wuffle came out of the darkness from Kalax as if she approved of that plan.

Seb stared at me, looking glassy-eyed, as if wanted to argue but couldn't think what to say. He finally nodded. I hated how it was taking so much out of him to deal with the wild dragons—were they worth it?

Seb scrubbed a hand through his hair. "If anything happens—"

"I'll come get you. I'll keep first watch, then Merik can keep second, and Beris third." To be truthful, I was loath to leave even the dying bit of light the fire was giving out.

But Seb didn't move, so I asked, "Is it, painful? Keeping the black dragons with us?"

Seb grimaced. That told me it was.

It was worse seeing him like this than it had been seeing him after the battle for Torvald, when the affinity had drained him but had helped to save so many lives. I had hoped the affinity would get stronger, making it easier for Seb to use it.

But now I could see he was sickening as if from some wasting disease.

"It's not connecting with them that's the problem," he said, his voice tired. I was sure he was lying about that. "It's how I have to keep stopping them from fighting all the time." He winced as if even now, in their sleep, he had to send the wild dragons soothing thoughts. "They fight over food, over who gets to fly first, over their status with the other dragons, and now they've even started fighting over us. I don't even think they really want to hurt anyone…they're just always trying to prove themselves."

Lips pressed tight, I kept a hand on his arm. I didn't know what to say. Did he still think this was a good idea? But if I started to argue with him, I knew he'd just dig in and wouldn't admit that he needed to stop.

Shaking my head, I asked, "By the First Dragon, how are we going to get more wild dragons if you have trouble handling just two?"

Seb pulled away from me, forced a smile and waved away my concerns. "I'm just tired. You're right. I'll feel better in the morning."

I watched as he stumbled wearily to Kalax's side.

☙❧

The next day proved even harder than the last but for different reasons. Seb rode in front of me in his navigator's saddle, high on the crest of Kalax's shoulder and neck, and I sat further back in the protector's saddle. The two wild dragons flew on either side of us.

Scratch and Hiss, I thought with a wry smile. I was coming to think of those as their names, even though Seb said they had proper dragon names that our human mouths couldn't form and pronounce. That made me wonder if Kalax had a dragon name of clicks and growls and croaks that she only shared with other dragons.

All names powerful.

Kalax's thought blossomed in my mind as sudden as a sea fog and just as elusive as I struggled after it. She didn't answer my question about if she had another name, but I laughed, feeling happy for the first time in a long time. Flying always made me feel that way—as if my troubles were far below, back on the ground that flew past us in pretty greens and blues and golds.

"On your left!" Beris yelled. He and Syl on their stocky blue Gaxtal swooped past us.

Kalax gave a rumble of annoyance and lifted her head. She wanted to show them just how fast she could fly.

I know. You can outrace any of them!

Gaxtal flashed over the forest, Beris and Syl on his back, heading for the horizon before pulling up and circling lazily. Gaxtal enjoyed showing off just as much as his riders did.

Behind us, Merik was navigating on Ferdinania with Varla in her protector's saddle the same as me. Beris and Syl were keeping a watch for any enemies while Merik was looking for this shrine to the First Rider that Varla had mentioned. As much as I wanted to tell Seb to let Kalax have some fun and swoop and soar like she wanted to, I knew we had to focus on the task. The longer it took to get help to the king, the greater the chance there might not be a king for us to serve.

At our side, the wild dragons tumbled through the air, playing a game of rolling over each other so they looked like a knot of whirling black storm clouds. Every now and then, one would snap at the other, or one would bite the air one tooth away from the other's throat. I had thought that they only did that when faced with us riders, but Seb was right in that they seemed to delight in trying to fight everyone around them.

Barbarians.

Kalax's scorn for the black dragons carried to me with a sharp sting. I wondered if the hatred between our dragons and the blacks was a very long-running one, or if it had only started when we humans started riding dragons.

Too much like younglings. Sniping at anything that moves. Biting what shouldn't be bit.

She blew a hot breath through her nose, and I suddenly understood that she hated the wild dragons. She just thought they were too dangerous.

Exactly.

"Hold!" Seb raised a hand into the air.

One of the wild dragons twisted and with a caw it suddenly tumbled downward and righted to skip the tree tops below.

No discipline. Kalax huffed again before angling her wings slightly and gliding downward.

This time, I felt Seb push with his mind when he held up an open palm in midair. *Dragons—here!*

The wild dragons jerked up their heads, stopping their play fighting to stare at Seb. Without taking their gazes from him, they rose back up, undulating like snakes with wings through the sky, flying just a few feet away from each other.

"You did it!" I punched the air. The blacks had reacted to Seb's command and had come back into formation. Seb glanced back at me and gave me a crooked grin, but I could see the beads of sweat on his face. All this effort to control these dragons and talk to them was costing him a lot of energy. How was he going to get them to listen to him in the heat of battle?

Seb turned to face forward again and held out his hand, pointing straight ahead. I could feel the air around me tingle with his Dragon Affinity.

To my amazement, the blacks didn't start fighting again, but came up and started flying straight. Kalax and Ferdinania flew in tandem with the two blacks, until a crow darted up from the trees below with a raucous cawing.

The wild dragons reacted at once, roaring at the interloper.

No! Don't! Seb shouted at the dragons, but their attention had already fastened on the crow as it dove down again, vanishing into the trees.

The black dragons drove down, hitting the trees like arrows.

Branches cracked and the trees shook and then the two black dragons burst out of the trees, once again tumbling and rolling, snapping and hissing at each other. They flew back into the sky, and I decided they were going to need a lot more work before we could ever take them into battle.

"There!" Varla shouted down to us from Ferdinania's back. It was still bright day, but the temperature had been dropping all afternoon. I wished now that I'd brought a thicker cloak or had some woolen scarves to wrap around me. We had been flying for a few hours, but now Varla pointed at a pinnacle of rock poking out from the forest canopy below.

That was the shrine of the First Rider? From here, it looked like a pile of gray stone and nothing more.

Seb waved at her and gave a thumbs up. Kalax circled once and chose her own approach to the outcropping. She crowed once and beat her powerful wings until she was level with Gaxtal, then swooped down, faster than a strike of lightning.

The thrill of a dragon at full clip was like nothing else. It always drove every thought from my head—I loved the cold air slapping at my face, the whistling of the wind and the feel of Kalax's muscles underneath me. It was both exhilarating and more than a little scary as the ground rushed up at us.

The shriek of wild dragons split the air. I tensed, reaching for one of my holstered javelins, but the two blacks fell past us, playing as they cawed and acting like kids. And they had passed us!

Kalax thundered with annoyance at being bested, but Seb gave a wild whoop. "We always knew the wild dragons were fast, but faster than Kalax is more than fast."

They cheat.

Kalax settled in the lower branches of a huge, ancient tree

whose thick trunk could hold her. She hopped from there to the grass of a clearing just below the rocks. She rumbled at the wild dragons, still circling the outcrop. Seb was trying to wave them in, but they were too caught up in whatever game they had started. Seb gave a shrug, leaving the blacks in flight.

"What do you mean, they cheat?" I asked, talking to Kalax.

It was Seb who answered with a question as we dismounted. "Do you see what they can do? Even though they're fighting each other all the time, they are flying with us. Well, sort of." He pulled his helmet. "They used their momentum and Kalax's slipstream to fly even faster with lesser effort. It's the same reason geese fly in a formation—each goose is using the slipstream of the one in front to fly with less effort. The wild dragons do the same, but just a lot faster."

"Apart from the poor goose up front," I muttered.

"Well, that's why we could change over who leads." Seb turned to Kalax. "Although I know you could always lead with no trouble, my girl." He cooed at her.

Kalax chirruped back, pleased by the attention.

Ferdinania and Gaxtal landed, and the others dismounted. Walking over, Beris asked, "Where is this shrine to the First Rider then?"

Frowning and looking around, Varla pointed to the back of the small outcrop where one standing stone—tall and narrow—stood at the very front of the large, gray boulders. "That looks likely."

I walked over to the standing stone. It didn't look like any kind of fine construction I had ever seen, so either it was older than anything I knew about or it was more an accident of nature that it looked like this.

"Uh, are you sure this is the right place?" I asked Varla.

She nodded, but she reached into a leather pouch and pulled out the scroll again, checking it over. She nodded at the standing stone. "Do you see...markings?"

Merik stepped forward, pushing up his goggles and putting on his optics. He had several pairs now that he could use to see better.

"What is it?" Seb asked, peering over Merik's shoulder at what looked like very faint scratches.

Merik said, "A man? A man with horns maybe? And that looks like a dragon standing up."

I was getting a bad feeling about this. Dropping a hand to the hilt of my sword, I said, "I've looked at a lot of old ruins so far, and none of them really looked like this. The Draconis Order built towers and temples."

"But it's on the map." Varla waved with the scroll. "And who else would build a shrine to the First Rider?"

I shrugged. "It just doesn't look much of a shine to me. More like a pagan site—something maybe the Wildmen would put up." I pointed to the standing stone with its odd scratches. "When did the Draconis Order ever leave any marks like that? It makes me think of rites and rituals held before flickering flames by strange and terrible people."

Varla was checking the inscriptions on the stones with those on the scroll. I was willing to bet none of it matched. She let out a long breath. "Maybe you're right."

I looked at Seb. He shook his head just once. That meant he wasn't feeling anything either—and we should have felt something. I'd always gotten a funny feeling when I was close to a Dragon Stone. It had taken me a long time to figure out what that feeling meant, but after almost missing it with the Armor Stone, I wasn't going to mistake it again.

Wouldn't the King's Dragon Stone—the thing that was supposed to be more powerful than all of them—feel even stronger?

I don't know why I could sense the stones. Maybe it was because I had been healed by one of them—maybe that left me able to feel the magic. Or maybe it had something to do with Seb's Dragon Affinity. I didn't really know and didn't want to know. It was one of those things that left me worried about magic. It had changed me, and that was unsettling.

I remembered too well the sensation like falling down and down and down into endless darkness…

Someone comes.

Kalax's warning knocked me out of my dark thoughts.

I looked up to see Seb and the others looking to the east. A moment later, the wild dragons stopped chasing each other around the rock outcropping and hovered in the air.

"Dragon!" Beris shouted. He and Syl ran for Gaxtal, buckling on their helmets. Ferdinania launched herself then swooped down to pick up Merik and Varla—she obviously wasn't going to ever lose another rider.

No harm.

Kalax's thought came to me with a warm breath as she

sniffed the air. But she stayed close to Seb and me, standing just behind and over us.

Seb pointed toward the distinctive dragon shape heading our way. "She's flying high. And she's not that big."

He was right. This wasn't a wild black. This was a smaller dragon that stretched her wings and neck out so we could see a pale underbelly. It was a posture all Dragon Riders knew. *This is my exposed belly; these are my vulnerable wings— I am no threat.*

Kalax whistled at the other dragons. Both Gaxtal and Ferdinania settled down again, but the black dragons disappeared into the woods to hide.

The shape grew larger, and Merik said, "It's a Messenger Dragon."

Messenger Dragons were easy to spot—they were much smaller than dragons we flew and they could change their color from sky blue to green to hide themselves.

Seb seemed to sense the trouble brewing before anyone else. He flung out a hand. In the next instant, the wild dragons had launched into the air, heading for the smaller, Messenger Dragon.

"No!" Seb yelled.

One black dragon snapped at the Messenger Dragon. It squawked, twisted and spun, changing color from white to blue to white again.

Seb threw his affinity at the black dragons away. They bucked and turned, and the Messenger Dragon changed to green and dove for the forest. Varla gave a yell, and Kalax roared her displeasure.

The two wild dragons flew in the air over us, screaming and roaring. I feared they would attack us.

"Seb?" Reaching out, I touched his shoulder. Under his jerkin, he was shaking, but he stared up at the black dragons. They hovered for a moment, and then headed to the top of the rock outcropping and perched there.

Beris strode over to where the Messenger Dragon had disappeared into the woods. He came back holding what looked to be a leather bag. "I don't know where the Messenger went, but it left this." He held up the leather pouch, the Flamma crest of flame and wings emblazoned on its side. "Seems to be for you."

Walking over, I snatched the leather pouch and glanced inside. One scroll lay at the bottom.

Hands held up, Beris backed away from me.

I rolled my shoulders, trying to relax them. "Sorry, I'm just..." I let the words trail off because I didn't know what I was. This couldn't be good news—why would anyone in my family send a Messenger Dragon after me? Taking out the scroll, I opened it. My hands were shaking. When I read it, I felt dizzy and my mouth dried. I had to read it twice before I could make myself take a breath.

I must have looked worse than I felt because Seb moved closer to me. And Varla asked, "Thea? Who is it from, Thea?"

"My family. My father and Reynalt. They want me to join them." I shook my head and kicked the sand. I wanted to throw the scroll into a lake or an ocean. But I had nowhere that I could get rid of it. I just had my father's words to me.

Silence fell. Everyone was staring at me. My face heated, and my stomach tightened into a hard knot.

"Thea?" Seb's voice sounded very low and worried. "If it's bad news and you—"

Slicing the air with one hand, I cut him off. Crumpling the scroll with one fist, I shoved it into my jerkin where it would stay safe until I could burn it.

"No. It's not…well, it is bad news, but my place is here." I tried to smile, but it felt stiff and strange on my face. I think Seb could see I was upset. Beris gave a nod and slapped Syl's arm and they headed over to check on Gaxtal. Merik and Varla went back to the shrine—or whatever it was, talking low and looking at the scroll again.

I glanced at Seb. "I should be asking if you're the one feeling well. That was a lot of work to control the blacks."

He was pale, but he nodded. "And you?"

I waved a hand. We were both lying, and we both knew it.

He was in pain over what his Dragon Affinity was costing him and I was in pain over what the letter had really said—that my father, mother and older brother Reynalt had thrown in with Lord Vincent, the true king, for he was strong enough to lead us all.

Now I must fight my kin, my blood, my family.

CHAPTER 10
BLACK CLOUDS
BLACK CLOUDS

We made camp not far from the shrine, or whatever it was we had found. Thea had been quiet since she'd gotten that message, and I didn't ask her again about it, but something was wrong with her family. I knew that much. A thin curl of smoke rose from the fire Varla had made. She had made only a small campfire, and we sheltered under tall pines where no one else would see us, but we still posted guards. Beris was taking first watch.

The wind ruffled my hair, and I leaned back against Kalax.

What now?

I sighed, not really expecting or even wanting an answer.

Thea's message from her family had me thinking about my folks. I didn't know where any of them were—if they were still safe in Torvald or if they had left the city. I wanted to go and find them, but I knew I was doing them more good here. My job was to end the war—that was the best way to keep them safe. If I could. And I hated that the message Thea had gotten seemed to be dredging up a lot of her old troubles, like was she a Flamma, a Dragon Rider or just plain Thea.

Be all three, Kalax thought, and I felt her confusion.

It's different for people. We have to choose one thing to get good at, if we want to get really good. And if everyone says you are a Flamma, then maybe she's thinking that's where her heart should go.

Kalax considered my thoughts quietly for a moment. *Is like asking a rock is stone or rock or boulder.*

I didn't understand, and I looked at her.

Kalax lay with her eyes half closed, her head resting on the ground. *Rock is all. Boulder must be stone and must be rock, too. Humans draw lines around things to say that is this and this is that and has to be so. All very strange.*

That was a piece of dragon logic I could agree with—although I didn't know what it meant for Thea the Dragon Rider or Agathea of the House Flamma.

"Hold!" I heard a shriek from across the camp and looked over. Merik was hanging onto the two largest of the swept-back horns of one of the black dragons as it undulated through the sky. I counted the times that he bounced in the makeshift saddle—visibly leaving the leather. How he'd gotten a saddle on the dragon I didn't know. I stood, cursing that I had let my concentration drop.

The dragon twisted, throwing Merik. His harness snapped and he grabbed for one of the many spines on the dragon's neck.

His hand slipped and Merik fell, but Ferdinania swooped in to catch him.

"By the First Dragon," I muttered and stood, heading over to where Ferdinania had dropped Merik to the ground. She hadn't set him down gently, meaning she wasn't happy he was trying to ride another dragon.

Kalax called up to the wild dragon, but it shook off its saddle and swooped out into the woods.

Merik stood up, dusting off his leathers. Over by the fire, Beris and Syl were laughing and slapping their thighs.

Merik shook his head and pushed up his goggles. "I was sure I was going to get it this time." Shaking my head, I turned my attention to the black dragons. I could hear them in the woods, growling at each other. I was sure that I sensed it had thought dumping Merik was a fun game.

Kalax sent me an image of all the boring drills and the training she had gone through. *Dragons not born knowing saddles.*

"Maybe that's it," I mumbled, reaching out to brush minds with the wild dragon.

I felt Kalax's annoyance, and she broke her thoughts off from me. It still hurt to use my affinity for anything other than Kalax —why it was so easy with her, I wasn't sure. But I was getting used to it.

The dragon Thea had named Scratch sent back actual thoughts for once. *Human hunt me? Drop and Ferdinania catch.*

Scratch gave a snuffling trill, and Hiss, the other black dragon, hissed back.

I saw that Scratch thought Merik and the saddle were trying to bring her down.

No, no! I thought at her, sending an image of how Kalax wore her saddle and let us ride her.

Scratch sent back an image of herself doing a double-roll in the sky with no rider on her back.

How do I say this?

And then had an idea.

Maybe the wild dragons would learn more from playing games. We didn't have time for the long process of earning and building trust with them. What if learning all of the complicated movements and signs that Kalax and the other trained dragons knew could be made into fun?

I could sense interest from Scratch—she liked the idea of fun.

I sent a memory of Thea skipping stones across the lake water and how the pebble stayed close and low to the waves, riding along them. I sent an image like that we had found on the standing stone of a man on the neck of a dragon.

How long can Scratch hold a human? I repeated the memory of the skipping stone, riding over the water.

Easy! Scratch hissed. The black burst up from the trees, rolled once in the air and flew toward Merik. Ferdinania hissed at it, as did Gaxtal. Beris and Syl ducked, and Varla scooted out of the way, but the black seized poor Merik with its front claws. Merik gave a shout. The wild dragon rolled in the air, throwing Merik up toward the clouds. The black rolled again and caught Merik on her back.

"Don't shoot. Merik's fine," I shouted to Thea, who was reaching for her bow. I hoped desperately that I was right.

I watched as the wild dragon rose higher. Merik—his leathers flapping and easy to spot against the black's gleaming scales—scrambled up the beast's neck and grabbed the horns. He had no harness and saddle, but it looked to me as if he might be better without them. The way that the wild dragons moved, bobbing their necks up and down, meant the harness straps that usually secured a rider to the saddle were thrown all over. Without a saddle, Merik was leaning into the dragon's movement. He could crouch low and use the dragon's scales to help hang onto the dragon by tucking his legs between the scales.

I was glad to see Merik had figured this out, but it might be hard to get any other Dragon Riders to ride without a harness and saddle. Our weapons and gear were all held to the dragon—what rider would want to do without those things?

The riders won't be able to fight.

I let out a breath. We'd deal with that later.

At least the wild dragon wasn't trying to throw Merik off. This time, whenever I brushed Scratch's mind with my own, I could see the image of the stone skipping across the wave tops, bouncing smoothly and cleanly, as the wild dragon focused on its chosen task. That was a first, too. It was flying fast, and Merik was only able to hang on.

The wild dragon flew low over the tree tops, bouncing like a stone.

Dragons fight.

Kalax's thought left me breathless. "By the First Dragon—

you're right!" Why would Merik need a bow or a spear if he was on a flying, angry ball of teeth, claws and fire? "Kalax, you are a genius," I breathed.

This would be a whole new style of dragon fighting. If the riders acted as little more than navigators, choosing targets and using the dragon as the weapon, we could fly faster and have double the amount of available riders!

But we can do things that they cannot. I remembered how I could work in tandem with Thea with her shooting other riders out of the sky and leaving the flying to me and Kalax.

We do both, Kalax agreed.

"Kalax, if we ever survive this, I am going to credit you as discovering a whole new type of dragon riding!" I told her.

Not new. Just different, Kalax corrected.

Now all we had to do now was to get Hiss playing the same 'game' and then we had to make sure that they could take commands from their rider.

Then find all of the other wild dragons.

I gave a short, dry laugh.

And there was still the King's Dragon Stone to find. Nothing but easy work ahead of us.

Still, despite how difficult everything seemed as I looked ahead, it was nice to know we had at least tackled one task. The next one was to figure out how to get Merik off the black.

Kalax suddenly lifted her head and swung it back in the direction of Torvald, her nostrils quivering as she snuffed the air.

And Merik shouted, "Dragons!"

From the back of the black dragon, Merik pointed to the eastern horizon.

A small knot of wild dragons flew toward us. Hiss screeched an alarm, and my mind raced. Were they Lord Vincent's dragons come to find us? Or just a wild band on the hunt? Should I try to capture them—and could I manage so many?

I tried to open up my awareness. As soon as I did, Kalax's thoughts wrapped around mine.

No! Feel more. The cold. The dark.

I could feel her concerned. The fact that she, a crimson red, one of the most dangerous things in the sky was worried sent a shiver down my back.

It was here—the Darkening.

Kalax kept her mind small, unwilling to connect our thoughts any more than that or the Darkening might sense us. I could feel the shadow of the evil coming closer, like black clouds against the edges of my mind. It seemed to me that the blue of the sky and the green and russet trees faded and paled, as if winter had deepened and the sun had dimmed.

A foggy panic crept through me, chilling my bones and locking my joints. I glanced over at Thea and saw her frozen. Beris and Syl, too, stared up, their faces pale and their expressions tight. The other dragons kept quiet—we could all sense danger.

The Darkening hadn't sensed us yet, but it would. I had been a fool to think we might be safe while we searched for and trained new dragons. Of course the Darkening would sniff us out. It used dragons—it even seemed more than half dragon itself!

And if a Flamma Messenger Dragon could find Thea, an ancient and powerful magic would surely find us, too.

Stop!

Kalax's thought crept into my mind. She had sensed the panic rising in my chest. The urge to run into the open, begging for mercy lodged in my throat. Kalax mentally surrounded me with her warmth. *Not you. Stop.*

I saw at once that she was right. The fear came from the Darkening itself as it rode the minds of the wild dragons. It was spilling out and hitting me through the Dragon Affinity. Sorrow for the wild dragons lifted inside me. They were being used as if they were puppets, their minds warped and molded to suit the wishes of the Darkening. The fear came from them.

Hide, Kalax thought.

Looking up, I waved to Merik and pointed at the foothills, to the deep gorges and ravines. He and the blacks we had needed to hide. Scratch seemed only too ready to do anything to avoid the fear coming our way. The wild dragon swooped low, flying close to the trees like a shadow, and Hiss followed, both of them quiet and fast. They were well adapted to sneaking and staying hidden.

Varla mounted Ferdinania and Beris and Syl were already on Gaxtal. Thea had our gear on Kalax and swept me up. We took to the air, following Merik, Scratch and Hiss.

I glanced back and saw Thea's tight frown. She gave me a nod, but I knew she must be fighting her own battles against the panic the Darkening spread before it. We'd both been too close to the Memory Stone and to Lord Vincent before this. I wondered how anyone could ever stand to be near the Darkening? How had

Lord Vincent even managed to raise it from its slumber—or was he too much part of it to ever notice?

The wild dragons led us past fallen trees and under bridges, doubling back along the ways we had come, pausing for a few breaths in caves I hadn't even seen. They swept around rock outcroppings and kept low to the ground, using the fading daylight to become almost invisible.

No wonder they're one of the chosen tools of the Darkening.

I could imagine what it must have been like for the first towns that had disappeared under the Darkening. They would have had no warning their doom was coming—one night they would be frozen in sheer panic.

After a long time of flying, Scratch chose a deep cave by the side of a waterfall. We each flew in through a spray of water before settling on the smooth, damp floor. It was crowded with five dragons, but the blacks weren't bickering. Our dragons turned to face the cave's opening and we waited, weapons ready, hearts pounding and no one saying anything.

※

"I think it's gone." Thea broke the silence and shivered. She stood beside me, and we both leaned against the reassuring warmth of Kalax.

You are right. Kalax snuffed the air. *Darkening gone now to search.*

"Why is it searching?" I said the words aloud, but I looked at

Kalax. The others needed to hear this conversation. "What is it searching for?"

"The King's Dragon Stone," Varla said, her voice soft. It was dark in the cave, and I could barely see her as just a dark outline. "That must be it. It wants every scrap of power or anything that could threaten it."

My stomach gave a lurch. I felt sick.

Thea put her hand on my arm. "I know that none of you are going to like what I am about to suggest, but I think...I think we should go after those wild dragons. Let's use them for once. Let's follow them."

I heard a shuffle of boots on the dirt and then Beris said, "Do you want to die?"

Thea's hand tightened on my arm, and I thought she was talking more to me than to Beris. "This is our chance to find out more about *it*—about where its camp is, about how powerful it is. And maybe it will lead us to the King's Dragon Stone."

"You felt what its mere presence did to us! To the dragons!" Beris' voice dropped lower. "And it wasn't even trying to use its magic against us! How do you think we were caught? It can freeze your soul and you just stand there, unable to do a thing. If the Darkening turns its full force on you, a dragon will even forget how to fly."

"I think Beris is right," Varla said. "It's too powerful."

Varla was right, but so was Thea. For the first time, we all pulled together—the Dragon Riders and the wild dragons. We all flew in unison. No fighting. That could give us an advantage.

Her hand tightened on my arm, and then she let go. She

cleared her throat. "Right now we're on our own—and we're on the run. In any military strategy, that is a bad thing. What if we find the King's Dragon Stone and have no idea how to use it? The Darkening could find us and take it from us. But if we know where the Darkening is, we'll be able to spy on them. We'll know where their main camp is, and we might find out what weaknesses they have. I think only one or two of us should follow. The others can keep on with the search. The two who follow the Darkening will be able to warn you if the Darkening comes after you again."

"Or we won't get any warning because whoever is trailing the Darkening has come under the influence of the Memory Stone," Beris muttered.

Next to me in the darkness, I felt Thea shrug and shift on her feet. "That'll be a warning, too."

The cavern was silent; even the dragons seemed to be listening to our plans. Wetting my lips, I gave a nod, even though only the dragons would see it—they could see in the dark. "I don't think this is a time for votes, but I'm with Thea. We'll go on Kalax—she's bigger and can fight if she has to—while the rest of you can keep on searching. You can send word through Ferdinania or Gaxtal if you find the King's Dragon Stone— Kalax will hear them."

Merik let out a long breath and said, "What about the wild dragons?"

I glanced back at them and could only see their eyes as just a gleam in the darkness.

"They'll probably come with me." Or not. The Darkening

had frightened them and I wasn't sure they wouldn't try to return to the wilds.

Gravel crunched and then Varla said, her voice gruff, "Just don't get yourself in trouble." I heard the slap of leather as Varla must have given Thea a pat on the back or a hug. And then it was time to mount Kalax and fly. But into what?

⚜

It didn't take long for Kalax to find the Darkening and its wild dragons. She could sense them long before I could. But it felt like we were chasing a storm—they moved fast, looking like a dark smudge of wings and scales, undulating in the way wild dragons do.

I glanced back at Thea who nodded at me, her helmet in place and her mouth set.

Darkening makes them slow, Kalax shared with me. That speed was slow?

She thought at me that the natural dragon senses of the wild dragons had to be dulled. I knew Scratch and Hiss had already smelled the other dragons. Even though we were miles away, they were acting skittish. But they had stayed with Kalax. Maybe the Darkening had to blunt the dragon senses in order to control them.

I was suddenly afraid for our two wild dragons. What if I was no better than the Darkening, using my affinity to control them?

Controlling those two? Kalax nudged me with the thought and a wry humor. But I sensed a shadow of pride that the two

175

wild dragons had helped us to escape and weren't leaving. They were bonded to Kalax it seemed.

Even so, I still felt uneasy for I was doing something similar to what the Darkening was doing—I was sending commands to the two wild dragons to betray their natural instincts.

As soon as all this is over I'll release them back to the mountains.

Seb thinks I am not free?

Kalax's question made me sit up straighter. She had a point. If she and the wild dragons decided to do something, I wasn't sure I could change their minds.

Behind me, Thea tapped my shoulder and pointed to where the Darkening-controlled dragons were now circling. I realized I'd been more right than I'd known to think of them as a storm. A very real, physical storm gathered in front of us.

Black clouds, thick and tall, swirled over a large, broken patch of land. Trees, shrubs and grass had been burned away by dragon fire. Mists and smoke rose from the ground. The land itself was similar to the dragon enclosure—hot water burst up from the ground, foul-smelling, bubbling mud-flats stretched out below us. So many dragons were gathered that every other animal— birds and small game—had been either eaten or driven away.

As we got closer, I could see dark tents made of heavy, purple cloth on the edges of the mud flats and bubbling springs. It looked a lot like King Justin's camp, but it was far bigger. Around the edges of the camp—where Dragon Riders in a camp would hang their washing and dry uniforms—there hung not clothes, but meat from kills. Food for soldier or dragon. All of it stank.

I urged Kalax down to the rocky gorges to the south of the Darkening's army. That would put us downwind and there were huge reddish boulders and land marked by colors that would easily hide Kalax. The wild dragons with us headed for a cave higher in the hills to the south—I couldn't blame them. That seemed a good idea. But we needed to find out a little more about Lord Vincent's forces.

Kalax settled silently onto the rocky ground. I slipped out of the saddle, but Thea was already on the ground with one of the long, extending optics to magnify the camp that lay in the distance.

Dragons!

Kalax didn't have to tell me that. About two-thirds of the dragons I could see were wild, black dragons. But Thea gave me the tellyscup and I saw greens and blues in the camp, hunched and looking unhappy.

But no crimson reds.

No, I reassured Kalax. *None like you.*

A few, new dragon colors stood out—burnt orange, sunburst yellow and even a few speckled dragons. They were smaller than our dragons, but not as small or fiercely spiked as the blacks.

"Southern dragons?" Thea breathed the words.

I nodded. "They must be. I fear for Commander Hegarty and Instructor Mordecai now."

"Uh, Seb? Look!" Thea tapped my arm and pointed to the north edge of the camp.

A dragon had lifted its head and spread it wings. It had grown huge, with rolls of scales that glimmered in the sunlight. The dragon next to it had six wings. Still another had not just one angered head, but two, and both snapped and hissed at each other. I shuddered. We had seen this before with the Darkening—dragons turned by magic into monsters.

They were all wrong—they'd been twisted by the Darkening. I could feel Kalax's intense hatred for such things, as well as her fear. But I wondered if the people under Lord Vincent would also become warped and strange?

How were we ever to fight such a monstrous, hideous army?

Thea pulled on my sleeve. "We've found out everything that we can from here. Let us be away to where the blacks are hiding. We need some distance from this foul place."

I nodded and we started back to Kalax, who suddenly stiffened.

She was alarmed by something, but she hadn't seen or smelled an enemy coming. Neither had I.

The figures burst out from the rocks around us.

Somehow—impossibly—they had snuck up on us. Holding their long spears pointed toward us, they eyed Kalax warily.

My heart sank. Wildmen. They wore cured leather armor, crudely stitched together with pieces of bone and fur. They didn't seem to be as warlike as others we'd run across. They weren't covered in the black paint of Lord Vincent's troops.

Kill them?

Kalax's thoughts hit me, deadly and ferocious. But I didn't

want her hurt by those long spears. Was there another way out of this?

"Seb?" Thea said the word low, and I could see she had tensed and already had her hand on the hilt of her sword. But then she moved her hand away and spread out her empty palms.

Was she crazy?

"Seb...hold," Thea said, her voice low and fierce.

Watching as one of the Wildmen took a step closer, I shook my head. That one was almost in range to thrust a spear straight at Kalax.

I felt Kalax echo my own growl with a rumble.

Next to me, Thea said, "Stop it. Both of you. It's not the time to fight. Yet."

CHAPTER 11
LADY OF THE FLAMES

S ometimes I wondered if Seb and I might have swapped places. It seemed obvious to me that no one here needed to fight. But Seb and Kalax wanted to attack. That was supposed to be my job.

But these Wildmen could have killed us at once or called Lord Vincent's army down on us. And they hadn't. Couldn't Seb and Kalax see that?

Muttering between clenched teeth, I said, "Seb, if you or Kalax attack, we all die!"

Seb had fisted his hands and I could see his knuckles whitening. "Looks like we're all going to die anyway."

I had to make a decision. The Wildmen looked very different from the ones I'd fought in Torvald. Of course, they could still be in the service of Lord Vincent, but they didn't have the manic stare of those under the control of the Memory Stone. They also wore slightly different clothing, and they looked a little scared.

Maybe it was my protector's training that let me see them as they were, or maybe Seb was so entwined with Kalax that he had picked up on Kalax's view that different meant a threat. I was trained to make quick judgments and I knew a fight I could win and what was a bad idea.

The Wildmen held their spears close, in defensive positions. They were exchanging nervous looks with each other in the way men and women did when none of them had command and they weren't really sure about the situation.

And they're being quiet, with the occasional glance past us, toward the enemy camp.

"Friends," I said and spread my hands even wider. Spear tips shifted in my direction.

"Thea," Seb warned, his voice low. Kalax raised her neck, getting dragon fire ready to spit.

"No, Kalax, Seb!" I held up a hand to them, and then pointed to Lord Vincent's camp. "We are not with them. They are our enemy."

A woman in the front with a tooth necklace called out with a thick, guttural accent, "Step forward, Dragon Rider, if you really mean us no harm!"

Well, here goes everything.

I walked toward her. The spear point shifted away as I approached. I stopped facing the tall, blonde woman who had spoken. She had painted her cheeks with green, making lines across her nose. She wore the same leather and hides as the others, but the tooth necklace and a thick, fur collar made her stand out.

She glanced at me, looking me up and down. "You carry weapons like our enemy carries." The woman scowled, pointing at the short sword on my hip.

I held her gaze. "What sort of fool would I be to walk this world as it is without some form of protection?"

The woman—who had to be some sort of chieftain or leader —laughed. I couldn't tell if she was laughing at me or if she really thought I'd told a good joke. "And what can you do with that little pig-sticker?"

Resting one hand on the hilt, I said, "You can try me and find out." I waved a hand at Kalax. "But my dragon might have something to say about that, too. She is not an enemy you want to make."

The woman scowled once more, her brown eyes darkening. "Dragons like yours come to our enemy."

A grumbling spread through the other Wildmen, but the women held up a hand and they fell silent again.

Behind me, Seb muttered, "Thea, be careful."

Ignoring him, I asked, "Do you really see any other red dragons?"

The woman's eyes narrowed.

This was going to get tricky.

My heart thudded into my ribs and sweat slicked my palms. I nodded back to the Darkening's camp. "If you wish to have a battle, we will fight. When the Darkening's forces come to see what this is all about, we will all die. Why not take this elsewhere and we can talk."

"That could be a trick. More lies of the Ghoul!" The woman

spat on the ground.

I shrugged and licked my lips. "My fellow rider, our dragon and I will be leaving now." I took a step back.

She must notice the same thing we'd seen in them—no sign of forgetfulness, clumsiness, hypnotism. No sign of being under the control of the Memory Stone.

Turning, I walked to Kalax. Behind me, I could hear the creak of leather as the Wildmen shifted.

The woman spoke up again, low and slow. "You are brave, lady rider. I can respect courage and a sharp tongue."

Seb was frowning at me, but I paused, then turned to look her in the eye. "You have to be brave if you want to ride dragons."

Her stare moved from me to Kalax, who huffed out a hot breath. She lowered the tip of her spear and gave me a crooked smile. "True enough. Come with us. I am called Thorri. We will share meat and talk of revenge against the Ghoul."

Seb leaned closer to me. "I think she means Lord Vincent."

I nodded. I also didn't like the idea of just me and Seb sitting down with the Wildmen. I wanted to show them there was more than just the two of us. And I knew Kalax could find where the others were camped. Chin lifted, I said, "There are others of our number with us."

Thorri frowned. One of the other Wildmen said something to her, but I couldn't hear what. She slashed the air with a hand and silenced him. "Good. Lead the way. We will follow."

"Done." I nodded before clambering up onto Kalax's broad shoulder.

Seb mounted into his saddle and asked, "What did you do? You're taking Wildmen to the others?"

I grinned. "You wanted allies, right? Let's show them how a real dragon flies."

Of course, Kalax knew better. She lifted into the air, but flew low to the ground to avoid attracting the attention of the Darkening. I was just glad to get away from that horrible stench—and I wasn't really sure the Wildmen would follow.

❦

Kalax found where Beris, Syl, Varla and Merik had camped. They'd found a spot in a small valley where they were tucked away. We had time enough to warn them that a contingent of Wildmen was coming. Syl jumped up, Beris reached for his sword, and Varla stared at me, her mouth hanging open.

I held up a hand. "It's going to be all right. They can help us."

"Into an early grave," Beris muttered.

I shook my head. "These are not like the Wildmen who have been fighting for Lord Vincent. They're just people who look angry that their families have been killed or captured. We all know what that feels like. The least we can do is talk."

No one looked happy with that idea, but Seb said, "We'll have our dragons for help if we need it." The blacks had followed us back to camp, and now they were perched in the cliffs above us. I liked that—they would give us a warning if any of the Darkening appeared.

By the time the Wildmen arrived, Varla and Merik had a fire and a meal cooking.

The Wildmen came into camp as quietly as they had come upon us earlier, but their dark skins looked sweaty and they were breathing hard as if they'd been running. They stayed close to each other, eyeing us.

I was pretty sure they wouldn't suddenly decide to attack us —they weren't in fighting stances.

Thorri stepped forward and started ordering her people around. She sent some to hunt rabbit for more meat, and some to get water from a nearby stream, and some to find more wood and some to see if fish could be had. Kalax lifted her head at that.

Slowly, the others started to relax. So did I. And so did the Wildmen. The meal helped. The Wildmen ate all of Merik's stew and he had to make more. They brought back rabbits they'd hunted, fish, and even a deer. After we'd all eaten as much as we could, the Wildmen entertained everyone by throwing bits of meat for the dragons to catch. Gaxtal was the only dragon who wouldn't play that game—he turned and left the Wildmen looking at his back and his tail, which twitched like that of an irritated cat.

And they seemed to know how to get along with the wild dragons. The Wildmen made a game of throwing bones and fish into the air for the black dragons to catch. It was clear they knew these black dragons well.

"Much bigger, your dragons," Thorri said, sitting down again by the campfire.

Seb leaned forward, his elbows braced on his thighs. "Do you ever ride dragons?"

"Seb?" Beris growled the word under his breath, scowling at the gigantic, bearded Wildman who sat next to him. "Do we really care?"

Seb pulled a face at him and turned back to Thorri. "Do you ride dragons?"

She shook her head. "You mean how you from the Middle Kingdom do?" She couldn't keep the sneer from her voice. Others of the Wildmen nearest to her gave low chuckles, and she said, "If any rode a black dragon—well, you could raise one from the egg and still have it bite off your arm as soon as look at you!" The Wildmen around us grinned at that.

Merik stood and said, "I'm going to check on the dragons." Varla stood and went with him. "We mean no offence," Thorri said with a grin and a shrug. "We just do things differently in the mountains."

The huge Wildman next to Beris said, "Those who manage to take an egg to their lodge and raise it may learn how to hunt with the dragons, but it is rare. Only a few are blood-tied to the dragons."

"Blood-tied. The Dragon Affinity," Seb said, the words only a whisper.

Beris gave a snort, stood and tapped Syl's arm. "We should help Varla and Merik."

Thorri glanced up at him and waved him to sit down. The huge Wildman next to Beris grabbed Beris' arm and pulled him back down on the log where Beris had been sitting. Thorri grinned and said, "Now we have eaten, it is time to share stories. This is a good thing. Some of our people have the old blood of the dragon family through their veins. But the black dragons, they are as wild as the wind and that is a good thing. Now, what stories do you know?"

I glanced at Thea. She looked back and shrugged. Varla had heard the mention of stories and had drifted back to the campfire.

"Come, Lady of the dragon flames," Thorri said, raising a skin of their strong mead. "You must have good stories of battle or of days gone by. Of your great king, the First Rider. You must know of him, for all the world does."

Varla edged up to my side, bent down and said, "The First Rider! Torvald—they know of him."

I waved at Varla to be quiet and said, "Thorri, it is strange to hear you speak of one of our kings. What do you know of King Torvald?"

I thought the question would be a good test. Did she really know that King Torvald—the first king of our kingdom—was also the First Rider?

Thorri stared at me, her dark eyes wide. She still wore the green paint on her face and in the firelight, it made her face seem strange and almost more like a dragon's narrow visage. "How could we not know of the First Rider? He lived with the old ones, the wise magicians. He had dragon blood in him. He freed the Wildmen from the Ghoul many long years ago, sharing with us some of his power so we might still hear dragons talk." She spoke as if explaining a well-known story to a child.

I rubbed my nose. "We have a few...different tales," I said.

The truth was that the old tales I'd heard recounted how the First Rider had fought against the Wildmen. "But I would like to hear your stories."

Varla squeezed in next to me and said, her voice eager, "Yes, please. I…well, I love a good story. It's going to be revealing to hear the story of our greatest king from another point of view."

Thorri glanced at Varla as if she wasn't sure about that, but she nodded and said, "You have asked for the story and so I shall tell you."

She stood up, raising her hand. All the Wildmen quieted and turned toward her. They obviously took story telling very seriously. Even the dragons seemed to want to hear this.

Voice low and melodic, Thorri began to talk. "Long ago, a pale man came to the north, to the Wildmen's village. The shamans and the wise ones could tell at once this was a ghoul in human form. His skin was too pale for him to have a real heart. His hair and eyes were blacker than the darkest night. But his words were fine and he brought with him gifts and great promises. The young did not want to hear the words of the wise —they wanted those gifts and they wanted the power promised. And such is always the way of the world."

A soft murmur went up from the Wildmen. I glanced around the campfire and saw they were all gathered close now, listening intently.

Thorri nodded and started to talk again.

"The Ghoul seduced our people with words. He said he would give us more land to hunt, rich houses and fine furs to wear. We would never know cold or hunger in any winter. All we must do is share what we knew of the wild, black dragons. It seemed too easy—too simple. But most did not want to think on such things. They were too ready to share all we knew. And when tales stirred of a strange sickness falling on others, of how people in the mountains and how the elders and the shaman were forgetting their families or were falling mad, it was said that was just what those who spoke out against the Ghoul deserved.

"And so the Ghoul learned to command the wild dragons, but they grew terrible. Strange and horrible dragons hatched, ones with no wings, others with many heads and some so huge as to blot out the sun.

"Soon, those who had welcomed the Ghoul began to fear. But the Ghoul said he was a prince and held the right to all the realms. It did not matter now if the Wildmen wanted to follow or not—we had to!

"The Ghoul became less of a man with each passing year. His power grew and his rule stretched out until it covered every tribe. The Wildmen had lost their freedom.

"And then one day a dragon appeared—a great gold dragon from the south. Upon it rode a man, and the Wildmen had never seen such a thing. A man riding a dragon? How was that possible?

"This First Rider was not alone—others rode dragons and came with him. He led his army and flights of dragons to the north, bringing dragon fire, his sword and bright magic to every- thing in his path.

"The Wildmen tribes fell back into the mountains. The Ghoul shed his mortal followers like leaves. Only the most terrible of his dragons—and those who had lost all the light inside them—stayed with him. From the hills, the Wildmen watched.

"A great battle raged for three days and three nights. Dragons broke apart the backs of the mountains with lightning and thunder. It seemed as if the world itself would break apart. But the First Rider came not just with dragons and his army—magic came with him. The bright magic spread over the land, freeing those who could not remember or who had gone mad. The Wildmen were free again to fight for their lands, for their people, and to drive off the Ghoul and his terrible army.

"Only the cost was truly great.

"Many fell—shamans and elders, warriors and even children. And just when it seemed as if the Wildmen would all die, the First Rider came to our aid.

"He and his dragon and his own wise men and riders stood between the Ghoul and the end of all. The First Rider held up a hand, and in it glinted a stone as blinding as the sun, as white as first snow, and as small as an egg. He held it high and the Ghoul and his army could not stand the light.

"At last the Ghoul ran and vanished, but when the Wildmen gathered to thank the First Rider for saving our lands and our people, they found him torn almost apart, weakened in his mind and as old as if had aged a thousand years in just minutes. He was near death. And so were his riders and his wise men.

"They lay on the battlefield like old men. Only the Wildmen of the mountains were left standing. But we knew we had been freed by the First Rider, for he had life enough to say his name was King Torvald and to tell us to carry his story with us forever so that this would never happen again.

'It is said he lived for three days and three nights—just as the battle had gone on for that time. But no one—not shaman or elder—could help him. In that time, he spoke of the dragons, teaching us how to heal them, how to work with them and be one with them. He gave us the blood-ties with his own blood.

"And then he died, and the Wildmen buried the First Rider by the shore of Lake of Hjolnir, the sacred center of the world, for never has anyone ever done so much for our people." Thorri ended her story with a soft sigh.

I looked around to see Seb, Varla and Merik facing her in rapt amazement.

"The First Rider's Tomb—that could be just what we need to find," Varla whispered.

"It could be close. It's been hidden in the north all along," Seb said.

Beris and Syl swapped glances, and Beris muttered, "Great— more wild chases."

I sat there, staring at the fire as it crackled. I couldn't quite come to grips with the fact that this was the clue we had needed. I'd sought to talk to the Wildmen because I thought we might at least be able to convince them to fight Lord Vincent with us. Now I could see there were much stronger forces at work that connected us.

The monks of the Draconis Order had never had the King's Dragon Stone. It had been lost in battle, and lost with the First Rider.

Varla sat up straight. "That's why that shrine we found to the First Rider had runes on it. Because the Wildmen knew him. He's their hero as much as he is one to us."

"Yes, the First Rider is a great hero to our people." Thorri nodded. "He showed us how to fight, how to be fierce, as well as freeing us from the Ghoul. But now it seems the Ghoul is returned, as our greatest shaman said he would one day, and despite all the First Rider did for us. That is what happens when the old stories are not told often enough."

"You are right, Thorri. The Darkening, or what you call the Ghoul, has returned. Only this time it wears the face of a noble called Lord Vincent. He has much of the old powers that you described—but just as in the old times, we have much as well."

That was a bit of a stretch.

I glanced around at the two dozen Wildmen, at our handful of Dragon Riders, and our mixed bag of trained dragons and wild ones. But I stood up and spoke to everyone. "Just like in ancient times, we have dragons of every color and we have the union of two peoples—the Wildmen and the Dragon Riders. We are all following the footsteps of the First Rider. To his example of bravery and tenacity we will be true. We can defeat the Darkening if we do so together!"

A mighty cheer rose up. It seemed the Wildmen appreciated a good speech. They were proclaiming vengeance on Lord Vincent even as I sat down.

"Good words, Flamma," Beris whispered. He stood, but leaned down to say, "But how are we going to do all of what you just said?"

I didn't know, but at least I had an idea of where to start. Turning to Thorri, I asked, "Could you describe the Lake of Hjolnir? Do you know where the First Rider now rests?"

Thorri frowned. "The Wildmen do not keep maps. We keep stories. I could tell you the old tales and rhymes. But some say the Lake of Hjolnir is nothing more than a myth. No one I have ever known has gone to the First Rider's Tomb."

I shrugged. "Well, now you know someone who is going to try."

CHAPTER 12
SCRATCH AND HISS

It didn't take long for Thea to work out a full truce with Thorri, and the Wildmen were eager to learn more of our Dragon Riding techniques. Beris wasn't happy about that—he kept grumbling that this could be all the Wildmen wanted—to learn from us and then they'd cut our throats. But we had two black dragons in need of riders, and these Wildmen really seemed to hate Lord Vincent even more than we did.

We started training the next day.

Merik and Varla had Thorri and a couple of the older Wildmen sit down with them to talk about maps and landmarks to try and get an idea of what lake in the north might be the Lake of Hjolnir. There were more lakes than were even on our maps—and we had huge areas of the north that had never really been mapped. Beris and Syl had no interest in training Wildmen, but they were willing to keep watch for the Darkening. That left me and Thea to do the training—and Thea just didn't have the patience for it.

At first, the Wildmen thought nothing of yelling at the dragons, who ignored them. It took some time for me to convince the Wildmen they could just ask the dragons to do things. The black dragons would only hiss back, but they would also fly better. They all reminded me of brawling drunkards after a night in the tavern. We spent most of the day just getting Scratch and Hiss to hold still long enough to let the Wildmen swing up. Usually one of the blacks would stand quietly and the other would buck up into the sky, dumping the rider.

At last, one bearded Wildman was able to cling to Scratch's back. And another Wildman—a man with an even longer beard that reached to his waist and who could growl and snarl fiercer than any dragon—actually started to make Hiss behave.

Maybe these Northern people and their wild dragons make the perfect match.

Kalax's thought came right after my own. *And maybe now three nations of Dragon Riders.*

Kalax was right about that. But she was also still wary around both the Wildmen and the wild dragons—she could smell the urge for blood on them and did not like how noisy they were at night.

Always drinking! Always loud!

She had grumbled that most of last night.

Ferdinania had decided to start teaching Scratch and Hiss some manners, and she would slap them with her tail if they got too wild or noisy. Gaxtal preferred to act more like Beris and simply pretended the wild dragons didn't exist.

At the end of three days, I was starting to feel good enough that I told Thea we could start the search for the tomb of the First Rider. And Varla had a direction for us to take—north, toward the higher mountains where most of the lakes of the north lay. It wasn't exactly a destination, but we might as well start since we were looking at several days of flying.

We rose early on the third day, broke camp and headed out. Merik took the lead on Ferdinania. Beris and Syl on Gaxtal followed, and Kalax with me on her back brought up the back to keep an eye out for the Darkening.

Below us, I could barely glimpse the Wildmen as they found paths through the trees of the foothills. They were as skilled at hiding as the black dragons. Thea and Varla had chosen to stay on the ground to keep the Wildmen with us, and the black dragons seemed to dart everywhere—sometimes flying up with Ferdinania and sometimes falling back to fly with Kalax.

I wondered if Thea was missing being up in the sky, but it seemed to me that Thea was enjoying her time with Thorri. The two had been staying up late every night, talking by the fire. I was hoping the friendship would hold, but Beris' worries bled into me. What if the Wildmen weren't to be trusted?

I heard a snarl of frustration and looked to see Beris' face tense as he glanced back. I was rather beginning to think he woke up annoyed these days. A tension rode his shoulders that wouldn't go away. Right now he shouted at wild dragon and the bearded rider who was following Gaxtal, "Get away with you! Not so close!"

I was sure that Beris was overreacting right now—the black didn't look that close. But I kept a sliver of my awareness connected with each of the wild dragons to remind them I was alpha leader.

You? Kalax's thought carried a touch of dry amusement.

Okay, we are, I thought back to her.

Now that the wild dragons had riders, I'd started pulling back from their minds. It was a relief to have someone else trying to get the ferocious creatures to do as they were asked, and these riders needed a chance to bond with their dragons.

"I said get back!" Beris yelled again at the Wildman on Hiss. I started to imagine either a mid-air collision or a spat between dragons was coming.

Before it could, Syl called out, "Down with your right knee! Like this!" He leaned down to one side.

The Wildman on Hiss copied him, and Hiss glided to the right, moving away from Gaxtal. It was a pretty basic, easy move, one every cadet learns. You have to use your knees, feet, heels and hips to get a dragon to move.

Do you, now? Kalax growled in my mind.

I grinned at her and scratched a spot on her scales that always seemed to be itchy because the saddle left it sweaty. "Not us— we move as one."

Kalax and I had become so entwined that it felt as though either one of us could just think the direction and the other would already be in motion.

"Good job, Syl!" I called out. To my surprise, he gave me a grin and a thumbs up

We carried on flying north and sometimes a little east, looping back every now and again so we wouldn't get too far ahead of those on the ground. Varla used flags to signal us, and toward sunset she marked the camp site for us.

Kalax and I were the last to land. I waited in the sky as long as I could, not just to enjoy the setting sun, but to make certain no trace of the Darkening was near. Kalax could sense them in the far distance, but it seemed Lord Vincent and his forces had other battles to keep them busy. I worried for those who might be caught up in his path. That had me thinking of my family—and of Thea's family, too.

Trying to shrug off the worries, I asked Kalax to land.

Our path was taking us ever deeper into the wilds, through rocky valleys and high passes, with white-capped mountains rising on either side. If the Wildmen were leading us into a trap, it would be a good one. For I had never seen any map of this area. We would soon need to figure out just where we were heading.

⚜

We made camp in the last scraggly lines of forest on the edge of a boulder field, right below a high pass through the northern mountains. The ground started to freeze at night, but the Wildmen had assured us it would be warmer on the other side of the mountains. We had seen nothing of the Darkening, so we felt safe to light bright, warm fires that illuminated the wind-stunted forest. It seemed as though we were the last people in the whole world.

And perhaps we are.

That thought was a little too grim, so I gave up searching the black horizon for any sign of life or light. We had flown so far north that I doubted anyone from the Middle Kingdom had ever seen what we were seeing now.

You forget the First Rider.

Kalax was right. I gave a laugh.

Thea looked up from the map she had spread out on the ground. "What? Did Kalax say something? Why do I miss all the good jokes?"

"I was just thinking we might be the first Dragon Riders from the Middle Kingdom to come this way since the First Rider and his army."

Thea groaned. "That is not a comforting thought. Come here and take a look at this, Seb. You know I'm useless at mapping."

"That's why you have a navigator." I happily gave up looking at the darkness and sat on a scrap of blanket beside her to look over the map. It was one of the few Varla had scavenged from the map tower.

"According to Thorri, the sacred lake and tomb of the First Rider is at the center of the world, but this puts Torvald at the center of everything. It just makes no sense."

"Well, Torvald is the center of *our* world, not theirs. Remember Arkady and his family? He said there are many lands, some that are even beyond the mountains and the seas."

That idea, which interested me, didn't look as though it had particularly pleased Thea. "Great. More places to search," she muttered.

"Not necessarily." I waved at the map. "The story Thorri told put this sacred lake at the center of the world. Well, for our world, Torvald is the center. That's the heart of the Middle Kingdom. So where is the heart of the Wildmen? What's the center of their world?"

Thea shrugged and glanced at the mountains. Firelight flickered over her face and put even more red into her hair. "The northern mountains, I guess?"

I turned back to our map. It was a Torvald map, so the Dragon Spine Mountains were the main focus, but it showed where the Dragon's Spine descended into the Southern Realm and reached up into the north. "If this really is the length of the mountains..." I walked my fingers over the paper to a point on the map where the mountains seemed like just faint lines. "Then I think that about here must be the center of the Wildmen's world." I walked my fingers back a little to a point where the map showed broad plateaus and the high pass. "We must be about here."

Varla came over with meat that the Wildmen had hunted and cooked. She held out a stick of roast to Thea, who shook her head, and one to me. I wasn't hungry either, but I took the meat. My stomach hadn't been handling food well, lately, and my leather jerkin was starting to hang loose on me.

Eyes bright, Varla nodded at the map. "I'm not sure that will help us. The Wildmen know this land better than any of our mapmakers ever did. And I've been listening to more of their stores and going back over our trusty Runes of Hroth the Druid."

I groaned. "I hope Hroth isn't going to send us to the ocean— or to the east now."

She grinned. "You should respect your elders a little more. Hroth never went to the Lake of Hjolnir, but he did write about it." She made a face, bit off some meat and kept talking as she chewed. "He didn't mention the First Rider in conjunction with it, but the lake is said to be on a plateau, high in the mountains, with sheer cliff walls that fall down from either side."

Thea and I swapped glances and I knew she was thinking that same thing—that did sound like the place we needed to find.

Varla finished her meat and threw her stick aside. Hanging out with the Wildmen was starting to ruin her table manners. "Now before you get too excited, there is a catch."

"Isn't there always?" I asked.

Varla shot me a sideways look, but she kept talking. "Hroth said the lake was guarded by enchantments and spells set down because this is sacred ground. The only way to gain entrance is to fly to the summit and have ten dragons roar all at once. Oh, and it must be under a full moon."

"What?" Thea asked, looking skeptical.

"I know." Varla let out a long breath. "Hroth didn't think much of that part of the story, either. He discounted that as just a tale to keep anyone away. And it sounds crazy, but considering everything else that has happened what with magic stones and ancient Ghouls and…well, everything, I think we had better listen to the legend and not Hroth."

"Let's just hope it isn't true," I murmured, looking up at the sky. "If it is, we're a little under five days away from the full moon and we only have five dragons, and that's including Scratch and Hiss!"

The night seemed suddenly colder. I gave a shiver and wondered if I could feed Kalax my meat. I just couldn't eat. Even if we found two more wild dragons, I wasn't sure I could manage them. Scratch and Hiss were doing better with their riders, but I still had to keep a thread of awareness with them. With another shiver, I got up and went to feed Kalax my dinner and try to rest as much as I could. But I knew the Dragon Affinity was draining the life from me.

CHAPTER 13
IN THE EYES OF THE DRAGON

I hadn't thought Seb would be up to the challenge, he was looking so tired, but he proved me wrong. It had been snowing for several days, but today the sun had come out—and Seb was still keeping the black dragons under control. I was flying with Seb and Kalax today. The cold air cut into my face and seemed determined to pull my hair out from under the helmet. I tried to ignore it so I could focus on the land below.

We flew north through wild mountains. Below us, every now and then, Thorri would signal with flags for the dragons to fly higher and stay out of the way, for she had come across other tribes, or something else. It wasn't very reassuring that even she was cautious about these frozen plains.

Glancing around, it seemed to me as if we had reached the very top of the world. Everything below fell away into mist and fog, or snowy white land. Ahead, I could see cairns in the snow

—tombs of black rocks and sometimes topped with human skulls and dragons' skulls.

The Wildmen had told us to avoid such places, claiming those cairns could put the evil eye on any who disturbed them. Beris made fun of such superstitions, but Seb and I frowned at him. We had seen much of magic—enough to respect these graves.

Thorri had said last night at the campfire, "Our people believe these are ghost wardens, set here to protect the center of the world. They are a warning. These were the dragons and riders who once rode with the First Rider."

With a yell, Beris kicked his blue into action. He, Syl and Gaxtal swooped up suddenly, into the clouds and beyond the line of ghost-wardens and cairns.

The Wildmen moved cautiously across the territory below us, avoiding the graves.

We were coming down the other side of the high pass and into the center of the Dragon's Spine mountain range. A low valley stretched out, dotted with short mountain plants that had gone brown under patches of snow. In the rocky meadow just below the summit, Gaxtal perched on the ground, Beris grinning and Syl glancing around nervously as if looking for either ghosts or the Darkening.

Well, at least the Wildmen will respect his courage.

The clouds that had been hovering ahead of us cleared, moving fast as the wind pushed them. Ahead, a wide plateau rose up at the far end the valley. It was like nothing I'd ever seen, as if the top of a mountain had been carved away by a great knife. The side I could see gleamed smooth and bright as if it had been polished by wind, snow and rain. That had to be the plateau we were looking for. It had to be.

Just as I thought that, the sky rang with dragon calls. Four wild black dragons rose into the air, pushing up from the plateau and blocking our path.

I looked at Seb, who held the reins tight in one hand. He had stretched out his other hand toward the oncoming wild dragons. It was going to tax his affinity even more to try and tame three more dragons.

"Hold!" I called out and held up a hand.

Merik and Varla brought Ferdinania up next to Kalax. Gaxtal launched into the air, swooping up to our left so we might catch the wild dragons in a pincer attack.

"No one attack!" I shouted. I pulled out the flag to give that command as well. Syl and Merik knew how to read such signals.

We need five more dragons, if the old legends are true. And here are four—but will they help us?

Seb had to control these new wild dragons.

The Wildmen riding the two blacks with us flew their dragons to just in front of Kalax. They stretched out long, sinuous necks at the three roaring, northern dragons coming toward us. For a hideous moment, an image of all of the wild dragons turning on us crossed my mind. If Scratch and Hiss reverted back to their wild state, five angry dragons could do a lot of damage.

Enough! Kalax kept her thoughts tight and focused. She was right. I shouldn't be looking to lose any battle before it had even begun.

Hiss lived up to her name with a hiss that rattled the air. A pulse of power followed it as Seb straightened and gave a low growl. The two black dragons at the front faltered, dipping lower in the sky. But the third—the skinniest and meanest looking— kept on coming.

Ignoring my orders, Beris and Syl on Gaxtal flew up and to the right, heading into an attack position, putting Gaxtal so the sun's glare would be behind them.

I swore. The third dragon had seen them and instantly flew higher, matching Beris' move.

Does Seb have a range for his power? How close does he need to be?

In front of us, two of the wild dragons flew in circles. Their calls sounded confused and they swiped at each other with claws extended. I had never seen any dragon act like that without a bloodbath soon to follow.

"Bring them," Seb said, his voice shaking now. "Bring them 'round."

Did he mean for me to bring the other dragons—*our* dragons —around in a flanking movement? Or was he saying he couldn't bring these new wild dragons around? I decided it had to be the former because it would at least put Ferdinania in a position to better defend the Wildmen below if the wild dragons attacked.

Far below us, I could see Thorri moving her troops to take up positions that were sheltered behind boulders. Spears jutted up and sunlight glinted off arrow points.

The two dragons ahead broke apart and careened toward us. Seb shouted out. Kalax swung to the left and Ferdinania to the right. But instead of Scratch and Hiss following Kalax, they charged straight at their two wild brethren, stopping just short of a collision.

The wild dragons croaked and peeled off, swooping around, exchanging chirrups with Scratch and Hiss.

Kalax? I thought at her. *What's happening?*

A sense of intense listening washed over me from Kalax before she said, *They are talking. Claiming.*

"They're telling the other dragons we're their food?" I said.

Seb yelled back, "They say we're their brood! Our black dragons choose us, and they're telling these interlopers to choose us as well!"

I wondered how Seb could know all that. A shiver chased down my back.

Just how powerful is he?

But Seb just pointed up to where Gaxtal and the third black dragon were swooping around each other, each of them trying to get into a position to strike "That's the drake of their knot. Come on, Kalax!"

With a lurch, Kalax flew upward, hot on the tail of the third dragon. Kalax gave a roar and the black roared back, dropping away from Gaxtal and heading toward Kalax.

Now see how Kalax flies!

Kalax roared with joy.

Seb allowed her to set her own pace. Her acceleration couldn't match that of the wild dragons, but the powerful beats of her larger wings gradually ate the airy distance between us while we watched the northern wild black get closer.

"Mine!" Seb roared. The word echoed in my mind. The pulse of power from him vibrated in my chest and my bones.

The black dragon croaked and fell from the sky. Kalax fell with it, rolling in time as Seb wrestled with the creature's mind, the veins on his neck bulging and seeming to burst before, with a vaguely contented chirrup, it pulled itself up and started to wheel back around and head for the confrontation behind us.

That hadn't seemed the same as the time that we had captured Scratch and Hiss, using diversionary tactics to 'surprise' them and even bargain with them, in a way. It had seemed more like Seb had claimed the dragon for his own.

Ahead of us, amazingly, Scratch and Hiss were hovering in the air, exchanging chirrups and crows with the two northern dragons that, uncertainly, looked from them back to the drake that now followed us uncertainly.

In a way, the wild dragons are like ours. They thrive on companionship.

Kalax's thoughts swirled into my mind.

Alone is death

The dragon Seb controlled hissed at the other two and a brief dragon argument began. Soon they were bowing to the pressure of the pack and of the brood, raised their wings, exposing their undersides and necks to show that they meant no harm.

We had done it—we had four new dragons to add to our small army, taking our force up to nine. I felt Seb sweep his own mind over theirs, almost as one might throw a blanket over an unsightly bench. They were claimed and added to his stable.

I looked over our shoulder, up to the where the plateau sat. If we were so close to our goal, why then did I feel so worried?

෯෴

We reached the plateau at the end of the day and made camp at the base of the cliffs to rest up and give the Wildmen a chance to catch up with the dragons. This close, it really did look like a mountain that had its top sliced off. No wonder the legend said that dragons had to take the First Rider to his tomb.

The sides of the plateau were not as smooth as they had seemed from a distance. The cliffs were actually more like scales of rock with thin shale forming cracks and layers across the surface. Even as we camped below, we could hear the thunder as some of the loose shale broke off and tumbled down the sides of the cliff.

"No one can climb that," Beris said, standing at the base of the mountain and pulling a flake of rock from it as if it was nothing more than rotten plaster.

Thorri and her Wildmen reached us after we had a fire going and Merik had made stew. The Wildmen ran into camp, hardly even out of breath, but they glanced around as if they wanted to be anywhere but in the shadow of this giant plateau. Everyone seemed quiet that night—no songs or stories, just everyone watching the skies and looking up at the wall of stone that seemed to block the stars.

In the morning, the Wildmen started fires early and sat close to them. Glancing around at the shadows under everyone's eyes, at the pale faces and the nervous looks that were being sent to the cliff, it seemed to me that at least half the camp or even more had had terrible dreams. I wondered if it came from camping under the shadow of that demon cliff. For myself, I had dreamed of swirling, flashing draconic eyes, flaring with flame and hellfire.

I shivered and not just from the chill in the air.

Coming over to stand next to me close by the fire, Seb gave me a nod. He looked like the rest of us—as though he hadn't had much sleep. "What is it?" he asked in a quiet voice.

"Just—just, you know." I nodded over to where Beris and Syl were checking over their saddles on Gaxtal.

Beris had volunteered to scout ahead. The air acted strangely here, Kalax had warned, curving around in unexpected currents and echoing our words in ways that made them sound more like the cries of an injured dragon.

Beris gave us a grin, and Syl pulled a face. They mounted up on Gaxtal and headed into the sky, disappearing into the clouds that hid the top of the plateau this morning. Frowning, I tried not to worry that we would never see them again.

Kalax had curled up near the fires—even the dragons needed more warmth this far north. Leaning against her side, and actually missing the porridge of the Academy and the fires of the Academy keep, I told Seb, "You did the right thing."

He glanced at me and I thought he looked thinner than when he had first come to the Academy from Monger's Lane.

"Sending Beris and Syl to scout first. That's the right thing. We don't know what could be up there."

He closed and then opened his eyes slowly. A frown pulled his eyebrows tight, as if he was having problems focusing. "Oh." The word came out flat and tired. "I thought you meant…" The words trailed off but he gave a small wave to the wild dragons who were currently wrapped around each other, grooming one another.

The Wildman had only just gotten used to having two black dragons around. Now we had four more that were far more wild than Scratch and Hiss. But the Wildmen who'd become riders— Dar and Temmi were their names—seemed ready to show off how they could toss meat to their dragons. Now we needed to find three more riders.

"Well, them, too. Good job!" I said, with a level of enthusiasm I didn't fully feel.

Seb gave a low chuckle. He nudged my shoulder with his. "Don't worry, Thea. I can do this. I've got more in me yet."

"We hadn't even started to think about how we were going to confront Lord Vincent with barely trained dragons as—"

A whoop from up above cut off my words. An ululating howl followed. I grabbed for my sword and so did Seb, both of us looking up and hunching down in a fighting stance.

Kalax just grumbled.

Beris came swinging out of the clouds. He didn't sit in his

saddle but seemed to be hanging by a rope tied around his middle. Gaxtal appeared next with the other end of the rope tied to Beris' saddle. Beris was laughing, but the rest of us couldn't quite see why.

"What under the heavens is he doing? And why?" asked Thorri. Her voice held a note of admiration. I glanced at her and shook my head.

Beris gave another shout. "We found it!"

Gaxtal hovered as Beris hit the ground, feet first. He untied the knot and moved aside so Gaxtal and Syl could land.

"You found the tomb of the First Rider?" Thorri asked, eyes wide and her voice hushed.

Chest puffed up, Beris nodded. "It's incredible up there. Pure dragon territory!" He pounded Gaxtal's side. Gaxtal gave a pleased-sounding snort, and Beris said, "Rock forms a perimeter wall, but on the inside there's flat land and a small lake that looks as if it could be made of crystal. Seems like there is a cave next to the lake, and that has to be the tomb, right? There is just enough room for a dragon to land, but I went down on a rope to make sure the ground would hold."

Syl swung off his saddle and shook his head. "Place isn't safe. Doesn't feel right," he muttered.

Thorri nodded and crossed her arms. "Of course The First Rider's magic is still strong."

Were we all feeling uneasy because of the King's Dragon Stone? That seemed possible, but why didn't this stone give me odd dreams as the others had? Was it because this stone was more powerful—or more dangerous?

I glanced over at Seb. He seemed to have perked up at the mention of a cave—maybe he was hoping the King's Dragon Stone would help us control the black dragons without leaning on his affinity so much.

Looking back to Beris and then to Thorri, I said, "So, we need ten dragons to roar at once and then a dragon can land? But we only have nine dragons with us."

Beris shrugged. He hadn't really believed that part of the legend—I wasn't sure I did either—but he said, "Ten or nine or five or two—does it really matter? You just better hope that roar unblocks the entrance to the tomb."

I turned on him, frustration chewing up my insides. "What do you mean?"

Resting one hand on Gaxtal's shoulder, Syl shook his head. "There's what looks like the skeleton of a dragon but it's encased in rock."

Varla and Merik had drifted over when Beris and Syl came back. Now she looked up, eyes bright. "What? Why, that's just how Hroth said how the body of the First Dragon was left. The waters of the lake were said to turn bones to something harder than rock."

Throwing my hands wide, I asked, "How do we tunnel through a stone skeleton? Why does there always have to be one more hurdle?"

"Wait," Varla said. She hurried away and came back with a scroll in one hand. The edges had been burnt and looked ready to crumble into dust. Carefully unrolling it, she pointed to three runes that looked like scratches of black lines. "You speak these words, that's what Hroth wrote. The stones will crumble to dust if you say them at the same time as the dragons roar on the full moon."

I groaned. "And how did Hroth know all this? What if someone was just telling him a story? Maybe Beris is right and it doesn't matter how many dragons we have."

Thorri glanced over Varla's shoulder. "I know those words —*fuathur pleathur dracon* is the old tongue. It means dragon rise first one."

Cold sank into my bones. Did we really know what we were doing here? What if we unleashed something we couldn't control? To me, it seemed as if everyone was uneasy here. I didn't know if that was because of the cliffs or because of magic that made you want to get away from here as fast as you could.

Seb broke the silence that had fallen. "Look, all of us here have felt or seen the effects the Memory Stone has…and some of us have felt how it is to use the Armor Stone or the Healing Stone." He shot me a look and turned back to face the others. "We know an ancient spirit or sorcerer that the Wildmen know as the Ghoul and we call Lord Vincent has called the Darkening back. If a few magical words can help us defeat that evil, we need to do exactly as legend says."

He was right. I had come to believe in a world of magic spells and strange powers. But I kept thinking of the cost of such magic.

Falling through the layers of darkness forever, of dying with no end.

I jerked back from the memory of that horrible moment when

Lord Vincent had struck me a mortal blow. It was only Commander Hegarty's use of the Healing Stone that had saved me. But it had also changed me forever. I could sense things now —I was different.

I knew the King's Dragon Stone would demand something from one of us—perhaps from all of us.

I don't want any of that to be true, but it is.

But we had a kingdom to save. And the lives of those I loved were worth any price.

Looking up to where clouds still shrouded the top of the plateau, I put back my shoulders. "Tonight is the last of the full moon. No matter what, we have to try this."

"Tonight," Seb said. His hand rested on my shoulder, and I wished it gave me more comfort.

* * *

Hanging suspended from a dragon was curiously peaceful. I hadn't been expecting it to be easy, but I was surprised when I had a few moments to relax and enjoy the view. But Syl was right—this place would leave anyone uneasy.

We had argued over if nine dragons would be enough, and then over who would be the one to say the words and go inside the cave first.

Beris said he should; Syl kept shaking his head over that.

Merik stepped back, swapping an uneasy look with Varla. She offered herself as the person to do this, but I could tell she wasn't really happy with that idea. Seb said he should do it, and Kalax grumbled over that idea. Thorri said she would—if she didn't have to climb on the back of a dragon. Dar and Temmi each offered to try, but we all told them we couldn't really trust their blacks not to spook and fly off.

Finally, Beris said we should draw lots, and I told everyone we should see who could actually say the words that had to be spoken.

That ended up being me.

Seb, Beris and Syl had the worst accent known to the Wildmen as they struggled over the words. Varla managed them very well, but I told her we needed her ready if this didn't go right to dig into the scrolls at once. Merik agreed with that and offered to help her. And Thorri turned white at the thought of having to get onto a dragon's back. But I could copy Beris' idea and get ready to land by swinging down from a rope—that way Seb and Kalax could remain in the sky, ready to swoop down and rescue me if I needed it.

Now, hanging suspended from a rope that attached on the other end to my saddle, I was hovering over a sea of silvered white. The lake. It covered almost all the top of the plateau, and if it really did turn your bones into rock, I couldn't afford to touch it.

Clouds rode the sky, covering the moon and then parting to revealing the pale, silver light and the sudden glinting lake. Above us, high in the sky, a sea of strange, northern stars glittered. I was really hoping that the moon didn't have to be both full and fully visible.

Kalax dipped a little as she hovered, and I yelled up at Seb, "Don't drop me in that lake! I don't want to find out if it's poison or not!"

He waved and guided Kalax a little higher and over toward the opening of the cave. I could hear the wing flaps of the other dragons; Ferdinania, Gaxtal, and the squabbling hisses and cries of the six wild dragons as they swept into position. We had nine dragons, spaced fairly evenly around the plateau, with Kalax in the middle and me hanging from a rope.

Ten dragons to roar at once.

That was what the old legends had said. I was really hoping this would work even if we hadn't gotten that part of it right. I wondered if others had found this spot and tried this—if they had they must have failed.

The rope cut into my underarms a little—it was tight and rough. I had a knot I could pull loose quickly.

Kalax started to glide forward, lowering me as my thoughts whirled. We were crossing the lake and, even in the cool of the mountain's night, I could see steam or something else rising from it.

By the First Dragon, it stinks.

No wonder Beris had been cautious about getting too close.

Up ahead loomed the cave. It seemed only a break in the rocky surface of the plateau, and stark, white bones rose up, blocking the opening like huge bars.

Kalax hissed deep in her throat. To be honest, I agreed with her. Goose bumps popped up on my skin. The shape became clearer and clearer. It was indeed bone, the vast calcified spine, shoulder blades, arms and wing stubs of a dragon of immense size. It looked as if the dragon had curled up and died right here.

I gasped. I had seen the huge, mutant dragon created by the Darkening, but I had never seen any other dragon of such a size as this. Kalax, who would one day grow to huge proportions if she lived her full life span, would only be two-thirds this size. And she was a large dragon indeed.

Seb's gasp carried to me. I knew he'd wanted to be the one to explore this site, but he had to coordinate the dragons and keep them in position with his affinity. I also wasn't really sure it would be wise for Seb to get too close to the King's Dragon Stone. His affinity was costing him enough as it was.

There was indeed just enough room for a dragon to land, but Seb and I had both agreed that we should not risk Kalax. It made more sense for her to be above me and able to sweep down to carry me to safety if need be. Whatever magic protected this spot allowed me to touch my boots to the smooth slate. It crumbled under my feet and I scrabbled for purchase. I steadied and stood still, heart pounding and my breath quick and uneven. I pulled on the rope to let Seb know I was secure and untied the knot.

Kalax gave me a gentle nudge of reassurance. *We won't be far.*

"I know," I whispered, waving as they swept back toward their location and turned back to the wall of bone.

My heart kept pounding. I wanted to be back in the air on

Kalax's back and flying away from here. I tried to tell myself I couldn't feel the magic, but I could. It shimmered on my skin and seemed to seep into my bones. It whispered to me that I wasn't welcome. That I should go. That I should run.

Gulping down a breath, I kept telling myself it was just the magic making me feel this way—someone had wanted to keep everyone from this spot, and they had done a good job with making it seem uncanny and unsafe.

Glancing up, I watched the moon peek out from the clouds. I swallowed, but my throat was dry and raspy. Would I even be able to say the words with my heart pounding like this, leaving me sick?

None of us were sorcerers—we were Dragon Riders and fighters. We would just have to hope for the best.

And hope this magic had no hidden surprises waiting for us —like backfiring because we didn't have ten dragons with us.

The dragons croaked and hovered in their own positions. It seemed to me that the blacks were getting tired of waiting. They kept sweeping away and back up into the sky.

I edged a little closer to the skeleton to get a good look at it. I didn't' want to touch the bones to see if they were really made of stone, but in the moonlight they seemed an odd, yellow-white type of stone, heavily pitted. But the old legends were true—this had once been a huge dragon.

The dragon's large and complicated knuckle joints stood out in the silver moonlight. I could see the long, connected rods of bone and talons that ended in cruel points. Something like a rust stain glinted between the knuckles. I stepped closer and saw the distinct shape and pattern of dragon scales.

Crimson red. Just like Kalax.

Arkady had said the First Dragon had been a red. Suddenly chilled, I stepped back and then checked the move. I couldn't afford to back into that lake. I knew now it really did change bones to rock.

A roar split the air, making me spin and grab for my sword hilt. The light that had been shining down dimmed as clouds slipped between me and the full moon.

Kalax gave a roar—it was time.

One by one, each dragon started an echoing roar that sent chills up my spine. Seb was having trouble getting them to all roar at once.

I had never heard so many dragons trying to call out all at once. It was terrifying, deafening, but also strangely musical, almost a cross between lion roars and the lonesome ululations of swans. The calls echoed around me, seeming to travel to the ends of the earth before coming back multiplied. It was time for my part in this.

"Come on, Thea, get it right," I whispered to myself. Straightening, I stood before the dragon bones.

"*Fuathur pleathur dracon,*" I called out, the Wildmen's old tongue feeling awkward and heavy on my lips.

The roaring continued around me, the full moon shone down and the skeleton didn't move.

Teeth gritted and tears stinging my eyes and nose, I shouted the words again, "*Fuathur pleathur dracon!*"

The dragons fell silent.

For a long second, I held my breath, fearing we had failed. We had gotten it wrong—we needed ten dragons and didn't have them. The world seemed very cold, and the old stories and scrolls seemed just that—dusty tales and nothing more.

But then, something started to happen.

A tremor started up in the very bones of the rock—small at first, and then growing louder. It was as if the dragon skeleton had taken up the dragons' roar. Was this our tenth dragon? It seemed to now be roaring, too, the soft sound starting to rumble low.

I crouched, one hand on the hilt of my sword, the other ready to reach up, the signal to Kalax to come and grab me and carry me away.

The nine dragons above roared again, this time calling out in one voice, and the dragon skeleton echoed back the roar. This was our tenth dragon—we had needed this dragon's voice all along. I didn't know how the dragon guarding the tomb was managing to roar with the others, but there was no time to think on it. The old words burst out of me as if some ancient force had closed around my chest. *"Fuathur pleathur dracon!"*

With a crack like the fall of a great tree, the bones snapped and fell inward in front of me. Dust choked the air. Coughing, I waved at it. The clouds parted and moonlight flooded the plateau so it seemed as bright as day. As the dust settled, I saw oddly shaped rocky pillars—and a clear path into a glowing chamber.

"I'm in," I shouted to the others. Drawing my sword, I

headed into the cave. Or what had to be the tomb of the First Rider.

* * *

A spectral, blue glow lit the chamber head of me. Crystals or fungus gave off an unearthly light. I couldn't be sure which, but the glow reminded me of the rare catch-crystals I'd once seen in the ancient mines near King's Village. The crystals could take any small amount of energy and create this vivid, blue light.

The tunnel ahead looked short and wide and opened into a wide, teardrop-shaped chamber. At the center sat a simple, stone sarcophagus and a rough-hewn rock statue. The light grew brighter, showing a carving of a winged creature on the stone sarcophagus.

"Torvald?" I breathed out the word.

I didn't have to be told to whisper or to tread carefully. This was indeed a holy site. I wondered what this king, the first to ever ride a dragon, had been like. Had there been a Flamma at his side as there was always a Flamma at the sides of the rulers of the Middle Kingdom? Had he had the same love for his dragon that Seb and I shared with Kalax?

Very lightly, I brushed my fingers over the lid of the coffin, hoping I wouldn't have to open it. "Sleep well, my king. You have earned your rest." I turned to the statue.

It looked very much like the standing stone we had come upon—a straight, tall stone. However, the shape of a man stood out. He was rough-carved, by axes I would guess. And I could make out a strong, square face with flows that suggested a short beard. Lines cut into the rock formed long hair. But this was no statue of some Wildman noble or god.

Whoever had carved the statue had formed the rough leathers and armor a dragon rider would need.

The man had been carved with one stone hand on the hilt of a sword at his side and the other hand held close to his chest. In that hand sat a large, dull-colored, rounded stone a little smaller than a dragon egg and a little bigger than my hand.

A tremble of excitement spread over my skin. My heart gave a hard lurch, thudding into my ribs. To be honest, the stone seemed oddly dark and faintly blue as if it was reflecting the light from the catch-crystals.

Reaching out a hand to touch it with one finger, I wondered if this was the King's Dragon Stone. Or had whoever fashioned this statue carved a likeness of the stone?

I couldn't sense anything from the stone—not as I had from the other stones of power. Was the stone sleeping? Or perhaps the First Rider had used all its power.

Touching the stone, it seemed cold to me—just another rock.

Something like lightning flashed up my arm, jolting into my heart.

Distantly, I heard the worried roar of a dragon. But I had no time for that. The stone was changing color. Red and orange glowed in the depths, pulling me closer.

Fire...fire in the sky and in the heart.

Thea!

I heard Kalax's thought mix with Seb's. But they sounded so very distant. Stepping closer, I closed my hand over the stone, feeling its colors swirl and bleed into me, watching my hand change color and form.

Fire in the depths of the earth.

Fire in the heart of the sky.

All things come back to the fire that begat them.

I had no idea where the words came from. They were just there...in my mind, falling from my mouth. They painted the walls of the cave in blue and yellow and greens so vivid I wanted to cry for the sheer beauty. The words fell into me, painted me with red, orange, green and blue flames. I suddenly knew I could feel the world the same way a dragon could—I was a dragon... and the mountain and the lake and the stones and the light that lived in all things.

For a heartbeat, I could sense them all—they were within me. The spark of that cosmic fire at the heart of creation was my heart—and the heart of every dragon.

Thea!

This time, Kalax's thought pushed aside the brilliant colors.

In a flash, I was Agathea Flamma, Dragon Rider. I was also kneeling on a dirt floor, a stone that seemed both icy and hot in my hand.

My head pounded, and my stomach gave a lurch. I put a hand over my mouth. How long had I been here?

Boots pounded down the tunnel behind me and Seb called my name.

I tried to stand, but couldn't. I also tried to call back to him, but only managed to open my mouth—words wouldn't seem to come out.

Seb bent over me. His hand on my shoulder made the world steady around me. Looking up at him, I thought I saw shadows of fear, worry and envy cross his features. "Kalax couldn't feel you for a moment. We thought something had happened to you."

It had. They had thought I had died, again—I wasn't certain that I hadn't.

Tuck away, Kalax growled at me. I knew at once what she was talking about. *Too powerful.*

I nodded, although I knew she couldn't see me. Head muzzy, the colors still lurking inside my mind, ready to burst loose the instant I closed my eyes, I slipped the stone into a side pouch. I slumped against Seb. My mind cleared a little, but I felt exhausted, as if I'd been through a battle.

"Thea?" Seb's face hovered over me, eyebrows pulled flat and his skin such an odd color in the blue light. "Can you understand me?"

"Of course." I frowned. The words had come out a groaning, sighing noise as if my lips spoke some other language. Tingles ran over my skin. My body did not seem my own. I should be standing tall, facing my red dragon, ready to do battle, to protect my realm.

Seb slipped an arm around me, helping me to stand. We hobbled back to the entrance.

Outside, the moon washed silver down on us. The lake sparkled. Kalax swept down and grabbed us both, carrying us up into the dark, cold sky.

"I'm tired…so tired. Can I sleep, Seb, and dream of flames and flying?" Seb didn't answer me. Looking down, I stared at the snow. I looked up again, but I couldn't tell if one dragon flew above me or if two red dragons sailed across the sky.

CHAPTER 14
FLY SOUTH

"Are you sure she will recover?" I demanded once again. The old woman sitting beside Thea, who lay on a stack of furs, made a clicking noise in the back of her throat.

The Wildman healer looked to be older than both her Thea and me put together. She dressed in a motley collection of rabbit and fox skins, with bones and feathers woven into lank, gray hair. She and her tribe lived in a tiny, secluded village on the edge of the high mountain pass that we had come through. Thorri knew of her and had said this woman was a good healer.

The healer's hut seemed far too simple to me, made as it was of reeds woven together. At least Thea was still breathing. She hadn't woken in three days.

"Whatever magic Thea touched, it still has her." Standing near the door, Thorri frowned. Her eyes had darkened with a troubled look.

I wanted to snarl and hit something. What was worse—if that was possible—than seeing Thea so still upon the furs was that this had happened before. I had carried her still-warm body to Commander Hegarty after Thea had been struck down. I should have found a way to prevent this—but how?

Coming over to me, Thorri tugged on my sleeve. "You have kept watch over her for days now. If you do not get some rest, you will collapse and pull the healer's attention away from where it should be—on her." She gestured to Thea.

I didn't want to leave, but Thorri was right.

Heading to the door, I gave a last look at Thea and then stepped from the hut.

The air outside seemed cold and clean after the smoke of the healer's hut. Varla had been hovering outside and now she looked over at me, clutching one ancient, thick book to her chest. "How is she? Any better?"

I shook my head. Merik, Beris and Syl had taken over training the Wildmen to ride the blacks. I was glad of that—and also that the wild dragons needed less and less of my attention. Right now I wasn't sure I could control myself, let alone a dragon. Kalax was also helping, taking the wild dragons with her to fish in any nearby lakes with good waters.

"Walk with me," Varla said. She took two steps, stopped and glanced back at me.

I didn't have the heart to resist—or the energy.

The village was just a collection of small, reed huts. From the sky, it wouldn't even look like a village. No wonder the Darkening had left it alone. Varla led the way through the narrow paths between the huts. Most of the villages—and the other Wildmen—were out hunting game.

At the farthest hut, Varla pulled aside a leather hide that served as a door. This hut was like the others—one room, no windows, furs upon the floor and a small fire burning in the center. The place smelled of smoke and goats, for the villagers kept a few scrappy herds.

Sinking down on the furs, Varla kept her book on her lap and said, "I think...I think we did the right thing. Thea would say that."

I could only stand there and stare at her.

"Getting the King's Dragon Stone, despite what happened."

I glanced over at Thea's leather pouch. It once again held the King's Dragon Stone. I'd glanced at it earlier. It had gone dark gray again—it had turned into just a stone again, cold and hard.

I glanced at Varla, who stared back with a stubborn tilt to her chin. "How can you say such a thing?"

"I've been doing some reading." She tapped the book in her lap. "There was a reason for the stories why many thought the Dragon Stones and your Dragon Affinity were bad news. The old magic is said to steal energy, to—"

"I don't need to hear this!" I scrubbed a hand into my hair.

Varla stiffened. "Yes, you do. We need to know as much as we can. If something happens to Thea, you know she would want us to keep going." Turning away from her, I shook my head, but Varla kept talking, her voice firm. "Thea is my friend, too, and I know her at least as well as you. She would want us to take the King's Dragon Stone to our king and use it against Lord Vincent. Despite the cost."

"So if she doesn't wake, another must take up the stone and use it? It killed the First Rider, didn't it? That's the legend. He fought the Darkening and he won—and it cost him his life, the life of his dragon, and all the other riders with him. Is that the price we have to pay? We'll use the stone's magic and all die. What kind of victory is that?"

Varla thumped a hand on the book in her lap. I glanced at her. In the firelight, her face seemed very pale and her long braid of red hair hung over one shoulder. "From what you described about what happened to Thea, I think the King's Dragon Stone must act like…like Dragon Affinity. You said Kalax told you that she felt Thea's mind disappear—and then appear again, but that it felt for a moment as if Thea was connected with all dragons. If it unites the powers of the other Dragon Stones together—and maybe even the power of dragons—it might not have any power of its own. It could be something that just pulls in power."

"We've seen what it did to Thea." I shook my head. "It almost killed her. It almost killed all of us!"

"And our other choice? We just let the Darkening cover the land? Kill or enslave everyone?"

Rubbing my eyes, I couldn't remember the last time I had eaten. My head ached and I felt hollow—and as if a wind could blow me away. "When I took it from Thea, it was just a stone. I wouldn't do anything for me."

Varla put down her book. Standing, she came over to my side. "If the King's Dragon Stone is like the affinity…well, we know you bonded with Kalax. Your affinity works better with her than any other dragon. It seems that Thea has bonding with the King's Dragon Stone. I'm also pretty sure she'll recover—the stone would have connected to you if Thea's injuries were fatal. And if the stone's power really is like the affinity, that means Thea can use its power and if she's careful, she'll be fine."

I nodded. It was true that if I tried to command too many of dragons at once, I'd start to have headaches and blackout. But the affinity had grown stronger in me, and so had my tolerance to the pain. I could command far more dragons now than I could a year ago. But still I worried.

Glancing at Varla, I asked. "You're sure about this?"

Varla nodded. "Pretty sure. I think Thea just needs some time to grow into her powers."

"Time isn't something we have a lot of." *She will survive,* Kalax said in my mind.

I could feel Kalax was nearby and had caught the scent of a mountain goat. She was wondering whether anyone would notice if she took just one.

First fire calls to Thea, but we guard her.

I wondered if all the dragons were helping Thea. I could sense Kalax's connection to Thea, but worry for Thea made it hard for me to focus on the other dragons. I was just happy to hope that what Kalax and Varla had said might be true.

Every moment Thea comes back toward Thea.

I wasn't sure what Kalax meant by that.

Glancing at Varla and with my shoulders slumping, I told her. "We'll fly south—after Thea awakes."

Varla shook her head. "That would be after you get some sleep and eat something…and then after Thea wakes. There's stew Merik made and skins to sleep on. I'll go sit with Thea."

I opened my mouth to protest, but Varla pushed on my chest. My legs buckled and I sat down on the furs covering part of the hut's floor. "Sleep…eat. If Thea wakes and finds you've collapsed and I let it happen, she'll have my skin."

With a tired smile, I had to nod. At least that was one thing I knew Varla was completely right about.

⚜

Thea awoke at first light. I knew that because Kalax told me. I wanted to go to Thea at once, but our dragon was far wiser, saying I should give Thea some time to eat and dress. I could do the same and then we would saddle up and be ready to fly.

I'd slept without any dreams, but I had little appetite for the stew the healer brought to me. It tasted bitter, and when her back was turned, I threw most of it away. Kalax sent me unhappy thoughts about that, but I couldn't force down anything.

Heading out of the hut where I'd spent the night, I found news of the plan to fly south had spread through the village. The Wildmen were letting out excited whoops and some were chanting. They'd daubed themselves in blue woad made from crushed leaves.

Coming over to me, Beris crossed his arms. "They're preparing for battle. They're acting like we're going to ride out and destroy the Darkening with the power of the First Rider."

"Aren't we?" I asked, trying to project more confidence than I felt.

"You and whose army?" Beris nodded at the two dozen Wildmen and our dragons—that wasn't even a full squadron of riders. "This one?"

I kicked at the dirt. "We're going to find the king, and we'll give him the King's Dragon Stone and then we'll make our plans."

Beris gave a snort. "And that would be the same king who lost the city of Torvald?"

Turning to him, I said, "I don't know what's gotten into you —maybe you just don't have much faith in the magic we've found. But if you—"

I broke off my words for Thea had stepped out of her hut. Beris and I both turned to stare at her as she walked over to us, nodded and offered a shadow of a smile. She looked pale still, but she wore her dragon armor of a leather jerkin, metal breast-plate and a metal, horned helmet. Her sword hung from her hip, and she had slung her bow and quiver of arrows on her back.

I looked her over, and said, "You don't have to fly, if you're not feeling up to it. You can travel with Thorri."

Thea rolled her eye. "I haven't flown for three days, Seb!" She headed for where Kalax sat on nearby boulders. I fell into step with her. She glanced at me and straightened her shoulders a little. "How would you feel if you hadn't ridden for so long?"

"I know, but—"

"But nothing, Sebastian Smith." Thea frowned. It was like seeing a shadow of her old self coming back. She punched my arm. "You use your Dragon Affinity all the time and you've blacked out on me, had nosebleeds and could barely walk at times. And still you flew. Give me the same respect, huh?"

"I, uh, of course. I'm…it's just…well, this is new. We don't know what the King's Dragon Stone did."

"It knocked me down, but I got back up. Now give me a hand with getting the saddles on Kalax."

When we were both strapped in and waiting for the other riders to give their signal that they were ready, Thea glanced me. "So we're going to take this to the king?"

I nodded. "But Varla reckons the stone's a lot like the affinity —you know how that bonds me more with Kalax than any other dragon. When I touched it, it was just a stone. It stopped sending out anything." I didn't add the other thing I was thinking—that it would stay bonded until that person was dead.

Thea gave a small laugh. "Come on, Seb. You can use your affinity with other dragons. If the King's Dragon Stone is like that, someone else must be able to use it. Maybe it takes time to recharge."

I wasn't sure about that. The Dragon Affinity seemed to work against me every time I stretched it too far.

It should have been me—at least I know how to cope with the Dragon Affinity.

A dry, mental chuckle came to me.

Do you? Or would magic use your thirst for connections?

Kalax had never been so blatantly honest with me. Had it been this obvious to her all this time? Was I addicted to using the affinity?

Thea was sorting out her harness and just said, her voice casual as if we had magic in our lives every day, "If we don't take this to the king, what was the point of all of this?"

I shrugged. But wasn't the point to defeat Lord Vincent and the Darkening? And did we have something that would let us do that—or would it kill us all?

I kept thinking about the First Rider—how he'd ended after his battle with the Darkening. It wasn't a happy thought.

"Ready!" Merik shouted.

Syl gave the same call. The Wildmen riders—we had three now, and two black dragons who still needed training. The dragons raised their heads and two of the blacks gave a roar. They were ready.

"Forward!" I called.

Kalax leapt into the air, spreading her wings to catch the air currents from the mountains. We were flying south—but I didn't know what might await us.

꧁꧂

We flew south for hours, and I had to fight the urge to keep looking behind me to see if Thea was well. Of course she was, I told myself again and again. Kalax would tell me if she wasn't.

We had agreed with Thorri that she and the Wildmen would head south as fast as they could. The Dragon Riders—who could fly much faster and further—would scout ahead. Hopefully, we could avoid running into any of the Darkening's forces without a true army to help us. The dragons would help us find King Justin and the dragons with the Middle Kingdom army—I was just hoping the king's army had grown, and that the king had not lost more troops to raids that might have gone against him.

By late afternoon, Kalax had become uneasy. I asked her what was wrong and she sent me back her thoughts.

Something wrong with the land.

Glancing around, I realized Kalax was right. No birds fluttered around the trees below us. No goats or sheep ran from the shadows of dragon wings. I couldn't even recall seeing deer or other animals darting out or into the woods—and the few villages we had seen had been empty. The north was a barren land, but by now we should be starting to see more signs of life. Uneasy now, I turned back to Thea to see if she was sensing anything. She did look tense, I thought.

Before I could say anything to Thea, Kalax lifted her head, snuffed the air and looked to the southeast.

Dragons there.

I signaled to the others to head lower—we would have cover in the trees. And I asked the Wildmen riding Scratch and Hiss to fly ahead of everyone. The black dragons might help us to pass as just a group of wild dragons out for some raiding.

Kalax had only just skimmed over a mountain stream when Hiss gave a screech.

Beris shouted, "Attackers! Defend yourselves."

I glanced to the southeast and saw a knot of black dragons flying toward us.

My throat tightened, and my heart started to hammer. The way these dragons flew—fast and straight, meant they weren't just wild dragons, looking for easy prey.

"I see seven," Thea shouted. I heard leather creak and knew she was already unslinging her bow. "We should fight."

That was always Thea's first choice, but she was right. I didn't trust I could control that many dragons with my affinity. I could also feel Kalax's surge of enthusiasm for Thea's words—she was eager for battle.

I glanced back at Thea. "We can't afford to lose anyone, but we also can't let any escape to tell the Darkening of us."

Thea gave a sharp nod and yelled, "Signal the others to fan out!"

I pulled out the flags and gave the signals. Merik took Ferdinania to the right with two of the wild dragons without riders. Syl took Gaxtal to the left, with Scratch, Hiss and one riderless wild dragon following him. I kept Kalax in the middle, so we could strike into the group of other dragons like the tip of an arrow.

Only it was not to be.

The wild dragons suddenly turned, rolling back and turning in the direction from which they had come. That kind of precision could only mean they were fully controlled by the Darkening.

"After them," Thea yelled.

With a howl, Kalax flew up and then swept down on our

prey. An echo of her ferociousness swept into me, setting my heart beating even faster.

Looking ahead, I saw the enemy dragons were leading us almost directly southeast, away from the mountains and back into the Middle Kingdom. That was Lord Vincent's territory now.

"We're close!" I shouted. "We can take them!"

Beris gave a whoop and a cry.

I knew then that we were all looking for a victory of any kind.

The dragon's urge for battle—for a fight—swept into me, and for an instant I lost what was me and what was them. We skimmed over fields, meadows and woodland—the greens and browns blending into a blur, the wind and scents biting at me. I gave another yell—this was why dragons roared.

Thea shouted my name. With a blink, I pulled away from the dragon's senses that had filled my mind.

Glancing at her, I saw her shaking her head and pointing up and toward the sun and a few clouds that hung in the sky.

For a moment, I saw nothing. But then the other dragons— not the blacks we were chasing but large Middle Kingdom dragons—came out of the clouds.

They seemed only dark smudges at first. An oily, smoky taste came to me on the wind. These were fighting dragons, I knew. And we were in trouble.

We'd been found by the dragons of the enemy.

Within minutes of us spotting them, the dragons turned and headed for us. Roars, shrieks and hisses filled the sky.

On one out of ten, I could see a rider. Metal armor like what we wore glinted in the late afternoon sunlight. I didn't know if they were rogue dragon riders or Wildmen riders. But if we were facing other riders trained at the Academy, we were in for a fight.

Thea pointed at the incoming dragons and shouted to Beris and Varla, "The riders! Aim for the riders!"

Arrows flew toward us, along with spears. Kalax ducked and swooped, and then it seemed as if we were caught in a whirl of dragons—tails and wings and claws.

How many were there?

I tried to breathe and remember my training. I could hear the twang of Thea's bow as she loosed arrows.

Dodging tail strikes and snapping jaws, I focused on trying to help Kalax to put Thea into positions where she could fight.

The sky had gone dark with dragons. Yells and shouts filled the air, along with dragon roars.

There's no way that we can win.

I clung to Kalax as she dove again, twisted and flew low over the fields, destroying fences with her tail. Splinters shattered behind us, smacking into the snout of the closest enemy dragon. It spun away from us only for four more to sweep in after Kalax.

Kalax rose up into the sky again, and I tried to help her put the sun at her back. We had a view now of the battle below. Ferdinania was running from three dragons—a green and two blacks. I couldn't see Scratch and Hiss or our other black dragons—maybe they were fighting or maybe they'd decided to hide in the woods below and to the north. I could hear Beris' war cry above us and looked up to see Gaxtal hovering as Beris got off arrow after arrow. I could hear the cries of enemy riders as Beris' arrows struck home.

Behind me, Thea gave a startled cry.

"Are you hit?" I shouted back at her. A large green dragon bore down on us, its eyes a milky white. I knew it must be caught under the magic of the Memory Stone. But I knew that green— the scar upon his shoulder. Glancing at its rider, I saw Thea's brother Reynalt.

"Agathea!" her brother bellowed.

He still wore his Dragon Rider helmet, but it looked scarred, the metal marked by twisted, barbed iron. "It doesn't have to be this way, sister!" he shouted at her as his green dragon hovered next to Kalax.

"Reynalt, you are not yourself!" Thea sighted down the shaft of an arrow pointed straight at her brother. "Lord Vincent has you under his control."

I almost couldn't bear to watch, but I couldn't tear my eyes away.

Reynalt shook his head. "There can be only one winner in this. The Flammas will be on the side that matters. Join us and live, sister!" He was shouting down at her, his voice full of pleading.

Slowly, Thea lowered her bow. She loosened the string, letting the arrow tumble from her grasp to spin and disappear below us. Suddenly, I knew what she was thinking.

Staring at Reynalt, she shouted, "For Torvald...for freedom! For House Flamma!"

"No, Thea—wait," I shouted, but it was too late.

Thea thrust her hand into the pouch at her side and drew forth the King's Dragon Stone.

For an instant, the stone seemed just dull, gray rock. But then sunlight glinted off the King's Dragon Stone. It turned brilliant white, light slipping through Thea's fingers, and power, as if a volcano had erupted, slammed into my chest.

CHAPTER 15
TEN AGAINST HUNDREDS

My ears filled with the sound of shrieking wind and screaming. Power spread through my body, tingling and sharp, leaving me unable to move. Around me, the sky seemed to flash white and then turned red as flame, as if the air itself had caught fire. White bolts shot from my hand, from the King's Dragon Stone, sizzling and bright. And then a voice whispered in my head, seeming to come from the King's Dragon Stone.

Fire consumes all.

Fire begat all.

Fire is the spark in the heart of the world.

Fire is the fury of battle.

The sensation of becoming something else…something larger, stretched through me. It was as if I had fallen asleep and had woken to a world of light. I could look down and see my arm holding the glowing stone, watching it pulse bright, white light in waves that crashed against all of us, against Reynalt and his green, against the mind-controlled wild dragons, against riders and Wildmen and even against the ground, striking into the hearts of everyone and everything within its reach.

Kalax gave a roar, stunned by the blast, but her shock seemed a far off thing. A gale whirled around me, but I was immune to the wind, to the force, to the fire. Dragons and their riders tumbled from the sky, but not me. The King's Dragon Stone spread a glow around me, and again that odd voice echoed in my mind.

There is a fire that forges all bonds or melts them. Everything must pass through the fire if it is to be purified.

The gale that had sprung up from my hand grew hot as an east wind and fierce as dragon fire. My hand burned, but I couldn't let go of the stone. I couldn't stop the fire I'd unleashed.

I was with the fire at the heart of the world and it was in me.

I heard Seb shouting and Kalax roared. But I could only stare at Reynalt on his green. My brother who had offered me a chance to join Lord Vincent. But it was not Reynalt making that offer— it was Lord Vincent, working through Reynalt.

Fury burned in me—in my heart—for such a thing.

Lord Vincent had worked his evil lies before into the ears of others—even into old King Durance, and even into King Justin. Through the flaming sky it was as if I could see Lord Vincent at the Winter Ball when last I'd seen him, smiling and dark, planning his treachery, working to bring down all I knew and loved.

Enough!

This was not my brother on the dragon hovering before me.

And I would bring an end to the disgrace of House Flamma. One way or another, I would free my brother.

Closing my hand around the King's Dragon Stone, I let loose the fire—and flew through the sky on bright, hot flame.

⚜

"Is she awake?"

From a distance, the voice seemed to pull me from dreams of flying through fire on a wind so hot my lungs hurt with each breath. I opened my eyes a crack. The light stung my eyes and I closed them again.

It hurt to breathe. Everything hurt—every inch of skin, every hair on my body and every last muscle. But beyond that, cool, sweet and blessedly calm night air brushed over my face.

Another voice chimed in. "Will she live?"

This time I recognized Seb's voice. He was worrying over me. At least that was familiar.

"I don't know. What she did—the magic she used was a lot stronger." That sounded like Varla. I must be surrounded by my friends—at least they seemed to have survived the battle.

But where was I? And where were Reynalt and the other dragons?

Struggling, I tried to move, but the heavy blankets seemed to weigh me down. A low moan broke from my lips.

"She's waking!" Seb's anxious voice filled the air.

Reynalt—I have to know what happened to him.

I meant to say the words but only managed another moan. It was as if my body was refusing to obey me.

Panic spread through me and knotted my stomach.

I thrashed at the blankets. I wasn't in pain. In fact, a comforting numbness had settled in my bones, like the heat of a summer afternoon lethargy. But I didn't want to be lulled back to sleep.

Easy, Thea-child. Kalax's thoughts settled into me. *Bodies must heal.*

The connection with her seemed very strong, and I asked her, *Where am I? What's wrong with me? What happened?*

Her presence wrapped around me just as she might curl her body around mine on a cold night.

I suddenly sensed the mountain air, sharp and sweet with pine and the smell of wood fires. I could hear the Wildmen as they made their meals and talked quietly. By the noise they made, they seemed to have grown in number. The other dragons were out hunting their meals—I could feel their hunger and that they were dizzy and not quite right. All this came to me in an instant

Less goats here, Kalax thought to me. She was allowing me to use her senses for a moment and letting me know the only important facts as far as she was concerned.

Somewhere, far away, someone was calling my name again, but I was drifting back into the warmth in my bones.

Sleep now, Kalax advised.

Underneath everything else, I sensed a dark cloud of pain from Kalax and the other dragons, but Kalax was trying her best to conceal it. I pushed a little more and felt how one side of her body had been bruised as if she had fallen from a great height and her wings were also aching.

Oh Kalax! Are you well? Were you hurt from the battle?

Sleep will make all better.

I knew when Kalax was being evasive. She was in pain, but it wasn't from the battle. It was from something I'd done.

The King's Dragon Stone.

Stretching out my awareness. I couldn't sense any of the wild dragons, other than Scratch and Hiss and two of the other wild blacks. Ferdinania and Gaxtal had suffered bruises and burns, and the wild dragons had broken bones that now had to heal.

What have I done?

My skin chilled and an ache seemed to tighten around my heart.

Enough. Kalax's annoyance came to me, clear and sharp. *Thea saved lives. We escaped. That matters. The magic is too powerful perhaps for humans.*

Oh Kalax...I am so sorry.

Kalax pushed at my mind, forcing me back into my body. She also pulled her mind away from mine, locking her senses away from my awareness.

For a moment, I opened my eyes to see fire again—but this was a small campfire. Smoke rose from it in a thin, white column. Seb, Varla and Merik huddled around the campfire, all of them looking bruised, with their flying leathers tattered. Beris and Syl stood at the edges of the shadows of a clearing. Sleep was trying to claim me again, but I fought against it.

"We won." I managed to say the words, but I heard them come out with a cracking, raspy voice that didn't sound like me.

Seb came over to my side at once, the lines easing on his face as he bent over me. "Not quite, but close enough," he said.

I gave a nod or tried to, and then I listened to Kalax and slept.

⊙⋙⊗

Kalax was indeed right.

I woke the very next morning and almost felt like myself again. Whatever I'd done with the King's Dragon Stone had left me drained, as if I was now recovering from a particularly strong bout of winter sickness. By midday, I was up and on my feet and getting worried glances from everyone.

They'd camped in the forest, letting thick, tall trees hide our small force. The Wildmen were keeping watch—they all seemed nervous around me now. I couldn't blame them. The smell of food—one of Merik's stews—pulled me to the fire. The Wildmen had been hunting and had added rabbit to the plants Merik and Varla had scavenged.

Sitting down by the fire, I ate three bowls. Syl and Beris were off tending to Gaxtal, Merik and Varla retreated to pour over the few scrolls and the old book Varla had recovered from the Academy—no doubt looking for information on how I, or they, could better control the King's Dragon Stone. I doubted they'd find anything. That stone had been in the First Rider's tomb for long, long years—and anyone who might ever have known how to use it had died in the first war with the Darkening.

Looking at Seb, who was still picking at his first bowl of stew, I asked, "How bad was it? At the battlefield, I mean."

Seb winced and looked up from his uneaten stew. "Well, no deaths—or none that we know of. You blasted the wild black dragons closing in on us. As well as your brother and every other dragon in the sky. Ferdinania has a torn wing, but can still fly. If we'd stayed put, we might have all been torn to pieces." He gave me a weak smile and a shrug. "You sure know how to pack a punch."

"And the King's Dragon Stone?" I asked. "What's become of it?"

Seb shook his head. "It was—it was like nothing I have ever seen. It looked as though the stone and then your whole hand became lit by an inner fire. It grew so bright it was hard to even look at it—and then waves of light and wind seemed to course from it. Dragons were dropping from the sky. If it wasn't for you losing consciousness and Kalax managing to get us to the ground without killing us—"

"Oh, Seb, I...I didn't intend that. I just wanted...I wanted Reynalt to be free of Lord Vincent."

Putting down his bowl, Seb picked up a stick and stirred the cooking fire. "At least we know the King's Dragon Stone works."

I glanced over at the Wildmen who were avoiding me now and then looked back at Seb. "What good is it, if it will destroy our own forces as well?"

"It gives us a chance." Seb looked up from the fire and forced a grin. "You have to believe that things will get better. Maybe in the king's hands it will be different—he is descended from the First Rider after all."

I let out a long breath and wrapped my arms around myself. "You didn't say where you put the…where you put it?"

"It's safe. Back in your bag. I told you it didn't do anything when I touched it, but no one else seems to want to get near it." Seb frowned a little.

"Do we know where the king is yet?"

"No, but there have been rumors and Kalax said she can sense dragons at the southern end of the Dragon Spine Mountains."

I shook my head. "We won't know if those are friends or enemies—it's all a mix. We'll have to do better to find the king." Seb didn't answer, so I leaned forward and said, "What are we going to do if Lord Vincent has control of all of our dragons and riders? Lord Vincent has a lot to answer for." Thinking of Reynalt, I sighed heavily. Had Ryan been turned as well?

Seb straightened. "Maybe King Justin and the last of the Dragon Riders went into hiding? They could be on the coast. All we have to do is find them."

"Your optimism is hopeless. How are we going to do that if our dragons can't tell an enemy from a friend anymore?"

"Slowly," he admitted, with a crooked grin.

It was such a ridiculous thing to say that I found myself smiling. "You're an idiot." I punched his arm.

"But an idiot with a dragon. And a plan. We'll go back to the Dragon Academy."

Hands tightening into fists, I stared at him. "Are you mad? That is probably the center of Lord Vincent's territory now."

"And, as such, it is the very last place the Darkening will look for us. If Lord Vincent can make his dragons seem like friends to us, we can do the same to him. It is also one of the few places where we might be able to find out more about how to control the King's Dragon Stone." Standing, he turned to face the south. I rose as well and stood next to him. He bumped my shoulder with his and said, "We don't need to lay siege to Torvald, but think about it for a second. Where else are we going to find out how to use this magic? Where else will we find any sort of defensible structures?"

"I should point out, Seb, that the Academy is half destroyed."

"That is the operative word—half." Seb put a hand on my shoulder. His touch seemed to help ground me. His voice dropped lower and he said, "We need shelter. We can sneak in. With black dragons and after the Wildmen show up, it'll just look like forces of the Darkening moving into the Academy. And… well, we have to find out how to use the King's Dragon Stone in a way that won't kill everyone, right?" He looked at me, eyebrows lifted high and his brown eyes soft and shining.

I could tell he was tired, too. Dark circles still stained his eyes, and he had hardly eaten any of his stew. But if there was a trick to using this magic, one that meant we could channel its power, we had to try for that.

Leaning against him, I gave a nod. And I wondered if any of us knew what we are doing.

After sunset, we started our flight south again. It would just be the dragons and riders—that meant there were ten of us. One of the wild, black dragons Seb had almost tamed had left us during the battle, fleeing with the other blacks.

That meant it was ten dragons against hundreds.

Thorri wanted us to keep scouting for her and her Wildmen to travel after the dragons on foot, but Seb had insisted we needed to get to the Academy as soon as possible. He argued that Reynalt or someone else who had escaped the power we'd use would take news of it to Lord Vincent. We couldn't risk the King's Dragon Stone falling into enemy hands.

That thought had my stomach cramping and my hands cold— I had feared that very thing all along. I vowed to myself that I would use the stone and its power to destroy myself and all with me before that happened.

But Thorri argued over the idea of being left behind, and Beris actually sided with her, strangely enough, saying we needed every fighter that we could get.

He wasn't wrong, but neither was Seb for thinking we needed to act quickly. We put it to a vote and the rest of us sided with Seb's idea of getting the dragons moving fast and ahead of the Wildmen.

Eyes snapping, Thorri folded her arms across her chest. "I'm still come to Torvald with any and all that march with me. We will not hide and hope you Dragon Riders will save everyone. We will fight!"

I had to admire her courage. She had no dragon at her side, no magical affinity or stone that would increase her chances. She and her forces were outnumbered. But she wasn't about to let any of that stop her. I hoped that I, too, would prove myself when my back hit the wall. And I couldn't shake the feeling that that would be happening sooner rather than later.

We were headed into the heart of our enemy's territory—this was not just our only chance, it was a wild and slim one, too.

⊗

To me, it seemed as if Kalax was feeling curiously settled, at peace with the thought of returning to where she had been born. She even chirruped to the other wild, black dragons with us, pleased by their presence and loyalty.

"She wants to hunt and fight. She says we've been hiding for too long," Seb told me. I could feel a surge of wild excitement pulse through me—it felt like that same beat of power from the King's Dragon Stone.

Fire...spark at the heart of every living thing.

Kalax's thoughts came into my mind. I wondered if we would have a later to talk about such things. After we'd won our victory.

Or would we end like the First Rider—given burials in tombs that would be made into sacred spots. I shivered.

We had wrapped every piece of armor, breastplate, or shoulder guard against making so much as a glint of light. We had daubed some of the Wildmen's blue on our faces, so we'd look more like Wildmen. Dar had grinned at such a thing. Even the dragons had seemed to mute their colors, something I hadn't known they could do. We looked like creatures out of myth and legend—bits of moonlight that skimmed the cloudy sky.

Seb had given everyone orders to make as little sound as possible. Kalax led the way, flying so low I felt as if I could lean down and touch the tree tops. The dragons worked hard to catch every updraft and current, gliding as much as possible. It would take a few hours to reach Torvald and the plan was to make it before dawn. I pulled my tattered cloak tighter around my shoulders and patted the leather pouch at my side where the King's Dragon Stone lay, heavy and seeming to hum softly. I tried not to think of what might have to happen if we were discovered—how I might have to use the power of the stone again to prevent it from falling into Lord Vincent's hands.

Instead, I focused on the flight.

We moved like hunting owls, as silent as death itself, stealing back into the country we had once called home. This time we were the invaders.

At one point, I looked back to see the long line of our ten dragons moving over the landscape like moonlight. Kalax was skimming over a river now, flying so low I could feel the spray of water on my face and smell the wet.

But I couldn't let the peaceful night lull me into a false sense of security. It might seem quiet, but this level of flying required constant vigilance from the navigators and the dragons to avoid snagging a wing tip or their claws on a trees or even on roof tops.

This would be a feat worthy of songs and tales, if any friend survived to write one about us.

It wasn't until the darkest part of the night, when even the stars had been obligingly covered by high, black clouds, that we spied a hump in the horizon ahead.

Dragons!

Kalax sniffed the air, her mind informing both me and Seb of what she had detected. I saw Seb lean down, confiding something in her and my hands tensed on my bow. Would I have to fight? Shoot one down?

The crimson red, daubed in the northern tribe's camouflage, slowed her pace, taking a long, meandering route toward the city, which spread out from Mount Hammal like the tiers of a cake.

"No dragons on the wing?" I whispered, and I saw Seb shake his head.

"No," he hissed at me. "I expect they're all asleep and don't expect an attack!"

"Won't they smell us?" I whispered.

Seb nodded, before indicating the wild dragons behind us who had joined our tiny force to make up our ten.

Of course, the dragons in and around the city would smell us, but we would just be more Middle Kingdom and wild dragons mixed together. There was no special feature that marked us out as enemy. Not yet.

"We get as close to the Academy as we can, and land where we have to." Seb waved at the rear of the city, which opened out onto Mount Hammal with its wild scrubby woods, meadows and the lake where I had once watched Kalax fish. It all seemed so long ago now. To think this had been my home, and now it stank of ash and blood. This was where I had become a Dragon Rider!

The moon set and the sky grew darker. I knew dawn would be coming soon. I could see the shape of Mount Hammal in the distance now. It looked old and scarred, even from here, and I felt a shiver through me.

What if Lord Vincent has burned the Academy?

I pushed the thought away and tried to remember the Academy and the dragon enclosure as it had been.

Usually, even in the middle of the night, we could hear the sound from the dragons—they would be grumbling, feeding or shuffling about in the old volcano crater that had acted as their enclosure. The night air had always been filled with the yips of foxes hunting, the screech of wild rabbits, or the soft hoots of owls. Tonight, I could only hear the wind in my ears. And I dreaded to think what we'd see when we got to the Academy or when the sun broke over the horizon.

Would the stones be blasted? The keep burned? The forces of the Darkening—the mutated dragons and the possessed Wildmen and Southern raiders—seemed to revel in destruction and death just for the sake of it.

Glancing below us, I could see that Lord Vincent hadn't bothered to rebuild any of the ruined bridges over the mountain rivers. Crops had been flattened in the fields. Villages had been burned. I would have expected an invading army to seize things of value, but the Darkening seemed to rejoice in pure destruction.

Kalax crested a ridge and Mount Hammal rose up in front of

us. Seb raised his hand and waved a white flag that could be seen. It was the signal to hold fast.

Kalax banked, swooping along the underside of the high peak, swerving back down a few hundred feet to the meadows. With an effort that would have earned us a medal from the Academy instructors, all ten dragons managed to copy the maneuver, coming to land on the barren ground. The one bit of good news was that the Academy walls—and at least one of the towers—still stood.

I had to admit, it was good to see it again. Hope lifted in my chest. Then I turned to the others.

They had already dismounted. We'd agreed that we'd go in on foot, just in case any forces of the Darkening were inside the Academy. It would be easier to break and run and have our dragons waiting to take us to safety.

I glanced around at all the faces, so pale in the early, pale light that came just before dawn arrived. Beris looked grim, and Syl fidgeted nervously with the hilt of his sword. Merik had his flying goggles pushed up and his optics in place, and Varla had her sword drawn. The three Wildmen grinned, looking eager for battle. I gave Seb a nod. He and I went first. We trudged over the ridge, finding the familiar path that led from the high meadow and down to the Academy.

It was much as we had last seen it, with scorch marks on every wall. A few more stones had been toppled from the upper walls, but two of the dragon platforms still looked solid, even in the weak dawn light. One wall-mounted trebuchet still stood. I wished again that the map tower had survived, but I wouldn't let myself think this might have been a wasted journey. We had to find something that might help us.

At the front gates, we paused. The Wildmen or others had put new gates back in place, but had left them open. Strangely, a dragon's skull, the bones bleached white, had been nailed to the top of the right gate. I recognized the skull as the one that had once hung from the keep's hall—it had been the skull of one of the earliest dragons to ever be raised in the enclosure.

"Some tribal ritual?" Seb asked, looking at the Wildmen.

Temmi shrugged, and I pointed at the dragons' teeth scattered along the base of the walls. Some were ancient and yellowed, but others held stains as if they'd been taken out only recently. "Looks more like a warning."

Remembering the skeleton of the First Dragon, turned to stone and guarding the tomb of the First Rider, I hunched a shoulder. "A warning to keep out—magic's here."

Seb nodded. "Good. That may keep others out." He headed inside the Academy, and I followed.

The training yard held little more than cold ashes and tumbled stone.

"Home sweet home," Seb muttered.

I patted him on the back. "It'll be that again." Glancing back, I saw the others had followed us in. Looking around us once more, I saw the walls held strong and thick, and we had front gates again. We could bar them and hold the Academy for a time, but if a large force attacked, we wouldn't be able to keep our defenses in place. Maybe Beris had been right and we should have waited for the Wildmen troops.

In my leather pouch, the King's Dragon Stone seemed heavy and warm. I wet my lips and resisted the urge to reach down and pat it, as if it was a pet. It was about as much a pet as was a trained fighting dragon.

I glanced up to the eastern sky—dawn was leaving pink and gray streaks across the horizon.

Turning to the others, I said, "Okay, Seb, Merik and Varla, let's see what we can find. Look for anything that might have been hidden or buried—maybe in a cellar or one of the instructor rooms. Beris and Syl, you'll take first watch, but stay out of sight. Post Dar, Temmi and Jal where they can be seen, so the Academy looks as if it's still under the control of the Darkening. There are certain to be others from Lord Vincent's forces about. Maybe they'll heed their own warning, but let's not take a chance that they won't."

Beris threw me a hasty salute and moved off with our Wildmen dragon riders. Merik and Seb headed for the keep, and Varla stayed by my side. I glanced around the training yard once more, thinking of all the mock battles I'd fought here. Now it might become the place where we made our final stand against Lord Vincent and the Darkening.

CHAPTER 16
THE FINAL LESSON

It was eerily silent as Merik and I crept up the stone steps inside the keep. Thea and Varla followed just behind Merik. Our footsteps echoed back to us but my heart was thudding so hard it seemed louder than our boots.

"Who put the dragon's skull on the gate? And why?" Merik whispered as he followed me.

I shook my head. I was just hoping we weren't about to find out that some contingent of Darkening sorcerers or something equally foul had taken up residence at the Academy and wanted others to stay out.

We passed by the arched stone windows that opened out onto the Dragon Academy, revealing the dawn just beyond the eastern mountains. The Academy was starting to look even worse in the morning light—you could see more of the scars on the walls. As we climbed higher, I could see the city below us. Large parts lay in ruins. The fires had all either gone out on their own or had been put out. The city seemed oddly silent, and I wasn't sure anyone still lived in it.

Reaching the top floors, we came upon an open door that had been left hanging from one hinge. The room looked as if it had escaped any damage—scarlet drapes still hung by the broken window, which let in a cool, morning breeze. A tall-backed, wooden chair stood next to a scarred oak table that still had all its legs and held a dozen scrolls and three books. How had this escaped the Wildmen?

I glanced around. This had been one of the rooms that led up to the lookout platforms. Pulling in a breath, I heard the sharp clack of metal bending. Was that from the metal stairs cooling? Maybe it was nothing more than a nesting pigeon.

Or maybe not.

I looked at Thea and put a finger to my lips. Slow and silent, I drew my sword and stepped over the threshold.

The windows had been smashed and so had the bookshelves that once lined the walls. I wondered how much lore we had lost —would we ever be able to recreate everything? But the scrolls and the books meant someone had saved something.

A raspy voice from above made me crouch low and look up. "So you, too, came back."

For an instant, I could see no one in the shadows above us. Dawn light was slowly creeping in through the broken window, but it left deep pockets of blackness. My eyes adjusted to the dimness, and a figure moved. He stood up in one of the viewing galleries where scouts used to sit, gazing through the wall-mounted tellyscups.

Moving slowly, the man came down the narrow, winding stairs and stepped into the main room. For an instant I didn't know him, he was so covered in dirt, but he took another step and his limp gave away his identity.

"Mordecai? Instructor Mordecai?" I could only blink. It seemed as if we were always coming across him here—as if he was as drawn to the Academy as we were. Perhaps even more so, for where else would he go?

"No instructor now, boy." Mordecai said and fell heavily into the chair. It creaked under his weight, although now I could see his face looked thinner. His gray hair also hung limp and long around his face. He gave a groan and started coughing, the sound a deep rattle in his chest.

After swapping a look with Thea and one with Varla—I wanted them to be ready in case this was a trick—I stepped forward to pat Mordecai's back. Merik came into the room and began to look over the scrolls and books.

Pushing my arm away, Mordecai glared up at me, his eyes blurred with moisture. He pulled in a raspy breath and said, "You thought me gone or worse! But you can't get rid of me that easily."

"We—we don't want to." Thea sheathed her sword. Frowning, she shared a look with me and wiggled her eyebrows. I knew what she meant. This was very unlike the sharp-witted Mordecai we'd known. Had he been badly injured? And where was Commander Hegarty—hadn't Mordecai gone to the Southern Realm with the commander?

Check him, Thea mouthed the words to me and I nodded,

motioning for Thea and Merik to keep watch. Merik frowned, but Varla stepped up, her sword still in her hand—she wasn't going to relax her guard it seemed.

"Come, sir. Let's take you to better quarters." I reached to take his arm. I could smell dried blood and stale sweat on him. How long had he been here? It looked to me as though he hadn't washed in days—but neither had we. Like us, he still wore boots and leathers, and like us they looked to be hard worn and becoming tattered. The gray cloak on his shoulders looked fit only for a vagabond, not for a Dragon Rider.

I'd no sooner touched him than Mordecai's hand snaked out to seize my wrist in a vice-like grip. He dragged me closer until he was staring into my eyes. His beard had grown shaggy. "I'm not dead yet, boy! Not yet!"

"No, sir. No." I twisted my arm to free myself and rubbed my sore wrist. He might look thinner and older, but he still had a grip like a dragon.

Behind me, Thea and Varla edged closer. Mordecai grasped the edge of the table and pulled himself to his feet. He swayed for a moment and I readied myself to catch him, but he glared at me, as if daring me to treat him like an old, infirm man.

Staring at Mordecai, Thea narrowed her eyes. "We keep meeting you here. But you and the commander were traveling south to get help."

Mordecai glanced at her and then back up at the viewing gallery. He was silent for a moment and then let out a breath. "Yes. Hegarty. He gave a good account at the end."

It was if I had stepped off of a ledge and suddenly realized there was no firm ground underneath me. "The commander?" The words came out unsteady even to my ears.

Commander Hegarty had been the only one who had really believed a boy from Monger's Lane could become a Dragon Rider. He had been more than an instructor—he'd taught me how to deal with the slights and insults from sullen nobles who thought I didn't belong.

"What happened to Commander Hegarty?" I asked. My throat seemed to clamp shut.

Mordecai straightened and faced me. He no longer looked just to be an old, sick man who had been through a hard time. His eyes sharpened. His boots and breeches might be caked in mud and grime with blood marking his leather jerkin and cloak, but he suddenly looked a Dragon Rider who had been through hard battles to get here.

How had he done that without Commander Hegarty?

And what of the others who had gone with them?

"What happened?" I asked, my voice sharpening. "Why are you here and not the commander? Hegarty is twice the fighter you could ever be."

With a nod, Mordecai said, "Yes…yes, he was. Which is why I'm here. He stood his ground to the last and told us to run. Said someone must get back. The rest of us scattered and I fear I was the only to come back alive. We found no help."

Grief cut through me, a deep sorrow. The commander dead. I couldn't believe such a thing.

Kalax sensed my sorrow and denial and brushed her heart against mine.

All men and dragons die.

"Seb?" Thea put a hand on my shoulder. "Let's get him some water and find if there is any food left in the stores."

I could only stare at her.

Mordecai stepped up to me. "You think I don't feel ten times worse than you, boy?" His voice firmed and gained in strength. "I've known Hegarty since we were both lads. We fought with the old king against raiders and the like. We shared the comrade-ship of long years, trusting our lives to each other's hands! We held the Academy for long years. His loss is one I'll not forget."

The pain of such a loss didn't lessen, but I realized I was not the only one who would miss Hegarty.

Elbowing me aside, Thea unslung her water pouch. "Sir, you must be thirsty. We should also see to your wounds."

He accepted the water and drank some down, but thrust the pouch back at Thea and wiped his mouth and beard with the back of his hand. "I've lasted this long. I'll go a day longer, I expect."

"But, sir…your wounds?"

"Will be there tomorrow if any of us live to see another sunrise. He turned to stare out the window. "I fear there will be none left to bury us."

Following his stare, I looked out the shattered window. I could see the ridge of the mountains, which sloped down to the dragon enclosure. From the top there, you could look down into the dragon enclosure, which spread out like a bowl. Beside the granite boulder that marked the path, I saw a fresh stack of rocks made into a cairn and topped with glinting dragon's teeth. That had to be the commander's grave—and now we knew that

Mordecai must also have put the signs up to warn others not just away from Hegarty's grave but from the Academy.

I glanced at him and crossed my arms. "You came back here to die? Why? What happened?" All thoughts of giving him comfort had fled—I wanted to know just what had happened to the commander. Why was he dead and Mordecai still alive?

With a heavy sigh, he sat in the chair. He shook his head and put his stare out the window again, looking toward the commander's grave. "The road south seemed choked with those fleeing Torvald at first. We sent them to try and meet up with the king's forces and soon parted from the roads. Everywhere we went, we ran into trouble. We took on the cloaks of raiders from the Southern Realm so we might pass. Any unfortunates not directly under the control of the Darkening seemed terrified. Some would attack any stranger."

He paused and turned away from the window. His shoulders slumped. "We pushed on and the days grew hotter and the woods thinned into the shrubs and grass of the southlands. It became harder to hide from the black dragons that flew the skies—the Darkening seemed to be everywhere. Every village we came across had been burned to the ground. So we headed for the high rocky mountains."

I frowned—it was sounding as if the Southern Realm had met with the same battles and war as the Middle Kingdom.

Glancing at me, Mordecai said, "At last we came across a small group of fighters—or rather their dragons found us. They were using herbs and strong potions to ward off the magic from the Memory Stone. Mostly, however, they were in hiding.

Hegarty talked them into flying north to join King Justin's forces, and so we started back."

His cough started up again. Thea offered him more water, but he waved her off, scowling at her, looking more like his old self.

Wiping his beard, he shook his head. "We had it all wrong. We'd faced a large battle here with the Darkening, but in the Southern Realm, they had seen a slow spread—they'd had manipulation and treachery. That cur Lord Vincent had been spreading the poison of the Darkening for years to turn the people of the south into his slaves. And we walked into his trap."

"There were no herbs and potions to avoid the Darkening and the Memory Stone," Varla muttered.

Looking up, Mordecai nodded. "We learned that truth too late. The dragons and riders we'd met up with led us straight to the Darkening. We did what we could to fight and run. Hegarty got us out only by giving up his own life. Only a few of the Southern Realm riders were still free of the Darkening. They… they helped me and then fled. I…I went back to find Hegarty's broken body. He deserved a decent grave and so I brought him home. If there are any dragons in the Southern Realm still free now, I fear they are in hiding…or they are dead."

His gaze seemed to turn inward and he fell silent.

Thea glanced at me, her eyebrows pulled into a tight frown. I was just glad that Hegarty lay near his beloved dragons. But we were still alive—and still in deep trouble.

"Now what?" Merik said, asking the question we were all thinking.

I glanced at him and pushed back my shoulders. We had no

time to mourn—we had battles to plan and fight. "We still have the King's Dragon Stone."

Mordecai straightened and his eyes brightened. "What? What Dragon Stone? The one that controls them all? You know where it is?"

"We do." Dropping my arms to my side, I nodded.

"Then why, by the First Dragon, haven't you used this…this King's Dragon Stone? Why is it not with the king?" Mordecai stood and looked from me to Thea and back again.

"We did use it," Thea said, her voice dry. "And almost died."

I lifted a hand and said, "Once, a long time ago, you were suspicious of what I could do—of the Dragon Affinity. You said it was too powerful for me and I didn't know how to control it. Well, the King's Dragon Stone is much the same, but even more so."

Thea huffed a breath. "Seb thinks it's bonded to me and—"

"We all do," Varla muttered.

"Bonded?" Mordecai frowned. "To you, Flamma? So it likes your hand and no other? Well, that is one bit of good news—you, Flamma, at least have a sensible head." His voice took on more strength and sharpened, so he sounded more like the cranky instructor we'd once known. "And, Smith, I was suspicious of you because the ancient power that runs through your veins and which comes out as the Dragon Affinity *is* dangerous. That is the same magic the Darkening pulls upon."

"Just as Lord Vincent does," Merik said, his voice barely a whisper.

I could feel my face warm, then chill. What if I had touched the King's Dragon Stone first? Could I have become like Lord Vincent—a ghoul who sought only power and more power? Was that how that prince of old had been corrupted—had he had the affinity and answered its pull toward the darkness of never having enough? He certainly wanted more territory, more destruction…more death.

"Much harm can come from dangers we have not foreseen." Mordecai's energy faded. Coughs shook him again and he slumped back into his chair. "But there is hope for us if Flamma here has the one Dragon Stone that controls them—the King's Dragon Stone. And you have each other." Mordecai looked from me to Merik, then to Varla, and finally to Thea. "That is true strength." He seemed to speak straight to Thea. "That was our mistake—to try and split apart. I should never have listened to Hegarty and left his side. Stay together and you will have the best chance any of us might have."

Mordecai gave a nod and looked at me. "I was suspicious of you, Smith, because you so wanted to master all of the skills we teach and you wanted to do it on your own. That was where I and Hegarty differed. He thought he could see a spark in you that would save others, but I feared that very thing. There are no heroes, only friends."

Only family, Kalax repeated in my mind.

I liked what the instructor was trying to say. I wanted to let him know I had learned that lesson. Before I could, a low booming shook the walls.

Low and powerful, it was a sound I would never forget.

"The Dragon Horns," Varla said, looking from Thea to Merik and then to me.

The vast, brass horns were each as big as a person and had been used by the guards to signal Dragon Riders. It was a sound of warning or challenge and meant someone at the gates was summoning the last Dragon Riders loyal to the true King of Torvald.

CHAPTER 17
CHOOSE SIDES

I was staring at Seb when the Dragon Horns sounded, vibrating in my chest and in my bones. My mind was still trying to grasp what Mordecai had been saying.

He believes in us. He believes that we can do this. Somehow his faith was reassuring—Mordecai had never spoken lightly. The Dragon Rider in me didn't see how anything had changed from a few minutes ago—in fact, with the Dragon Horns blowing an alarm, our life had just seemed to get drastically worse.

And now we knew that one of our best leaders, Commander Hegarty, was dead.

From the looks of him, Mordecai seemed not far from collapsing. I couldn't think on what he must have endured, bearing the broken body of his friend back to the Academy. If any man was spent—it must be him.

Which meant our army had the king, Ryan as a commander,

and the rest of us who hadn't ever been given as much as a squadron assignment.

And yet, we've probably seen more battles than any but Thorri and her Wildmen.

Striding to the window, I scanned the horizon for possible danger. "Beris must be sounding the Dragon Horn," Tightening my hand into a fist, I cursed. "We told him to stay out of sight. He'll bring the whole of Lord Vincent's army down on top of us!"

Seb stepped up to my side and pointed to the southwest. "Look south by southwest."

I followed where he was pointing, shading my eyes with one hand and squinting against the early morning light. On the horizon, I could see dark, almost black, clouds rising up. Colors— reds and yellows—flashes in the distance. Was that lightning?

The line grew in size and shape—I was seeing dragon wings as they cut the light and cast shadows. I could see reds, greens, blues and even the orange and yellow of some Southern dragons at the head of a cloud of black dragons.

"The Darkening?" My mouth dried. Was my brother riding with them, along with other Dragon Riders who were now controlled by the Memory Stone?

Muttering something, Seb headed up the steps and to the viewing gallery. He put an eye to the brass tellyscup.

Merik clambering up beside him and elbowed Seb aside. "I was always better with these than with any viewing glasses. You're the better pilot."

Seb didn't argue but came down the stairs again. Merik

adjusted the internal panes of glass and tube lengths—it was as much an art as a science to be a good spotter, and Merik was better at it than any of us.

Turning back to the window, I watched the approaching dragons. They seemed to be gaining speed and headed straight for Torvald.

Merik was mumbling, talking to himself, but then he spoke up, the words clear and loud. "I'm seeing a large force of black dragons, some with Wildmen for riders. That's got to be Lord Vincent's forces." He licked his lips. "They're chasing another group—Middle Kingdom dragons and what looks like a few Southern Realm dragons."

"Southern Realm? A few joined the king! Ah, Hegarty, old friend, you did not die in vain," Mordecai said, standing and limping over to stand behind us. "How many are with the king?"

"Uh, wait, hard to tell." Merik's voice faded to almost a whisper as he calculated. We had practiced enough when training, learning how to guess numbers in a flock of birds, a swarm of bees or a pride of dragons.

Guess the number in a small area and multiply how many areas there might be and then you have the number.

"King's forces approximately a hundred," Merik said. It sounded like he was trying to be enthusiastic.

"Enemy forces?" I asked, my heart thudding in slow beats.

"Not good," Merik said.

"Enemy numbers?" Mordecai barked out the words. He still could summon that instructor's voice that could strike terror into the spine of any cadet or Dragon Rider.

Merik let out a breath. "At least seven hundred dragons. I can't tell how many ground troops."

My mind blanked at such numbers—seven to one. No wonder the king's dragons were fleeing. Despair settled into a hard lump in my chest. Reaching down, I touched the leather pouch that held the King's Dragon Stone. It seemed very warm, but I couldn't use it at this distance—could I? And what if I did and killed everyone?

Varla nudged my side with her elbow. "So we can do anything if we do it together? Wonder if that includes dying together."

I glanced at her. "Enough of that! Don't think about failure. Think about fighting. And surviving." I gave her a smile, hoping she would take my rebuke as one of encouragement. She gave a shrug and I glanced up at Merik. "How long until they reach the city?"

Merik frowned. "They're holding back. The enemy, that is— Lord Vincent's forces. They aren't really trying to engage the king's dragons or bring them down. It looks like they're just driving them on—not letting anyone break away or turn."

"That's just cruel," Seb said. He shook his head, his mouth pressed into a thin line.

"No, it makes good battle sense. When you are so sure of winning, why not push your enemy? Hound your foe to the point of exhaustion and then you can have done with the lot of them with few casualties to your own forces. This is it. This will be the final battle. And I think Lord Vincent wants to see the king defeated over the capital of the Middle Kingdom."

"I don't know." Shaking his head, Merik looked away from the tellyscup and glanced at Seb. "The enemy is holding quite a bit back, letting the king's forces get further and further away."

I could hear the screeches and roars of the oncoming dragons now and see them as more than just a moving line. To me, they looked tired with wings that beat slow and heads that drooped ever so slightly. The scent of blood carried to me. Our dragons were flying lower and lower, and I sensed alarm from Kalax—these were her kind and kin. Which left me thinking of my other brother.

Where are you, Ryan? Are you there? Are you still alive?

"Come on." I signaled to the others. "Let's get the gates closed and the dragon platforms that still stand cleared as best as we can. We might as well make it easy for them to land. If we're going to have a last stand, let's have it here."

"I'll summon Kalax and the other dragons here," Seb said.

"There is one trebuchet working. I'll man it." Mordecai turned and limped to the door, moving faster than any of us.

As I ran down the stone steps, the heavy lump of the King's Dragon Stone bounced in my leather pouch at my side. I patted it and held it still.

Soon we'll see just what you can do.

And that might be was the last thing I ever did.

※

As the king's dragons flew over the city, a few dark arrows shot up from enemy forces inside the city and fell back to the ground.

We worked fast to close the gates and get rubble from the fallen tower stacked up to help them hold. Mordecai, as he'd promised, manned the one working weapon we had—the wooden trebuchet that could launch stones or balls of fire into the sky. But the enemy forces held back.

Beris and Syl blew the Dragon Horns again, trying to signal the king's forces they could safely land at the Academy.

Sweaty now, my hands skinned from lifting rocks and getting the gates closed—they creaked and groaned as if they'd never before moved—I looked up at the sky. Kalax and our dragons had come at once and now sat within the Academy, perched in the training yard. How would we get a hundred dragons in here? I didn't know, but we'd have to do it somehow—and then we had the problem of feeding everyone. Were we safe here or trapping ourselves within stone walls? At least the Academy had its own well—no one would lack for water.

Within a short time, the air stirred with dragon breaths and wing beats. The king's dragons whirled and wheeled over the Academy. Some perched on the landing platforms, others came down to land on the fallen towers, the ramparts, or even on ruined roofs.

I had never seen the Academy so filled with dragons. Ironically, this came at a time when this was perhaps the smallest number of Dragon Riders the Academy had ever boasted. Usually, only two squadrons of fifty dragons would be active in the air over the city, while the other dragons rested in the enclosure, and another four squadrons patrolled our borders. Now, we had no dragons in the enclosure—it had been destroyed when Lord Vincent's armies had taken the city.

The few Southern Realm dragons with the king seemed to know nothing about landing platforms. They came straight down to the ground and landed with dusty thuds. Riders climbed or almost fell off the backs of their dragons. This close, I could see the marks of battle—wings torn, arrows sticking out of saddle leather and harness, blood stains and torn leathers. The Academy stank now of blood and dragon sweat. The dragons all seemed too tired to even roar or bicker—and our wild, black dragons huddled close together, glancing around as if they feared attack.

That had me thinking of the enemy.

I glanced up at the sky but it hadn't filled with enemy dragons. Arrows didn't pour down on us. There was no challenge at all.

"Why are they not attacking?" I muttered, asking no one in particular and everyone in general.

Heading up to the top of the wall, I could see the enemy dragons hovering over the southern half of the city. They circled there as if they had nothing better to do. What were they planning?

From the top of the wall, I glanced down. I had a better view here and could see the mix of dragons—a few from the Southern Realm, their riders distinct by their light armor and their dark skins. The glint of gold caught my eye—the king's crown.

Pushing through the crowd of riders, I headed to the nearest landing platform, for I had seen Ryan.

I called his name.

He's safe! Thank the First Dragon, he's safe!

He saw me and caught me up in a hug and spun me around. I slapped his shoulder. "I knew you were too much a Flamma to die!"

That remark left him frowning. He put me on my feet, and from behind him, a tired voice I knew said, "Lord Vincent gave us one day to surrender or die."

I glanced over Ryan's shoulder and saw King Justin.

He looked as battered as any other rider, his armor stained black from dragon fire, his face lined as if he had aged a dozen year in this short time.

Bowing, I muttered, "My king."

Justin put up a hand. "Don't." He sounded almost as old as time itself. For a moment, I feared the mind sickness still lay upon him from his time under the influence of the Memory Stone. but his eyes seemed clear and sharp, and full also of misery. "What sort of king am I, to lead my people to this?" he asked.

I shared a look with Ryan—kings and princes were not meant to indulge in such talk. Mouth pressed tight, Ryan shook his head as if it all was already lost.

I heard an uneven step behind me and Mordecai pushed through the crowd. He had obviously heard the king's words for he said, "You are my king, and that is all that I—or any—need to know, sire." Reaching out, he clasped King Justin by the shoulders in a traditional Dragon Riders' embrace. Mordecai leaned forward. "You are a king and your people need you. Do not fail them at this time. Remember your father and all who have died in protecting your realm."

Justin stood a little straighter, nodding to himself.

Walking to the edge of the landing platform, high on the walls of the Academy, the king stretched out his hands and called out, "My people—my troops."

Everyone—dragon and riders—fell silent. Even the groans of those wounded were bitten off.

The king pulled off his helmet with its golden crown. "We have suffered much…some would say too much. But we are come home. The blood of dragons runs through each and every one of you, and it is fitting that here, in our birthplace, we shall make our last stand! Our enemy would see us grovel—would see us beg on a bended knee to be made into slaves. Our enemy would see us serve the Darkening and become something foul. But I say we stand free—we will die free if we must. Each and every woman, man and dragon has done me proud this day and every day before it. I am glad to call myself your king, and prouder still to call myself a Dragon Rider of Torvald!"

Following his words, an echoing, ragged cheer rose from all of us and even the dragons roared approval. For the first time in a long time, our king sounded like a true leader.

Justin lifted his hands again and the riders and dragons quieted. "For now, take your rest. See to it that your brothers and sisters and steeds are well cared for. Sharpen your arrows and your swords and bind your wounds. Tomorrow we face our enemies over the skies of Torvald."

Silence fell. I glanced at the faces around me and knew

others must be thinking what I was—tomorrow we rode to our deaths.

A distant voice called out, "All hail Torvald. All hail the king!"

The shout sprang up from a woman's voice—I didn't know whose. But I took it up and then I heard Mordecai start the chant. Soon the words echoed from every Dragon Rider.

The chant continued as Ryan put a hand to the king's elbow, guiding him down from the platform. I could see the king was half dead on his feet. Mordecai and I followed. Back on the ground in the training yard, Seb found me. We headed into the keep, filled now with riders, most of them wounded.

Ryan led us from the main keep and into one of the smaller chambers off to the side. Bookshelves and tapestries had been ripped from the walls, but the wooden table and chairs had been left, thanks to Mordecai, who had set out the warnings that had kept the Wildmen from the Academy walls.

Ryan helped the king remove some of his armor, and Mordecai helped the king out of his heavy boots.

"Thank you for that, Mordecai." The king groaned and slumped into a chair. It was strange to see him like this—battle weary, but with an air of authority about him now. It was as if the war had matured him. "The dragons of the Southern Realm came to us just a week ago. At first, we feared a trick or some new form of enemy attack, but they told us they had heard of brave Dragon Riders who had come to find those who would fight the Darkening."

Mordecai nodded and sat. He spoke to the king of

Commander Hegarty's death—how they had thought they had failed to find any dragons or riders to help.

King Justin put a hand on Mordecai's shoulder. "You did not fail. Nor did the commander—but his loss is a great one."

Varla and Merik came to us with water and the little food that some riders still had and were sharing—stale bread, dry cheese and bits of meat. Water skins were passed around. We ate and drank, and the king began to talk, his voice low and tired.

"We did what we could to try and attack Lord Vincent's forces, but for every raid we managed, we lost dragons and riders. And troops." Leaning his elbows on the table, the king shook his head. "We saved a few villages from attack, only to find more and more of Lord Vincent's forces following after us. They harried us and baited us, instead of us doing that to them. Every time we charged, they would turn and we would follow. I didn't realize what they were doing until the third day—they were leading us west and north, bringing us back to Torvald." He groaned and covered his face with his hands. "I have failed you. I pulled our forces together when I should have scattered everyone as far as I could. Lord Vincent will sweep in tomorrow, kills us all and then he will control the whole of the known world."

"He told you this?" Mordecai asked gravely.

"No." Justin shook his head and put his hands flat on the table. "He told me nothing, but I wish I could see his face for I would like to smash it with my fist. They say that he rides an immense black dragon with four wings and two heads now, larger even than Erufon was." He glanced at me and looked away. "No. Lord Vincent sends messages to me through my former Commander of Dragons, Reynalt Flamma."

I swapped a glance with Ryan, but he was staring at the floor and would not look at me. Face burning hot, I said, "I am so sorry, my king."

King Justin straightened. "This is not your fault. I do not hold Reynalt accountable. He is doing his master's bidding. He said we had one day and night to surrender, for tomorrow the armies of the Darkening would swallow the world." He gave a hollow laugh. "He was never that melodramatic before."

Shame washed through me along with a burning anger that my family stood with the enemy. Why hadn't I been able to free Reynalt from the Memory Stone with the King's Dragon Stone? Wasn't that supposed to control all the stones? Did I have to hit Lord Vincent with its power directly? I tightened my hands into fists—I needed to know what to do.

The king's hand fell onto my shoulder, warm and heavy. "I know what you are thinking, Flamma, and I forbid it. I speak not as your friend now, but as the last true king of the Middle Kingdom. Your place is here with me. Unless, of course, you wish to flee. There are still, sadly, many refugees who will need protecting in the dark years to come."

"But we might win, sire!" The words seemed to burst from Seb. He had been quiet so far, but now he waved his arms, looking as if he could not hold in his frustration one more instant. "We have the King's Dragon Stone. We found it! We found the tomb of the First Rider!"

As I looked at Seb, I realized what Hegarty had seen in him.

His simplicity of spirit, a goodness inside him that was refreshing to be around.

Like a dragon—what he feels is what he shows.

Moving slow, frowning, the king blinked, glanced at Seb and then turned to regard me. "The King's Dragon Stone?" He held out his hand.

Ryan stepped closer to me. "Thea?"

Breathing slowly to calm my heart, I wondered if I could bring it forth. The last time I had done so in the heat of battle, I had almost killed myself and our dragons. What if it once again flowed with an energy that would kill us all?

Be still in your heart.

Kalax's awareness drew closer. In the same movement, Seb stepped up to me to put his hand on my shoulder.

I breathed steadily, trying to do what Kalax had said. With trembling fingers, I reached into the pouch at my side and closed my hand around the egg-shaped stone. It seemed cold at first, but that voice whispered in my mind.

A fire in the heart of the world.

Pulling out the stone, I stared at it. Heat kindled in my chest, growing brighter with every heartbeat.

Steady, Thea! Kalax breathed her thoughts into me.

The stone began to glow. I held it on my open palm.

King Justin reached out and took it from me. Suddenly, it was just a dull, gray stone again. I let out a breath.

The king frowned and held up the stone. "It doesn't seem to want to glow for me." He stared at me. "You've used it? It works?"

I shook my head. "I have, but it's…well, it's very powerful"

"And not really in control," Seb muttered.

King Justin looked at the rock in his hand, before handing it back to me. Instantly, I started to feel the heat and the stone started to glow. Hurriedly, I dropped it back into the leather pouch. The heat faded at once.

"It could kill us all," I said.

The king stared at me and then gave a laugh. "That might be a kindness, for the Darkening will certainly do worse to us. With a wave of his hand, the king commanded, "You have this day and one night to master this weapon, but sharpen your sword at the same time."

He waved us from the room. Seb followed me out and we headed into the keep, which seemed full of wounded men. Outside, the Academy was at least being put to rights. Riders and dragons had cleared the rubble from the fallen towers. Walls were being patched. Guards now walked the top of the walls. From the look of it, a group of riders were even repairing the other trebuchets. The practice yard seemed filled with dragons— you couldn't turn around without bumping into a tail or wing.

We had barely gotten three steps out of the keep when the Dragon Horns sounded again.

I glanced up to the tower above the gates and saw Beris waving and pointing to the south. It couldn't be an attack—not yet, could it?

And then I knew just who would be sent to cause division in the ranks of the king—Flammas were coming.

"Seb?" I said, through gritted teeth, suddenly terrified of

having to confront my brother again. I was determined to get it over with. "Get Kalax. I will ride out to greet them."

"We will ride out," Seb said, his voice grim. The shimmer of his Dragon Affinity rose in my mind and Kalax gave a long, battle roar that echoed against Mount Hammal.

※

Kalax flew down from the Academy to slowly circle in long loops, heading toward the large, black dragon heading for us. From up high, I could clearly see Lord Vincent's forces, which had camped just past the south walls of the city. Wild dragons hovered in the air before landing and then flying up again. Other dragons sat on the ground, looking far too passive to be anything but under mind control of some king. Tomorrow we would face them all.

Looking away, I glanced down at Torvald. The city looked ruined, large chunks of it blackened by fire or tumbled down. Looking back up, I watched the black dragon that now matched our slow, circling glide with its own.

I'd expected to see Reynalt, but the rider on this dragon's back wasn't my brother—I saw my father's lined face and his bristling, red mustache.

"Agathea!" he called out across the distance that separated us.

"Father." I stiffened my back. I didn't really want to give him any more greeting or grace than that.

I had never seen my father ride a dragon—he had long ago

retired from the ranks of Dragon Riders. But I had seen the painting that had hung in our house and I'd heard the stories of his time with the king's army. He'd fought in the Pirate Wars, had been at the Battle of Dragon Pass, and his tales had inspired me to become a Dragon Rider. I'd thought it was a life of adventure. Now I wondered about that.

Had the stories been lies? Exaggerations? Would I have been happier listening to my mother and only focused on being a lady who could dance and stitch and arrange flowers? But that would not change this day—my father would still be on the wrong side.

Kalax had chosen me and Seb as her riders. Now it was up to me and Ryan to carrying on the Flamma tradition that had been forged back in the depths of time.

As close as an egg to fire, the Flammas and their dragons. Close to our dragon and our king. Why did Father think he could sway me to his side?

His dragon flew closer and hovered in front of Kalax. "My daughter, there is no need for this battle, not between us, or between Lord Vincent and Justin. Lord Vincent does not wish for the fine traditions of Torvald and the Academy to be destroyed. A future is in front of us—one of the three kingdoms united as they were meant to be. We will see peace. The time is now to turn away from that usurper, Justin!"

"King Justin, Father," I yelled out. "And how can you be such a fool as to believe those lies? Did all of those years at the old king's side mean nothing to you?"

"Old King Durance is dead, and he was wise enough to name Lord Vincent as his rightful heir. Tomorrow will see Lord

Vincent crowned high king of the three kingdoms—right here in Torvald. Stand with me. Bring Ryan home to us. Let us see peace again."

I shook my head and called out, "We'll have peace—after the Darkening is defeated. You are the one who needs to stand aside before it is too late!"

He bowed his head for a moment, but then looked up again. "Stop this foolishness, Agathea. Come stand with your family. Your blood, your kin."

I swayed in my saddle, hating what I must do. But my mind was made up, even as my vision clouded with tears.

"I am with my kin, Father." I tapped Seb's shoulder, the signal to let Kalax know we had to leave—fast. She tucked her wings and dropped her head in a sudden dive.

"Agathea, daughter!" I heard my father shout after us as we fell.

Kalax unfurled her wings to catch the thermals that surrounded Mount Hammal. She soared over the Academy.

I did not look back at my father. I would not. I wanted to think his words had been a trick of the Darkening, that the Memory Stone had a hold on him. But I feared that my father might have been speaking only because he saw how House Flamma could survive this war. Tomorrow, I would face him in battle. Him and perhaps Reynalt as well.

Tears stung my eyes but I would not let them fall. I had to find a way to save not just my king and his kingdom—I had to find a way to save my family.

CHAPTER 18

ENDGAME

The blaring Dragon Horns woke me, and I stumbled to my feet without even opening my eyes, thinking it must be training again and I was late. Thea would yell at me again. But as soon as I moved, the aches shooting through my joints told me I was no longer a cadet. I dragged open my eyes and stared around the practice yard.

Next to me, Kalax was already awake, but I didn't see Thea.

The Dragon Horns sounded again. It wasn't even dawn yet and the air still held a cold bite. Other riders and their dragons were stirring.

I glanced around, wondering if this would be my last day alive—and happy at least that I would spend my last moments with dragons.

They had always filled me with fascination and wonder. I'd grown up watching for winged forms in the sky above the city, stealing time away from stoking my father's smithy so I could watch for the dragons.

When Kalax had swooped down to Monger's Lane—the last place anyone thought could produce a Dragon Rider—my dreams had come true. I'd had no idea my journey was only just beginning.

Glancing around at the dragons stirring and stretching, I wanted to grin, but I knew others weren't feeling what I did—they dreaded this day. But I was with dragons. The only thing that would be better would be to have fewer dragons in the sky facing us.

Stretching out my affinity, I could sense the enemy dragons that outnumbered us almost seven to one. Most of them were the faster, more ferocious black dragons, but I sensed blues and greens with them, and a few of the Southern Realm dragons, which seemed to glow almost with an inner heat. It would have been an awe-inspiring sight to see so many different kinds of dragons, if not for the fear and anger that came with them.

It was not natural for dragons to gather like this. I could sense the wild dragons wanting to pick fights. Other dragons were unhappy and wanted to leave but were held back by magic.

This magic, clearly, was of the darkest kind.

I shuddered, for I could sense that magic in the dragons, twisting their minds as well as their bodies. The mutations Thea and I had seen at Lord Vincent's camp weren't just changes to how they looked—the dragons sent out a sense of bitter anger that left them ready to lash out at anything or anyone.

The Darkening had done this. Even now, I could feel it

through my Dragon Affinity, settled inside the deformed dragons like the stain of ink. It made my blood chill.

Even worse, I could sense changes in our dragons that were now with the enemy, and I wondered what the Darkening was doing to the people who had been forced to serve it.

How long before the magic of the Darkening starts to change not just dragons but everything?

Even if we survived this day, would all of those who had come under the spell of Lord Vincent be forever changed? Was there no hope for any of our futures, no matter what we did today?

Always hope. The future comes.

Kalax seemed so certain. Just the feel of her mind against mine was soothing, like wearing a favorite set of clothes. It made me feel…well, more like myself.

It pushes back the fear from the enemy dragons.

That is a surprisingly human thought, Kalax! I didn't know that dragons were philosophers.

Kalax more than most, because of Seb, and Thea. Become more alike.

I wondered at that. Was what we did with dragons really any different from what the Darkening was doing? We tamed dragons and rode them. The Darkening did the same with black dragons. But if Kalax was becoming more like me and Thea, were those dragons now becoming more like the ancient evil? Suddenly, I needed to know something.

Kalax? What made you choose us as your riders, so long ago?

Choose? As if Kalax or Seb or Thea could choose against your heart? Why wish to be a Dragon Rider?

Good point, I thought.

It had always just felt natural. It was a dream I wanted and something I couldn't give up—no matter what.

From near the keep, Thea called out to me. "Seb!" She ran over to my side. "Have you seen Beris?"

I glanced around. Merik, Varla and Ferdinania all stood near Kalax, along with our other black dragons and Wildmen riders. I didn't see Gaxtal or Syl or Beris.

It was still dark out. Around us, dragons and riders were gearing up for battle. I wasn't certain if Lord Vincent's forces would attack at dawn or after, but the plan was to hit them first and hit hard.

Looking past Thea, I saw Mordecai limping toward us. "He's gone. Him and his dragon. Deserted us! The plan is off! The king has ordered it for that fool will have told all to our enemy." Mordecai started to turn away.

I stepped in front of him. "What do you mean? What's wrong?"

Thea glanced at me, her face pale. "Beris is gone. Beris and Gaxtal. We can't find them here."

"I should have known we couldn't trust him," Mordecai grumbled.

I glanced around, but how could anyone find just one stocky blue in all these dragons? "Where's Syl?" I asked.

"Up on the ramparts, trying to spot his dragon and his flying partner." Mordecai cursed once again.

I turned to Thea. She was shaking her head and muttering, "He can't have gone. He just cannot have."

"You think he ran away? Beris may be arrogant and can hold a grudge longer than a dragon lives, but he's no coward."

She glanced at me, her eyes troubled. She looked at Mordecai. "Beris isn't a traitor."

"Then where is he? We can only hope he did run—and didn't run to the enemy. The king has said he will take lead and fly in front. Look for him to signal you for when it is time to unleash the stone's power."

The Dragon Horns sounded again. I turned to Thea, who was pale-faced, but had her mouth set in that determined look I knew.

"I have a different idea," she said.

We threw our saddles on Kalax took to the sky. Kalax circled once over the Academy. I glanced at Thea—and I knew exactly what she was planning and that I wasn't going to like this one.

Below us, Mordecai was shouting orders, yelling for us to return and fall in with the other Dragon Riders.

"Are we going to listen to him?" I asked Thea.

She looked straight ahead. To the east, the sky had lightened to a pale gray. Thea shook her head and called out to me, "We're going to be the first to engage the enemy. But not the way anyone else is planning."

I gave a groan. I didn't know which were worse—Thea's bad ideas or mine.

From the sky, we watched the enemy react to the Dragon Horns and it was like watching someone kick a wasp nest. The sun had only just touched the horizon, and the air was chill as we flew. Below us, enemy dragons squawked and roared. Riders ran about between them. They looked as if we'd woken them and I was glad of that.

Glancing back, I saw Thea pulling out a square of white cloth that looked like something left from her days as a noble when she must have had silken sheets. She was making a truce flag.

I frowned at the sight of it but asked Kalax to fly as slowly as she could, giving the enemy more time to see that we were alone. Thea started to wave the flag.

The sun was beginning to rise, revealing more of the enemy's army—it wasn't just dragons now. Wildmen and Southern raiders had come out of the city to join Lord Vincent's forces.

Faces turned up toward us and I could see gestures being made. No arrows flicked past us, so I guessed our truce flag had been seen. I was hoping we looked as if Lord Vincent had won.

But I was also hoping that Thea didn't really want to surrender.

Behind us, I could hear roars from Ferdinania as well as from Scratch and Hiss. I still kept a thread of awareness with the black dragons. I found it terribly difficult trying to control the impulses of just a few dragons—how was the Darkening managing with hundreds?

"He's not coming," Thea said.

"Wave the flag higher," I told her.

Glancing back, I saw the sky over the Academy starting to

fill with dragons. We didn't have long. I shook my head. "The king is going to be so angry with us. If we live, we'll be thrown out of being Dragon Riders."

"Not if this works," Thea said and pointed to the ground. "There! Look!"

In the center of the enemy dragons, I saw smaller dragons lifting from the ground and flying away.

An immense black dragon with four wings and two snapping heads. It pushed its way out of the mass of dragons, obviously not caring who or what was in its way. It snapped at everything, it's tail lashing out. There was no mistaking the giant beast that Lord Vincent himself rode.

"Ready?" Thea asked again.

"For what? And whatever you are planning, this better be good and if it can't be that, at least make it work."

"Of course." She waved the truce flag once more before patting the leather pouch that hung from her side. "Just concentrate on your flying!"

Fair enough, I thought.

Turning, a sudden chill washed over me, as if we'd hit one of the cold, north winds. The Darkening itself was here...the Ghoul, as the Wildmen had called it. It rode the body of Lord Vincent and the dragon underneath, just as Lord Vincent in turn used the Memory Stone to ride those he controlled.

Is Lord Vincent a victim, too? Before all of this—before he sought the power that the Darkening could offer, was he like me...just someone with the Dragon Affinity?

The black dragon flew closer, dwarfing the sun, blotting out any view of the army behind it. A sense of uselessness and terror washed over me.

We should give up. What can we do? We should bow down and just do as we're told.

No, Seb.

Kalax's voice in my mind warmed me. I shook my head. Lord Vincent was trying to use the Memory Stone against us— the Darkening was trying to bend us to its will.

A spark kindled in my chest. Glancing back, I saw Thea had tucked her hand into her bag. She had touched the King's Dragon Stone. She pulled her hand out again, but that one touch had been enough—she looked impervious to the waves of fear and doubt still washing toward us.

I wet my lips and tried to act as if I felt the same.

On either side of Lord Vincent's huge dragon, a host of dragons had taken to the air. My heart seemed to stop as I saw Gaxtal and Beris. I also saw Thea's brother, Reynalt, and an older man on a black-- Thea's father.

What was Thea planning? I had no idea, but suddenly I wished we could just run, or really could surrender.

"Truce!" Thea shouted. I tried to focus on Kalax and on flying. With this many dragons in the air, the possibility of a collision was very high. Beris and Reynalt seemed to want to circle us, blocking any possible escape.

Whatever you're going to do, Thea, better do it soon.

CHAPTER 19
THEA'S HUNCH

From the massive dragon's back, a measured even voice reached Seb and me. "You have seen sense at last."

The black dragon's wings moved in a blur. Looking up, I could see Lord Vincent, with his pale skin and his trimmed beard, looking paler and even more skeletal than before. He seemed tiny on the huge dragon's back, but I wondered if the Darkening was sapping him of all real vitality and natural life. Or was it that he was trying to control too much?

"Lord Vincent." I gave a small bow that helped to hide the disgust that was crawling inside me. Whatever he was, he had been the cause of far too much heartache and pain.

"Little Flamma, heart full of fire as always." Lord Vincent gave a low laugh as if he sensed my revulsion and it meant nothing to him. "Pride, always such pitiful pride in your frail, weak bodies." I knew then it was not Lord Vincent talking, it was something else, something that inhabited his skin. I could feel it in the darkness that crept out from him, stealing the very warmth from the air, pulling the life from all around.

"We wish to discuss terms," I called out.

Lord Vincent smiled. "You have those already. But now I will give you new ones. Surrender is not enough. Lay down all weapons, and you will kneel before me with the head of the usurper upon a pike."

I cleared my throat and leaned forward to put a hand on Seb's shoulder. "Lord Vincent doesn't see what you do, Seb. Perhaps you can make his dragon see?" I hoped Seb would get my message.

He did.

A sudden wave of nausea gripped me as Seb gathered his Dragon Affinity. He blasted it out in a wild punch that left me reeling.

Lord Vincent started as if prodded, and his dragon swayed. He turned to look at Seb. "Is that really the best that you can do, little man?" I could feel him gathering his own dark strength.

Lord Vincent reached a hand up to the three chains around his neck—the Memory Stone, the Healing Stone and the Armor Stone. He wore all three and thought himself invulnerable. He thought he was protected from harm—he was the arrogant one here, the one filled with too much pride.

But his focus had slipped to Seb and away from me.

Reaching into the leather pouch, I touched the King's Dragon Stone—now we would find out if it really did control the other stones. I send an image of fire melting armor—and then I let go of it and grabbed for an arrow.

The truce banner was in fact my long bow. I nocked an arrow, drew back the string and loosed it.

The arrow flew straight and true, crossing the shortened distance in a second before lodging in Lord Vincent's neck. We'd done it—we'd gotten past the powers of the Armor Stone. But Lord Vincent still had the Healing Stone as well.

"Now, Seb. Strike out now!" I shouted.

Seb put out his hands and reached out with his Dragon Affinity. The call to every dragon to our aid echoed in my head.

A terrible, whining scream broke from Seb.

Kalax roared and I heard the sound echoed by other dragons. I wasn't sure it would be enough help. I started to reach for the King's Dragon Stone, but I checked the move. I could end up killing Seb and Kalax, as well as my father and brother, and myself. And I wasn't certain it would stop the Darkening.

The First Rider had only managed to defeat the Darkening— but it had returned. I had to make certain I ended this forever.

With a flash of a white hand, Lord Vincent pulled the arrow from his throat. He clutched at the Healing Stone on his chest, using its power to close the wound, which was gushing dark, red blood.

Seb was calling out and sending waves of affinity, luring some of the wild dragons to us, breaking the hold over the other dragons. I glanced down to see fights breaking out in the ranks of the enemy as dragons suddenly switched sides and started to attack those still with the enemy.

Lord Vincent gave a laugh. I looked up to see his dark eyes fix on me. "You think you can hurt me? A girl with a bow and a boy who thinks he can talk to dragons." His voice echoed, deep and dark. "I have lived for millennia. I am the ghost that haunts all your nightmares! The kingdoms are all rightfully mine—and will be again forever!"

I knew it must be the Darkening speaking, incensed now that we had struck at it.

But I had something else in mind.

Concentrating, I thought of Beris' name.

I had no natural Dragon Affinity, but Seb had taught me that the affinity could be learned. We had flown together, and I could sense just a little of Beris and Gaxtal. I sent an image of the Memory Stone that hung, even now, around Lord Vincent's neck.

A whisper of thought returned back to me from Beris. In that moment, I knew he had not betrayed us, not like my father had. He'd sought to do what we were doing now—to get close to Lord Vincent.

Gaxtal suddenly lurched, his neck stretched forward. With a twist and a sharp lash of his tail, Gaxtal snapped at Lord Vincent like a darting snake. Lord Vincent turned, but too late. Gaxtal snapped the chains from around Lord Vincent's neck.

Two of the stones tumbled to the ground, but I had no idea which two of the three. And would that be enough?

Lord Vincent gave a sharp cry and the black dragon he rode twisted one massive head and snapped at Beris. Gaxtal closed his wings and dropped, trying to save Beris, but I saw the blood flow, and then they were gone from sight, tumbling to the city below us.

Seb continued to reach out with the force of his Dragon

Affinity. I could see other wild dragons start to rise from the outskirts of the city, flying toward us. I glanced at Lord Vincent. He was turning on us now, pulling his sword—ready to kill us if he could.

With a roar like thunder, the king's dragons reached us and smashed into the enemy dragons. The sky seemed filled with dragons—with teeth and roars and slashing tails and claws.

"Thea—flee!" I heard the shout and glanced over and saw Reynalt's green dragon descend to attack Lord Vincent's huge black dragon. He was no match for that immense monster, but Kalax twisted away, wings spread, heading for Mount Hammal.

Fly, Kalax, fly! I urged her on.

She roared in response. But I could sense something was terribly wrong.

Below us the towers and rooftops of the city swept past. A shadow fell hard against Kalax's mind—even I could feel that.

Glancing at Seb, I saw he was clinging to his saddle. From what I could see of his face, he'd gone pale as winter snow. Blood splashed back at him—his nose was bleeding. I'd seen this before when he'd stretched his Dragon Affinity too far. The effort to break the Darkening's control over the dragons was taking its toll. Glancing back, I couldn't tell who was winning— the sky seemed filled with dragons, dragon fire and death.

We've lost.

The thought hit me hard, but Kalax's thoughts struck me even harder. *The King's Dragon Stone—all must act, not just you.*

Suddenly, I knew just what she meant.

Mordecai had said that together we could do anything. The

Darkening wouldn't understand that. It was alone—it wanted control of those around it. It didn't want to share anything with anyone.

And the First Rider—he had used the power by himself. That was why he'd died—why I'd almost died, too.

I glanced around, looking for Varla and Merik on Ferdinania. The other dragons were converging on Mount Hammal, circling over the dragon enclosure, summoned by Seb's affinity.

Together, Kalax thought at me again.

She landed on the ridge above Mount Hammal, not far from Commander Hegarty's grave. A shadow fell over us. I looked up to see Lord Vincent on his huge dragon. I didn't know where my brother Reynalt or my father were, but Lord Vincent still clutched one stone of power.

"Thea!" Merik shouted at me. He waved at Seb's limp form. "Is he hurt?"

"I'll kill you all!" The scream came from Lord Vincent.

I waved for Ferdinania to land next to Kalax and shouted out, "Together. We have to act as one." Dropping my bow, I pulled out the King's Dragon Stone. I no longer feared Lord Vincent would take it from me. But he would indeed feel its power.

The stone changed at once from gray to glowing, pulsing with waves of heat and light. I reached over to grasp Seb's shoulder.

"Thea." Seb's voice was weak, but I could feel his courage, strong and bright as the stone. His Dragon Affinity flooded into me. Beside us, Ferdinania landed. Merik and Varla swapped a glance, then swung out of their saddles and came over to press their hands against Kalax's side.

I glanced over and saw Gaxtal, barely able to fly. But he came for us, carrying Beris and Syl, too, now. With a shudder, Gaxtal landed. Beris stayed in the saddle, unmoving in his harness, but Syl, eyes bright, swung down and put one hand on Beris' leg and one on Seb's.

Together. Family.

I didn't know if the thought came from me, or Seb, or Kalax, or the voice of the King's Dragon Stone itself. But this was how it had always been meant to be used—the Dragon Stones and the Dragon Affinity, and even the King's Dragon Stone. We were a part of one thing, one world...one life. We had to learn to act together—or we would all die.

A roar made me look up. The huge black dragon was driving down onto us—we had but one last chance. Closing my eyes, I gave myself to the fire.

Fire...fire in the sky and in the heart.

Fire in the depths of the earth.

Fire in the heart of the sky.

Fire that binds us all. Fire that lights the day and banishes dark.

My hand burned, but the fire spread out from me this time, filling me, spreading to Varla and Merik, to Syl and Seb. It washed into the dragons.

Even with my eyes closed, I could see the King's Dragon Stone pulsing. Waves of heat and light exploded outward.

I heard a scream, which I knew to be Lord Vincent's last cry.

Fire brighter than the light surrounded him. It flashed as it struck the Dragon Stone he held. The wind hit, spilling out from us, sending every dragon in the sky tumbling.

Kalax and Ferdinania wrapped their bodies and tails around us, pulling Gaxtal into that circle, sheltering us under their wings. I felt as if I was fire—fire and light and as if I might forever fall into that brightness.

But I could feel Seb stir under my touch, and Varla shifted and muttered something, and Merik gave a soft groan. Syl slumped against Kalax.

The world became quiet again. Slowly, I opened my eyes.

The sky was blue and the sun shone.

The Darkening had been vanquished.

Forever, I hoped.

EPILOGUE
A NEW PATH

O ne of the many problems of surviving is trying to figure out if it's time to rejoice or time to mourn? Thea didn't seem to know any more than I did. We also faced the question of what should be rebuilt—the old life, with all of its faults, or should we start anew?

After the battle, all of us stood on what was left of Mount Hammal for a long time, too numb to talk or do anything but sway in the breeze. For the first time in ages, I couldn't feel any dragons—it was as if the affinity had been burnt out of me. Or used too much. At least Thea hadn't passed out from using the King's Dragon Stone. It, too, had stopped glowing for once. We all swapped looks and, without saying anything, Thea went over to Commander Hegarty's grave and tucked the King's Dragon Stone into the pile of rocks that made up the cairn. It looked like just an ordinary rock there.

Then we went to look after Beris.

There was nothing we could do for him, and the Healing Stone was not to be found—although later, we discovered the Memory Stone and the Armor Stone in the ruins of the city and gave them to the dragons to hide and keep, since the riders had not done well with that. Without the Healing Stone, we could only give Beris a hero's grave. We built a cairn next to Commander Hegarty, and Gaxtal stayed beside Beris for three days and three nights.

The rest of us trudged down to the Academy.

With Lord Vincent and the Darkening gone, the king's forces were able to run off a confused group of Wildmen and Southern raiders who no longer wished to fight. It took weeks, still, to clear the city. It was taking even longer to rebuild. The king wasn't all that happy with how we had acted on our own —but he couldn't exactly punish the people who had saved his realm. Besides, he had bigger problems. The nobles turned out to be one big headache. For too long, they had been allowed to live in their manor estates, while others struggled to make a living. It was an inequality that no longer existed—everyone had to work to rebuild the city, or they could go elsewhere. That was one decision that King Justin made that I approved of.

Dealing with the Wildmen was another problem that arose.

Thorri arrived on the day after the second battle for Torvald. For all their rough ways, the Wildmen set to work at once to help with the rebuilding. They were strong and once others got over their fears, the Wildmen proved to be not just skilled hunters, but they had all the old stories we had lost. They had them in their memories and now it was just a matter of writing them down in books again.

But the Wildmen weren't looking to move back north, not until they had better access to trade routes and access to the rich farmlands. The king didn't seem inclined to deny them our friendship—a wise move.

But more than a few grumbled.

Trying to sort everything out, King Justin put Commander Ryan in charge of the Dragon Riders, and we were put in charge of both nobles and refugees. Life seemed to become endless meetings to attend and arguments to sort out. All the time, I kept looking for my family—just as I knew Thea was searching for her own.

It had been my idea to open the terraces in the city where the worst of the war had hit, turning them into parks, farms and communal orchards. It took a full year, but the trees were now blooming with their first buds and it seemed a step in the right direction.

A few noble families had either died out in the battle or fled, never to return. The king ordered the land to be farmed and worked to feed anyone in need of a meal. That went a long way to helping settle a few more Wildmen and gave the refugees something to focus on other than those they had lost.

One refugee I had not been expecting to ever see again had been none other than my father. He had fled the city and stumbled upon the king's forces when they were heading north. He'd been with them during the Darkening's attack. By what I heard, he'd devoted himself to mending what armor he could, repairing harness for the Dragon Riders, and even forged new blades from scrap metal. The work seemed to have done him good, for he had not touched a drink in all that time. When I met up with him after finding my stepmother and my sister again, my father seemed a man I could admire, and that was a strange, new feeling.

There was much sadness we couldn't avoid, and the biggest loss was that of Beris.

Both Gaxtal and Syl were still mourning. For a time, it seemed as if Gaxtal would head to the enclosure, which had been reclaimed by our dragons, never to fly again. But Mordecai urged Syl to find Gaxtal a new rider. And Ferdinania, who had bonded with Gaxtal on our travels, pushed at the blue to do what she had done and choose again.

It was a happy surprise when Syl's dragon sought out none other than Beris' younger sister, who was now old enough to learn the ways of a protector.

Thea was helping her with that—and she had almost given up on searching for her father and brother. No one really wanted to speak of them. The king said Thea's father and brother had died trying to save Thea, and that was that. But Lady Flamma had been found alive and still living in the Flamma household. She was not quite as boisterous as she had once been, or so Thea said. But Lady Flamma installed herself as advisor to the king, acting as something between a godmother and a steward, running the royal household and organizing state affairs. It was a role perfectly suited to her and it seemed to ease her grief, although, she, like Thea, often took long walks along the ruined mountain paths.

The top of Mount Hammal had been blown apart by the King's Dragon Stone, it seemed. Something none of us had noticed at the time. Those who had seen it said it was like the heavens opening and every storm happening at once.

I didn't remember that, and Thea wouldn't speak of that day. Varla kept saying one day she would write a story, but Merik and Seb said they didn't want to remember much of it.

Gradually, my affinity came back to me and when I asked Kalax about that day, she simply said, *Together*. That was all she would say.

That was probably enough, for we had work to do to rebuild the Academy.

Mordecai became the new commander, and he didn't let a day pass without telling us we were lucky the King's Dragon Stone held within it the power to heal and protect. He didn't see how else we could have survived. No one, thankfully, asked where the King's Dragon Stone had gone.

For myself, I often went to Commander Hegarty's grave just to sit. Dragon eggs had hatched and new cadets had been chosen by the young dragons. Training would soon take up most of our days.

That pleased me.

On this morning, Thea had come up with me to see where the dragons were digging out new tunnels and caves. Scratch and Hiss had decided to stay with us and were arguing over their new caves. Scratch kept carrying in dried branches and Hiss kept throwing them out. Kalax had dug herself a new cave, closer to the hot springs.

Come next spring, another choosing would take place. Only this time, we'd have a batch of black dragons in the mix. A few Southern Realm dragons had also stayed, making Commander Hegarty's dream of someday adding new bloodlines into our dragons a reality.

As I stood on the ridge, looking out over the new enclosure, one of the new cadets—just chosen by his dragon—called up to us from the path below. "Instructor Seb? Instructor Thea? We have a question about rebuilding the Dragon Academy and just where the foundations for the map tower should be placed."

I glanced down. The cadet wasn't alone. He had two other cadets with him. Their faces looked pinched and a little worried. The winter wasn't quite ready to let go and the air still carried a bite of cold. But they also looked as eager as we must have once looked.

For now, I slipped my hand around Thea's and pulled her closer to my side. Together we headed down the path. And in my mind, I heard soft amusement from Kalax as she thought of us as teachers for the young.

THE END OF DRAGON BONDS

BY AVA RICHARDSON

Keep reading for an exclusive extract from Ava Richardson's
dragon-filled epic adventure, **Dragons of Wild.**

THANK YOU!

I hope you enjoyed this book! If you'd like to let other readers know this is a book they won't want to miss out on, please leave a review :)

Receive free books, exclusive excerpts and be kept up to date on all of my new releases, when you sign up to my mailing list at AvaRichardsonBooks.com/mailing-list

Stay in touch! I'd also love to connect with you on:

Facebook: www.facebook.com/AvaRichardsonBooks

Goodreads:
www.goodreads.com/author/show/8167514.Ava_Richardson

AVA RICHARDSON

DRAGONS of WILD

BLURB

In a time of darkness, unlikely heroes will rise.

The once-peaceful kingdom of Torvald has been ravaged by evil magic, forcing Riders to forget their dragons and their noble beasts to flee to the wilds. Now, anyone who dares to speak of dragons is deemed insane and put to death. Into this dark and twisted land, Saffron was born sixteen years ago. Blessed with the gift of dragon affinity, she has been forced into a life of exile, secretly dreaming of a normal life and the family she lost.

Scholarly and reclusive, Bower is the son of a noble house on the brink of destruction. His mission is to fulfill a mysterious prophecy and save his kingdom from the rule of the evil King Enric, but all he wants is to be left alone. When he meets Saffron, Bower gains a powerful ally—but her magic is too wild to control.

Their friendship might just have the power to change the course of history, but when the Dark Mage King Enric makes Saffron a tempting offer, their alliance will be shaken to the core.

Download your copy of Dragons of Wild here!

EXCLUSIVE EXTRACT

I leapt off the cliff. The branches of the trees and small shrubs whipped and snapped at my bare calves, biting into my skin. Stray twigs snatched at my hair. I didn't care. I should have trembled with fear, but I didn't. Holding my arms outstretched in a perfect imitation of the diving, shrieking seabirds that flocked to our shores, I was flying like a dragon.

Blue sky. White sun. Cold air.

Time seemed to slow. The pounding of my heart proved I was still alive even as it drowned out the haunting calls of the birds behind me.

Below me the broad expanse of the Great Western Ocean spread out like a blanket. The distant islands seemed little more than dots in the distance. No ships rode the waves. The sea was flecked with white spray and I could even pick out the smaller shapes of the seabirds, which seemed the size of butterflies beneath me.

How high up was I? Panic tricked though me. This was the highest I'd ever dove from, only I wasn't diving anymore. Looking around had caused my body to shift and turn. I started to spin and tumble. I was falling.

With half a scream, I twisted and righted myself. I let out a whoop as I dove again for the water. Energy surged through me. I was like one of the great dragons. I didn't have time to question why I was doing this as the water and rocks rose at me, faster and faster.

What had old Zenema told me?

The crashing froth of waves lashed into the rocky coastline of my island.

Hands forward. Breathe. Be like the gulls.

Zenema, the matriarch-dragon was always wise. Despite the years that lay on her, she could still dive as elegantly as any seabird. I tried to shape my body as she had instructed, but the wind pulled my legs and my arms out of place. It tugged on the clothes Zenema insisted I wear and whipped my hair across my eyes so I couldn't see where I was aiming. And there were rocks down there!

Foolish child! A female voice rang in my ears and heart. A shape swooped down like an arrow out of the sun.

"Jaydra!" I gasped out the word, but the wind tore it away. Flipping first one way and then another, Jaydra, the blue-green sea dragon, my den-sister, sought to match my dive. She was trying to save me. She was my closest friend and ally on the island. I'd grown up with her, and she even brought me food when I was ill. But could she save me now from my own foolishness.

Blue skies. Gray sea. Black rock.

I was falling faster now and almost out of control. If I hit rock, I was going to die. Closing my eyes against the onrushing sea, I felt for the crystal-clear moment within my heart I knew was there. It was the same feeling I got on the back of Jaydra, or when I ran as fast as I could. The power of the magic that coursed through my veins was always waiting to bubble up. I didn't really know what it was or where it came from—only that, in some extreme situations, it could pour out of me. I had only moments before I would be dashed on the rocks below. I willed my mind into the trance, and my hands moved in complicated patterns of their own accord.

Jaydra snarled and gave a low roar.

My eyes flew open as power poured from my fingertips. A bolt that looked like golden light hit Jaydra squarely on the chest. Power erupted from my fingertips, blowing both of us apart. My fall became a slow arc away from the rocks, and Jaydra flew back, spiraling across the sea like a skimmed stone.

"Jaydra!" I screamed at my sister-dragon seconds before I hit the water.

Cold slammed into me, knocking the air from my lungs. Salt water gushed into my nose and mouth, bitter and chilled. I tumbled head over heels, every muscle straining and every joint aching.

I knew Jaydra had been thrown across the waves, but in my mind, I could see her with her leathery wings wrapped around her protectively as she plunged into the waters, sending up a wall of water in her wake.

White water. Warm water. Pain.

Download your copy of Dragons of Wild here!

Printed in Great Britain
by Amazon